SOCIALLY DISTANT

The Quarantales

COREY MARTIN   SHANNON BRADY   KOJI A. DAE

MAX CARREY   ANGELIQUE FAWNS   M. A. LANG

B. L. BATES   DAVID MANFRE   A.R.R. ASH

HANNAH J. HART   FRANCES PAULI   E. E. KING

CHRISTOPHER NADEAU   NAYAS BANERJEE

GRACE MILLER   MORGAN BARBOUR

CHRIS WHEATLEY   DORIAN WOLFE

SHAUN AVERY   DAVID ANNAN   ELLA ANANEVA

Edited by

FROG JONES & MANNY FRISHBERG

Impulsive
Walrus

This anthology is dedicated to Christine—
and to her black-market hairdresser whose name I will not disclose.
It is your fault that we did this.

CONTENTS

INTRODUCTION

FROG JONES

I LIVE A SIGNIFICANT PORTION OF MY LIFE via a digital interface.

Most of my social interactions happen through my computer. Whether I'm hanging out with my guild on World of Warcraft, or simply speaking to friends and colleagues via Facebook, or Twitter, or any number of other social media platforms, a very large chunk of my life is and has been digital since long before COVID-19. Some of the best friends I've ever had I rarely, if ever, see face-to-face.

So when the pandemic first hit, I have to admit: it was sort of nice. I know that's terrible. I know the virus kills people, and I know I shouldn't have taken comfort in it. But the early days of quarantine were an introvert's dream. *You mean I can't leave my house or meet people face-to-face? Sold!*

Apart from making me a dreadful person, this also meant I was missing something. Because, in the midst of quarantine, interesting things began to happen. Society began to shift and warp rapidly. For a speculative fiction author, it became a ground of fertile ideas.

This crystallized for me as I was speaking with one of those online friends. She told me she had an appointment to get her hair cut later that day. Mind you, this is during the absolute height of quarantine. There were no hairdressers open. None. And yet, she had an appointment. With her stylist. For a haircut.

I had many, many questions.

What I learned, actually in retrospect, makes complete sense. But it hadn't occurred to me that, in the wake of all in-person business becoming illegal, that a black market would form. An illegal trade in coffee, in haircuts, in the normal commodities of everyday life. Some people relied on the income from those things to pay the rent, the bills, to eat—simply forgoing that income *was not an option* for them.

And so, like bootleggers in prohibition, a silent, illegal network had begun to spring up. Of businesses operating in the shadows, selling products to those who wanted them.

This. Fascinated. Me.

As I write this, it is July of 2020. And if you'd asked me in January if I'd be writing about black-market hairdressers in six months... I probably would have said, "Oh, that's an awesome idea. Might make a good *fiction* story." If you'd suggested black-market salons as the non-fiction introduction to an anthology, I would have told you that you were *completely out of your mind.*

You see, in my day job, I'm a public defender—and I have been in criminal law for a decade and a half. I am intimately familiar with black markets—drugs, guns, sex, child porn, etc. Most of a public defender's clients participate in a black-market economy of some sort or another. And an interesting thing about those economies is the way they take on a life of their own.

You see, as soon as your business is illegal, one central fact defines how you operate: you cannot call upon the police to protect you. Someone decides to steal from you? It is on you to either prevent that or retaliate so hard that the next person doesn't do that. Violence is prevalent in the drug trade because a drug dealer who is *unwilling* to apply a large amount of violence is going to get ripped off.

So the mere existence of a black market service means that there is money that is unprotected from theft by normal law. The more successful the business, the more likely it is to be victimized. Organized crime is, in part, a way to regulate criminal activity that has nothing to do with the law. It's one of the interesting evolutions that businesses go through when they're cut off from a society's protection.

And against this backdrop of experience—against this knowledge of how black markets operate and the risks they embody for the businesses engaged in them—I learn about someone opening a black-market hair salon.

A hair salon.

What happened next in my mind, happened in a matter of a split-second.

Because *in the second* I learned of the existence of a black-market hair salon, I knew that, given time, that hair salon would become mired in a world of violence and retaliation. I pictured a stylist who'd stab a bitch with those scissors for cutting in on her turf. I pictured back-room deals bristling with guns in order to schedule a perm. Imagine everything you ever saw gangs doing on *The Wire,* and then apply it to hair stylists.

The concept was at once hilarious...and intriguing.

Because I knew, in that moment, that while what I was imagining was bizarre, I also knew that, given enough time, *it was inevitable.* It's how black market economies work. The longer the restrictions go on, the more likely it was that successful hairdressers would become hardened, violent criminals. That's just a simple fact of how society works.

Now, I'm sure this hairdresser in particular was quite a nice person. In fact, I'm sure she's going to read this introduction and laugh at how preposterous my ideas are, because my mental image of what she was actually doing is so far off the mark as to be inapplicable. And maybe—but really, that's a secondary issue.

Because moments after I thought about all this, I had a second thought. And in many ways, this second thought is more dangerous. I recognized it for the trap that it was, recognized that the inertia in my brain was railroading me towards an inevitable catastrophe.

But I couldn't help it, couldn't stop myself. I couldn't say, "NO FROG! THE LAST THING YOU NEED TO BE DOING RIGHT NOW IS WORKING ON ANOTHER ANTHOLOGY!"

The cat had escaped the bag. Because by the time I realized all of that, I'd already thought: *If this was what my mind did with the quarantine, I wonder what other speculative fiction authors would come up with?*

And as soon as that occurred to me, I had to know.

I had to know.

And so, resigned to my fate, I posted the call for the book that you now hold in your hands. I was smart enough, this time, to involve the amazing Manny Frishberg in helping me edit these stories.

The response I got to the call was, by the way, overwhelming. Well over a hundred e-mails flooded my inbox with submissions; authors whose own creativity had been sparked off in just the way mine had. What you hold in your hands is a collection of the very best of those stories. Some of them are humorous. Some of them are tragic.

But all of them explore the idea of the quarantine. What does our life look like if we continue to compress it? What happens if social distancing is just... how we have to live, from now on? What happens when digital interfacing replaces face-to-face? How do we get our day-to-day necessities? How do we have fun? How do we love, and how do we live?

These are all hard, hard questions. And people from around the world have come together to answer them. The sun never sets on the authors of this anthology – from India, to Britain, to Canada, it's truly an international volume as we all explore the ramifications of this new world that we might, just might, have to live in.

This anthology isn't going to make you feel *better* about things. It'll give you a laugh or two. But it will make you *think*. It'll ask some hard questions, and I'm not sure it will answer many of them. That said, I believe that getting as many people looking at these questions is, in and of itself, a worthwhile endeavor. And it has been my absolute privilege and honor to curate these stories into this form for you.

So kick back, relax, and prepare to wrestle with the future as you read... the Quarantales.

ODE TO T.P.

COREY MARTIN

About the Author:

COREY MARTIN lives in Greenville, NC, where he freelanced as a food columnist for the Daily Reflector and music critic for *Mixer* magazine. He sold his first story to *Nothing Ever Happens in Fox Hollow* where readers can hear the audio stories on their YouTube channel.

When not working his day job, he grinds out stories of suspense, horror, and dark comedy in the hopes of entertaining as many readers as possible.

You can contact him via email: vivaldi86@yahoo.com

Ode to T.P.
Corey Martin

NEARLY A YEAR HAS PASSED SINCE THE ECONOMY WENT UP IN smoke. To be more precise, it went up in smoke then fell into a shit-filled diaper emporium and choked to death. That's how bad it ended for us.

And still no toilet paper.

We were divided, you see. Most believed it would simply disappear like a fresh pimple on a horny teenager, while others speculated and warned the officials something needed to be done, lest the world suffered the consequences. Guess what they decided to do? The riches jumped ship with their dough, and people like myself are still out of work; unemployment stimulus stopped coming a few months ago...

And still no toilet paper.

Grocery stores ran out of food a few weeks ago. Evening meals have consisted of canned meat and vegetables, except when I want something fancy and spoil myself with a TV-dinner. That's only for special occasions like Sundays and holidays. I'm down to my last three dinners, so I've been snacking on nuts and inventing soups with whatever condiments haven't expired in the fridge. Take if from me, ketchup, mustard and sriracha spread over wheat bread—or crackers, if you're lucky—isn't that bad once you accept the inevitable fact you'll pay for it in the john for ten minutes with your pants around your ankles and an aching butt-hole, left to suffer...

Without any fucking toilet paper.

I've used my free time during lockdown to work on my novel, but haven't gotten very far. Since stepping outside has become a dangerous undertaking, the ideas don't come as easily. The muse really is gone these days, almost as if she too deserted us all who are left to fend for ourselves.

The dark circles under my eyes have deepened. I've avoided

the mirror so I don't see the reflection of someone who looks like they were knocked on their ass by their alcoholic step-father. And, of course, there's the hair. I've heard about the underground salons but refuse to do my own hair, even though I resemble Bob Ross more and more each day. Haven't seen any happy little clouds in my sky lately.

And definitely haven't seen a single fucking roll of toilet paper.

Today was different. I decided to go against regulations, and go out for a walk. The city consisted nothing but highways, but I could avoid them and take side roads. Not that it mattered much; with most people out of work, you could play hopscotch in the center lane and come out without a scratch. There wouldn't be as much to see on the side roads except apartment buildings, but the fresh air would build my spirits that this lockdown would one day be over. I grabbed my hand stitched face mask—made by a sweet lady that didn't survive the pandemic—a travel sized bottle of sanitizer, and headed into the new world we've been forced to live in.

As I walked down the sidewalk, heading for the side street a block from my apartment, I absorbed everything as if seeing it for the first time, things I took for granted in the past. Ever notice how the clouds in the sky really do resemble objects? Look at that one, the one that looks like an angel with its wings stretched out. I pretended she was my mother watching over me as I continued my journey, and it made me smile for the first time in months. I missed her, but was grateful she didn't have to battle her cancer during the outbreak, in a world where doctors were as stumped as their patients, the only foods sustainable were crackers, bread, and canned meat...

And there's no fucking toilet paper anywhere.

It wasn't long on my little stroll before I saw another person in the distance. I couldn't be certain from this distance, but I guessed it to be a man. He waved at me. I waved back and continued towards him. As we walked in opposite directions we would eventually meet in the middle, but it seemed from my line of sight I was doing most of the work. Honestly, it looked like the man stood stood on the side of the road and waved at passersby. Nothing wrong with that. Perhaps it was his way of supporting the medical workers who risked their lives each day to help those infected; a kind gesture to show we supported all they did for society—what was left of it.

The incident still seemed peculiar, especially when I noticed an severe glare from the sun on the man's face. Maybe he wore shades. This made sense for the sun's reflection, and I continued, getting closer and closer.

At this point, I started feeling like a real idiot. The cardboard cut out looked so real; I stood for nearly a minute, gazing at this thing I mistook for a person. The features were spot on, down to the receding hair line. Poor guy. A bright smile plastered all over his face (at least he was optimistic). Taped to the center was a black box with a small speaker. I nearly dropped dead on the street when a wave of static erupted from it, and the man's voice started talking to me.

"How are you?" his voice reminded me of Sesame Street, overtly kind and happy.

I wasn't sure whether to respond, but no one was around so I wasn't worried about a passerby thinking I'd lost my marbles talking with a cut out piece of cardboard.

"I'm good," I said. "Is this cut out supposed to be you?"

"Yeah," the man's voice said. "If you look closer into the eyes, you'll see tiny cameras installed. This is my only venture outdoors these days. Speaking of which, what the hell are you doing outside your home?"

"Needed some fresh air. Do they expect us to stay in like hermits forever?"

I took his silence for pondering what I said. Maybe my words would give everyone courage to leave their homes and take a chance at living life again. Adjusting is one thing; communism is completely different, and I wasn't having any of that shit.

"Well," the man's voice said, "good luck. Keep your distance and be safe."

I nodded, then continued down the road. I turned my head a few times, catching a few glances at this new form of human being, and prayed it wouldn't be the new norm.

Also, if the man never goes outside, how the hell did he manage to set up a print out of himself?

The side street would come to a dead end, and the only views I had were the grassy embankments and pine trees in the distance. It's better than looking at four walls every day, and some days deer could be spotted grazing near the trees. At least that's what I remembered coming driving down this road. I kept my eyes opened in case a doe was spotted. When I came to the dead end, I'd turn back and head home. There wasn't a need to overdo it on the first day; I felt better to be outside, breathing fresh oxygen. It puzzled me why no one else risked the adventure, but I wasn't naive. Maybe I was the dumbass—very likely.

My breathing grew heavy from the constant hot air I huffed into my mask. I lowered it and relished the coolness of the air kissing my face and lips. Just a few breaths, then it was back on. What was the point of wearing it right now anyways? The rustle of the trees were my only companion, and my sole interaction I had thus far was with a man made out of cardboard. It was a visit to the Land of Oz. At any moment I expected to run into the scarecrow, with no mask due from the lack of brains to know any better. Maybe instead of straw, he'd be stuffed...

With fucking toilet paper.

The thought to remove the face mask crossed my mind because I was running out of reasons why I shouldn't.

Once I slipped it off, I balled it in my hands and shoved it in my pocket. For the first time in nearly three months the world started feeling normal. Just a nice stroll on a brisk spring day.

Until the sound of tires on pavement forced me to turn around. I stepped towards the curb strip to avoid a hit-n-run.

The sand colored SUV pulled up beside me. The tinted window in the backseat rolled down, and a pretty blonde poked her head out. Her neon pink face mask drew my attention, as well as some glittered letters I couldn't make out.

"What do you think you're doing?" her attempt to be Valley girl sickened me.

I glanced in both directions of the road as if it were obvious. "I'm walking."

"Yeah, I see that. Got eyes, ya know. Don't ya know how dangerous that is for everybody?"

Again I glanced, and told her nobody else was on the road other than the SUV that felt the need to interrupt my exercise.

A door opened from the other side.

Then, the driver stepped out.

Before I knew it, a group of college students formed a semi-circle around me, all of them wearing decorative face masks. The pretty blonde stayed in the car, and turned the interrogation over to whom I guessed to be her boyfriend. Based on his choice of dress—shorts hiked enough to pass for swimming trunks, knee-high socks and Sperry's—this young lad already peaked in high school and tried to maintain that image since graduation. What I wasn't prepared for were the large letters etched on each of their masks: SJW4LIFE.

Fuck me.

"You think you're the only one allowed to be out walking?" the preppy leader said.

If I've learned anything dealing with this gang, it's the ability to turn their words around. That's how you defeat them: with logic. I've never tried it—never been a huge fan of confrontation—but age made me older and wiser, and I was ready to test my skills.

"Never said that," I said.

Some giggles from his merry band of misfits. I couldn't make out their smiles but I saw it in their eyes; windows to the soul, you know. They thought they had me as they waited for their fearless leader's next scorching.

"I think if you're out for a stroll, we should all be allowed," Preppy said.

"Fine," I said. "Wanna tag along?"

He stumbled his words. "No...we can't...not supposed—"

"No one is out here," I said. "Who's gonna tell?"

The group eyed each other, and while they thought it over, I kept my eye on the pretty blonde in the car, who was too busy on her cellphone to notice me staring hard at her perky breasts pushing against a too-tight pink top. Whoever invented nipple piercings should be knighted.

"Hey," Preppy said. "Where's your mask?"

I reached into my pocket and pulled it out. "Right here."

"Oh, so you don't have to wear a mask either, huh? Must be nice to have that kind of privilege."

"I suppose."

"I feel offended you're not wearing your face mask. You could be contaminated. You should think about others, you know."

"Aside from seeing you guys, I haven't seen another group of people."

"So, you're saying we're not good enough to protect from a serious virus?"

"Look..." The anger rose in my voice, but I took breaths to keep the tension down. That's how they get you, and I wasn't going to let them win. "It's a public street. You have as much right to be on it as I do. Park the vehicle and let's all go for a friendly stroll. I'll wear my mask the entire way."

"No," he shouted. "That makes no sense. We can't go against our values."

"And what values are those?"

"I mean we can't just get along and have nothing to fight about. Otherwise, what's our purpose?"

I shook my head. Did he want an answer, or merely thinking out loud?

Far as I was concerned, this kid's purpose was merely to exist, and he should be damn grateful for that. I've said it before, the virus took all the wrong people.

Should've taken the ones who hoarded all the fucking toilet paper.

A few awkward moments of silence passed between us before the blonde girl whined she needed to use the bathroom. The group returned to the vehicle, but warned me I should learn a thing or two from them. I promised I'd try, and flipped them the bird as they sped back to the highway.

I hated pointless arguments, but was glad I stood my ground. Well, not *my* ground...but you know what I mean.

As pavement started turning to gravel, I glanced at the dead-end sign's warning. Rather than take a chance and see what was beyond, I turned back and headed home. I slowed my pace in case I caught a quick glance of a grazing deer, but no luck. Maybe another time.

Once I stepped back on the sidewalk that would take me back to my apartment building, a horn honked behind me; the SJW4LIFE gang. I thought round two would commence, but they drove by. No shouting, no whining. Maybe if I'd played their game, they would have offered me a ride.

Fuck it; I could use the exercise.

A window rolled, and a hand appeared with...

Oh, could it be?

Yes, a roll of fucking toilet paper.

When the SUV was close enough, the hand hurled the roll at my head, but I didn't mind at all. I snatched it off the ground before it unraveled completely.

The day ended well enough. I wanted to celebrate my outing, and I knew just the thing. A nice hot bowl of condiment soup, extra sriracha with crackers, and a huge glass of soda. The festivity would conclude with an aching butthole crying out...

For the fucking toilet paper.

DANCING ON THE RAZOR'S EDGE

SHANNON BRADY

About the Author:

SHANNON BRADY is a fiction writer who lives in New York with her family. She graduated cum laude from Purchase College and holds a BA in Creative Writing and Screenwriting, and specializes in fantasy and horror. Her work can also be found in *Italics Mine*, *Jerry Jazz Musician*, *Queer Sci Fi*, and *Ink 2 Screen*. When not writing, she can be found baking, reading, and looking for new horror movies to watch.

Dancing on the Razor's Edge
By Shannon Brady

JAXINE AMINTA HADN'T GOTTEN A DECENT NIGHT'S SLEEP IN ten years.

It was just another entry on the list of things that had become the norm in the past decade, and that she hated so fiercely it made her stomach turn. Which helped about as much with the sleep thing as the fact that melatonin pills were one of the many medicines that had fallen into dire shortage.

She had to admit she'd been luckier than most, she thought as she tossed and turned in bed, determinedly keeping her eyes shut. She still had a *bed,* after all. A roof over her head, food, and a kitchen to cook it with, and fresh, clean water. That was more than thousands — *millions* — of people were lucky enough to have nowadays. Jaxine wasn't hopeful or dumb enough to feel certain that tomorrow it might not all be stripped away, so she gave thanks every morning and every night for what she did have, trying so hard not to hate the three hundred square feet that had become her whole world.

Like many, Jaxine had no friends left, and she barely knew, let alone liked, her neighbors. But she wished that she could still talk with them face to face because she was sure they would say the same as her about it all. Her laptop had broken four years ago, and she still had her old phone, but she had never been very good at communicating with people via technology, even before all this. Maybe it was a new incentive, but being tinged with fear it didn't exactly help. In fact, it did the exact opposite.

In the past, they had been cautious about getting too honest too close to anything with a mic. It had never been directly stated that government surveillance and tracking had increased, but most people had seen too many spirited away by police vans (at the luckiest) to take those kinds of risks. But Jaxine thought that she was beginning to figure out the pattern: it was anger that put the target on your back. Not just hopeless frustration, true and righteous fury that could lead to violence, to a way back up the slope instead of further downhill.

Depression, terror, pain, weariness...that was the point of all this, and they didn't mind hearing it if they *were* listening. It kept you thinking only of yourself, and possibly a select few loved ones, and how you could scrape together enough to stay healthy, off the streets, *alive,* just for one more day. And the struggle for survival sapped everyone dry, made them empty husks, turned them into cogs in the machine.

Before the pandemic, she'd heard it all about their country's way of life. Other countries had recovered, but the aid they offered was being refused. Doctors and soldiers alike were being fought off at the borders, still. Transportation and news weren't exactly reliable, even at the best of times.

The world of her childhood hadn't been *great,* but at least it had been alive. Now her city was silent, no longer frozen in fear, but limp and exhausted with despair.

There was no way out. But that didn't kill the urge to try and find one.

The annoyingly chipper tone of her alarm made Jaxine jump a few feet in the air, eyes flying open, and she blearily scrambles out of her tangled sheets to slam the off button. The volume was low enough that she didn't think anyone can hear, but she hurried anyway.

One o'clock in the morning. Time to head out.

She would never forgive the people who had ruined the quarantining efforts at the very beginning of all this, the one chance they'd had as a country to nip this in the bud right away. The maskless crowds that had spread the virus everywhere without a care, the corporations and business owners willing to sacrifice working lives for blood money, every last politician who'd immediately rushed to worsen the situation or had been too spineless to stop the rest. Far too many of those had survived, even flourished, while countless innocents died lonely, painful deaths.

Her greatest fear was that she was becoming just like them in doing this, Jaxine thought as she crept around her dark apartment, gathering her outfit piece by hidden piece: the gloves under her mattress, the shirt in the cabinet under the sink, boots at the back of her closet's top shelf, pants under her couch cushions. All of it was thick, long, and dark blue. She wrapped duct tape where her sleeve met her glove and where her pant leg met her boot, and after she pulled on her hood, around her neck as well. There: not a single bit of skin showing anywhere.

Not the tiniest microbe could get in, she reassured herself. And she would carry nothing to anyone else, she could never risk infecting a single other person. She had to believe that that was what set her apart, made her selfishness different.

The only visible part of her was her eyes, through a thin strip of the plastic embedded in the hood. It was another heavy navy-blue garment, that also came with a solid filter between its layers of fabric to wholly shield her mouth and nose. Jaxine always thought of it as a more form-fitting version of the sort of hood that used to be put on the condemned before execution. She figured it was fitting; she had enough will left to risk doing this in the first place, but she wasn't sure she'd have enough to resist if she were caught and punished for it.

She'd been terrified the first time she tried this, and four months later, a healthy fear lingered in her bones. But now, her head didn't spin and her fingers didn't shake as she eased the window by her bed open, off-white paint chips falling onto her covers. Hesitant as her movements were, she didn't freeze for a second as she slipped outside, onto and down the fire escape. She hadn't lived here her entire life, but it had been long enough for her to know how best to stick to shadows, not be seen by cameras, and most of all, how best to avoid people.

Lucky for her, the place was only a few blocks from her apartment building. But it still felt like sneaking across the whole continent. The security cameras were old hat by now, and she made sure not to pass by any stores that used retinal scanners around their entrances, just to be safe. She longed to see the signs of a local bodega or restaurant or just one more advertisement for a movie or a play or *any* new entertainment at all. Something friendly or warm, at the very least.

As things were, she had long ago learned to just tune out the scrolling news signs, garish corporate billboards, and huge screens, which blew up the faces of their subjects larger-than-life, and blared their voices to all in the vicinity. Every last one of them made Jaxine's blood boil: the various politicians spouting lies about their prosperity, the church officials bleating about the will of God and punishment of sinners, and most disgusting of all, the President rambling about his own brilliance and glory, mentioning several times his upcoming fourth term.

Not once in ten years had any of them offered condolences for the hundreds of thousands of dead, even insincere or backhanded ones. Her friends had dropped like flies, organs destroyed from the inside out by the storm of infected cells; her uncle and aunt had each died alone and choking, ventilator tubes down their throats; and on the opposite coast, her parents and younger brother looked thinner and sallower every time she managed to get video chats working long enough to see them. Hers was the most commonplace story in the country. And it meant *nothing* to any of them.

Never. Jaxine would *never* be like them, would never get anywhere near that evil. The thought fleetingly fired her up, made her move faster, more like she had used to before all this. Out of the corner of her eye, she saw an armored van with the city police department's logo painted on its side, roving at the end of the long street. Once, she might have panicked and frozen in terror at just the thought of them. Now, she just narrowed her eyes and darted off deeper into the backstreets like a fox, heart burning.

One of her two cousins had been killed by the virus after

someone had spitefully coughed in her face. The other had been shot to death when his local police force had raided his neighbor's apartment, grinning and laughing and putting hundreds of bullets in every room. It had never been made clear to the family what crime, exactly, was supposed to have been committed.

Everyone but the most hardcore bootlickers knew that it was either one so minor it shouldn't even be on the books, or none at all. She wondered what the bastards responsible had stolen from the houses, if they hadn't been there just for the thrill of another hunt, for their machine guns to make them feel powerful. If there had ever been any such thing as a good cop, there wasn't anymore.

A few blocks, several alleyways, and two flights of basement stairs later, and Jaxine was finally there, at a thick metal door at the very lowest level of this warehouse building. The stairwell's sickly light was flickering, casting things in odd shadows, and it was this, and her police sighting earlier, that had her eying the stout man watching the door with more suspicion than usual.

"Hey," she said gruffly, trying to make herself sound much tougher than she really was. "How's the weather down here?"

"Depends. How d'you feel about acid rain?" The watchman was dressed in an outfit much like her own; she couldn't see where, but somewhere on his person was a handgun. And, somewhere else, was a remote control he could use to shut down the lights and sound, and open all the exits. He wouldn't escape if the cops found them here, but it was part of his job to give them all a chance to. His hazel eyes betrayed no emotion as they studied each other, taking a long moment to figure out what an undercover cop's eyes might look like. If he recognized her voice, she didn't recognize his.

She snorted. "Why would I be bothered? It's beautiful, isn't it?"

He nodded solemnly and unlocked the door for her with a long copper key from a ring in his pocket. The cement hallway that it scraped open into was pitch black, but Jaxine strode through it without any more hesitation, head held high.

"Much obliged, friend." The noise of a door clanging heavily behind her was her only answer, but she did not look back and her step did not falter. By now she knew how to make her way around without seeing — left, left, right, right, and left again — and knew that the light was not far away. This time, it was a gentle, hypnotic purple that guided her to the final entryway, like a moth to a flame.

Acid rain. Jaxine didn't know who had come up with the code word for entry to the basement (indeed, no one knew exactly who the higher-ups were here), but she had never found it terribly fitting. The colors she found here could be acid-bright, sure. However, they didn't hurt.

Being bathed in their light wasn't like being caught in poison, or even like the visual assault that the screens and billboards made on her eyes. In this city that was either deathly dull or luridly painted, it was the only remnant she knew now of the beauty that it had once proudly shown off.

The music, hard and loud like a racing heartbeat, was familiar, but the overall scene here was like no club she'd ever been to before all this. The lights moved in waves and ripples instead of flashing, and in so many rich and gorgeous colors that she didn't think she could name them all. The dozens of bodies that they illuminated looked almost fluid as they moved beneath them, winding and twisting into each other, every inch of them wrapped tightly in the usual soft black and dark blue fabrics. No skin, no lips, and voices were lost in the overpowering sound.

If Jaxine stood there and focused for too long, she'd forget that these were even other humans she was staring at. So, she wasted no time; she slid into the mass of dancers like a snake into water, and let herself be moved by their movements, reveling for the first few minutes in the long-lost sensations of being *among others*. And it wasn't long at all before her gloved hand found another that fit around it perfectly, as if by magic.

"Hello, there," Jaxine said to the person behind her. Between the masks and the noise, she had learned not only to speak up quite a bit more than she was used to, but also to enunciate as hard as she could. "What's your name?"

Her dance partner's voice was deep enough to send a shiver down her spine. "Justinian."

She purred low in her throat at the unfamiliar name, and wondered whether it was his real one; most people used a fake name and simply assumed that she did too.

"Ooh, *regal*. Do you have a last name too?"

"Not here. What about you?"

"Jaxine. Pleasure to meet you."

Nothing that happened here was like before. Neither their dance nor the dances around them were anything like the high-energy runarounds of their grandparents' age or the sexually charged grinding of more modern times. She wondered if any displaced onlooker, past or future, would recognize it as a "dance" at all, the way their bodies weaved around and against each other.

It wasn't exactly fun, but it wasn't strictly supposed to be. Instead, it did what it was meant to do. It satisfied a person's most primal need: to have another human close by, enough that you could feel their warmth, to feel protected and cared for, and *together* with them. It soothed the lonely chill in the marrow of her bones, and made her think, for just a little while, that there was some lingering purpose to society, to living on in this place, after all.

Some were perfectly happy making this a silent affair. But Jaxine craved the voice of another just as much as she craved their touch. And as unfortunate as the social norm had become, there was only one subject that every stranger could relate to.

"Are you lonely?"

Justinian nearly laughed. He took Jaxine's arm and guided her around in a slow spinning motion. She could almost picture a smirk behind his mask.

"Isn't everybody?"

"Nowadays, sure." Jaxine snickered.

Sometimes the fabrics they wore here felt like thicker barriers than her damn apartment walls. As she pressed up once more against her partner's body, feeling his lean, hard muscles through the heavy woven cotton, half of her was satisfied, and the other half craved more, craved *skin*.

"For me, it was a whole lot. My uncle, aunt, cousins. My grandma. She was in one of those homes, and you know how it spread like wildfire there. They didn't even tell us she had it, or she was dying, until the autopsy was already finished."

Justinian *hmmm*ed understandingly. "I never had that big a family. We didn't know my dad had it 'til he collapsed on the kitchen floor. Brain bleeds, big ones. Mom was a nurse; she was never the same: always thought she gave it to him. My brother was studying abroad when it hit, and they wouldn't let him back in."

"Condolences. First time here?" Head rubbing against his chest, Jaxine felt his heart skip a beat at the question.

"...Second. How could you tell?"

"You're talkative. Don't worry, it's a good thing. Keep everything bottled up and you'll burst, like...see, like this guy who used to live in the building across from me. Top floor. A few years ago, he threw himself right out the window and busted his head on the street."

Justinian's heart was thumping faster and faster, and she heard him swallow dryly before he spoke again. "Doesn't it bother you? Talking about these things like they're normal?"

"If I think about it, it does. But you can't think too much, it'll wear you down until you snap, too. You've got to talk out loud about it. You've got to feel that other people are there, remember that the rest of the world is real, and that you're not alone."

If she hadn't been so close, she wouldn't have heard the

muffled click of his tongue as he mulled it over, and decided: "Nice. Were you going to be a therapist?"

She found herself *laughing*, running a hand up his arm and wondering what *he* did to keep muscles like steel cords. "That might have been the plan, if the fucking plague hadn't hit."

A laugh of his own rumbled deep in his chest, and he wrapped his arms around her as their movements slowed, closer to the outskirts of the crowd. "Will I see you here again...Jaxine?"

"Yeah, you got it right. And maybe. I won't ask for you, but I'll be glad to dance with you again."

She glanced into the clear plastic stripe that revealed Justinian's eyes. In the rush of lights and colors, their irises were obscured, though she was fairly sure they were dark. More clearly, and more importantly, she could see the friendly creases at the corners of those eyes. Everyone had to be viewed with suspicion nowadays, even here where you no longer had to hold them further than arm's length. But Jaxine felt in her gut that this was a man she could trust.

A pity, really. Tragedy, if she was feeling melodramatic. She really did hope their paths would cross again — in a good way, she clarified, for anything that might be listening and hoping to jinx it. But you didn't come to places like this to make unnecessary attachments.

Those arms loosened around her at her slightest movement forward. Part of her rebelled at the loss of contact, the rest of her was eagerly gravitating back towards the heart of the crowd. "You've been a good partner."

"You too." Tall as he was, already he was fading into the crowd as well. They were partners no longer, only two more parts of the whole. "See you."

It felt like slipping into a warm bath, to return to the center. Under the fabric every inch of her skin was tingling, every nerve electrified and hungry. Each body part she found brushing against hers was a joy: arms, shoulders, knees, fingers. It wasn't long until she could reach out, just a little further, and find another hand ready and waiting to entwine with her one.

"Hello," she said, looking her new partner up and down. One only a little taller than her this time, more thickly built, fingers longer, and eye color completely indiscernible. "And what's your name?"

Their arms were draped around each other, their footsteps small as they avoided tripping up other dancers. The voice that answered her question was too weak to make it through the mask at first, and she didn't catch a name.

"Speak up. Sound it out?"

It came stronger now, and more decisive too. "I'm *Rosa.*"

She smiled and hoped that the other woman could see it around her eyes. "I'm Jaxine. May I have this dance, Rosa?"

"Of course. Your hands feel strong."

"I hope so."

Like with Justinian before her, and whatever partner had held Rosa before she had, they couldn't seem to get close enough to each other. Jaxine hoped that she would always be happy to be held like this, that she wouldn't come here one day and be unsatisfied in the arms of another. Touch and voices weren't supposed to work like a drug, but still...

No. No worries, not here. Only happiness, the most natural that they could scrounge up nowadays.

"One question, Rosa...are you lonely?"

THE STEALTH MISSION BACK WAS ALWAYS EASIER THAN THE ONE there.

Like any other club, the underground closed up for business a bit before dawn — the darkest hour, as they used to call it. Nobody ever went out the same way they came in, and they were told to leave at staggered times, as well as how to use the several floors of the building and the service tunnels underneath to make the getaways. Just like everything else about the operation, she wasn't sure of the specifics, but she had heard that there was somebody paid to make sure all the security measures were looking the other way. When her thoughts wandered in daily life, which was fairly often, Jaxine wondered how involved it was, how deep it really went.

The moon was still shining by the time Jaxine shimmied back up her fire escape and in through her apartment window. She touched as little as possible as she ripped off the duct tape and shed her outfit, but she still felt a frisson of fear run over her when she saw her own bare skin again, when her mouth, nose, and eyes were unprotected.

Before the plague hit, she had invested in a compact washing machine and dryer for her apartment, and it was arguably the thing she was most grateful to Past Jaxine for. While her outfit was going through the wash, she was in her tiny bathroom, furiously scrubbing every inch of her skin, being as thorough as she could underneath the pathetic trickle that was all she got out of her shower.

She'd cut her hair incredibly short at the beginning of all this, in a fleeting panic over possible contamination, and had simply never let it grow back out. She knew, obviously, that it was a virus and not a parasite, but she couldn't put her finger on why the idea of having hairbrush the back of her neck again still unsettled her.

The first pale rays of dawn were sneaking past her shade by the time Jaxine crawled back into bed. She pulled the covers over her shoulders and put her pillow over her head to block out the light. Honestly, she assumed she wouldn't have any more luck falling asleep now than she had a few hours ago; her body was still alight inside.

She had danced with several partners tonight, and spoken to most of them, confirming that she was far from alone in loneliness and sorrow. But her mind kept jumping to the first pair, Justinian and Rosa. As she hugged herself, it was them that she thought of, that she wished fervently were at either side of her right now. (She had been too young, too anxious, before the plague hit to have ever shared her bed with anyone else.) Her imagination supplied scents, eyes in plain light, voices that were clear and loving, and reassuring. Unafraid, more than anything.

The sleep Jaxine finally fell into, head clouded with yearning, was restless. Troubled dreams chased her around through it all, like dogs after a fox. She would still wake up exhausted, as she had for the longest time.

But, at the very least, it was sleep.

DIVISION OF RESPONSIBILITY

KOJI A. DAE

About the Author:

KOJI A. DAE is an American writer living longterm in Bulgaria with she/her pronouns and anxious depression. She has work published with or forthcoming from *Daily Science Fiction*, *Third Flatiron*, and *Luna Station Quarterly*, among others. When not writing or stuck at home, she enjoys blues dancing and cycling.

Division of Responsibility
Koji A. Dae

"WE'RE IN THE ROARING TWENTIES ALL OVER AGAIN. BACK then it was speakeasies." I click purchase on my smartphone. My eyes flick from the blue of the screen to Nick's shadowed face. "There are so many rules these days."

He takes my phone gently from my hands and turns off the wifi before setting it on the nightstand. Then his lips are on mine, his arms around me. I melt into his warmth. But, too quickly the warmth becomes heat. His kiss presses from sensual into demanding.

I push him back. Not hard. Not final. Not a no. Just enough to consider whether or not I have the energy for this. These days he seems to have a surplus of sexual energy, and it's all aimed at me. The only target he can access during the city-wide lockdown.

As if he can read my mind, he whispers, "Please, Mandy. I'll do all the work."

It's not that simple, but I let him tease me until I respond. He knows my body well enough that he can always awaken bits of lust in me. Enough for me to meet him a quarter of the way, if not in the middle. The sex is decent, but not mind blowing. It doesn't even lull me to sleep.

After cleaning up, he nuzzles into my neck, kisses me sweetly, and asks, "See? Worth it, right?"

The question hangs heavy between us. I don't want to get into it again. Instead, I pick up my phone and turn the wifi back on. A message comes through.

23 Lark Street. I was feeling blue, so I thought I'd swing by.

He rolls away, and I stare at my glowing screen.

Hurt radiates from his back. My heart sinks into guilt. I spoon him, wrapping my arms around his chest, nudging my knee between his thighs. "Are you mad?"

He grunts. "I'm scared for you. What if you get caught, or worse, sick?"

I almost laugh. For years I was the one worried about him bringing home an STD. He always had more partners than me. But now, fear of the virus has made him domestic, satisfying all his needs in me. My laugh dies.

"I need this." I kiss his shoulder. "I wish you would call Sandra."

He tenses. Things were going well with Sandra before the lockdown. They were headed towards something meaningful. But like work and non-emergency doctor visits, their relationship got put on hold. Then the lockdown continued, and the hold dissolved.

Before he can remind me that sneaking out to see his girlfriend would be against the law, a soft mewling starts from Lacy's room. We both freeze. Waiting. Hoping. But the mewl grows into a full cry and we sigh together, united in this, at least.

I glance hopefully at Nick, but he either doesn't see my look or ignores it. I throw the blanket off and say "I'll go" as if I have a choice.

Honestly, I'm relieved to get out of the room — out of our bed — and he knows it. I can sense his hurt as I escape into the darkness.

I make my way to Lacy's room. She's sitting up, still screaming, tears streaking her face.

"Shhh, honey, it's okay. I'm here. Mama's here." I stroke her soft hair behind her ear, dry the tears from her still closed eyes. She settles.

"Lie down, baby." I pat her pillow.

She drops her head to the bed and I tuck the blanket around her. Her breath comes even, but as I turn to tiptoe out of her room, her hand reaches for mine. "Stay."

I bend and kiss her forehead, then lift the blanket and scooch onto her too-small single bed. She throws her arm over my chest and falls into a deep sleep. I lie awake, desperately wanting to inch away from her. But it's easier to squish myself into her tiny bed than to go back to Nick's embraces.

NICK SPENDS HIS MORNING SULKING IN THE HALF OF THE living room we've labeled "outside." Work calls. Plenty of Counterstrike between them. He sinks into his virtual world.

I pick up the leftover plates in the clean half of our living room.

"No eating outside!" I singsong to Lacy and Nick as I scrape the breakfast dishes clean and put them in the dishwasher.

Lacy rolls her eyes, opening the refrigerator. "It's not outside, it's just our living room. Can I have some juice?"

"For now, it's all the outside we've got." I kiss her forehead. "And no juice before school."

School is a Zoom call with twenty other first-graders who don't want to listen any more than Lacy does. I glance over to make sure outside is arranged neatly. The last thing I need is Lacy's teacher judging us for how much takeout we order.

I kick Nick out of the room so her classmates won't hear him swearing with his buddies. He tries to keep the colorful language down around Lacy, but he's not always successful. Then I get the call started for her on my laptop. I'm about to retreat to the kitchen when she tugs me back down into the papasan chair.

"Oh no, not today, little lady," I say, trying to stand. She crawls onto my lap, as if she's still three.

"Look," I point at the screen. "All your friends are here."

But she won't let me go. It's my own fault. When the lockdown started, I sat with her during class every day. Life was changing so quickly, and I wanted to make sure she was comfortable. I also may have wanted to make sure my computer was safe in her six-year-old hands. Of course, that was nearly a year ago. None of us expected the habits we formed that first month would last a year.

The day is filled with making countless snacks and cleaning up. All tasks that were so much easier before lockdown, when Lacy was at school and Nick was in the office. Folding clothes used to be my favorite chore. But now I can't get any seams to lie straight and listening to a book in my headphones isn't as relaxing as having it play on the speakers. Everything feels so muffled. Claustrophobic. And Lacy keeps interrupting.

The darkening of the sky brings freedom. I pull on clean jeans, a t-shirt, and a hoodie. Not that an oversized cotton-blend will protect me from a microscopic virus, but it feels like I'm doing something. That's what's important these days: feeling like we have some sliver of power.

Or privacy.

"Mom, where are you going?" Lacy stands in the hallway, crumbs falling from the peanut butter toast she munches. I check my Fitbit. Seven p.m. Nick's on duty. I glance frantically to the living room, as if I can make him magically appear.

"I have some things I need to do. I'll be home after you're asleep tonight."

She frowns, then steps forward and flings her arms around me, burying her head in my stomach and getting peanut butter on my jeans. "Can I come?"

"No, baby, you know it's against the rules."

I try to peel her off, but she clings. I call for reinforcement. "Nick?"

Nothing.

I call louder, frustration lowering the pitch of my voice to a growl. "Nick!"

He shows up, assesses the situation, and tickles Lacy until she lets go. Before she can latch back on, he scoops her up. "You and me, missy. Movies and pizza. What do you say?"

"Pizza?" Her eyes light up.

Of course, they'll order in. Far be it for him to make an actual meal with her. But I'm too grateful to be angry. I mouth a thank you and sneak out while she's distracted.

In the stairwell, I tie on a freshly ironed mask. Kittens and balls of yarn—leftover scraps of material from Lacy's infancy. The mask is lopsided and doesn't have a great seal, but it turned out better than any of the blankets. God knows I've had time to practice keeping thread in straight lines as my clientele slowly dropped off my schedule.

A big orange cat stares at me, as if asking me what I'm doing. I shrug and reach out to pet it. Just in time, I pull my hand back. Even pets can carry the virus, and it's not like they practice social distancing.

I check over my shoulder as I leave the building. The streets are a place of semi-legality. Not quite forbidden, but the police can stop me to ask where I'm going, and I need to supply an appropriate answer. Grocery store or pharmacy, I chant in my head. I pull my hood up and tighten the strings to hide my face. Please, don't stop me. I suck at lying.

Down Lark Street, I slow. The damp pavement reflects the lights as they come on, creating an almost magical scene. There's a person standing on the stoop to number twenty-three. I walk past, keeping two meters of space between us. But our eyes meet.

He's younger than me, maybe in his twenties, with a scruff of a beard. He lifts his eyebrows in greeting. I duck my head back down. Circle around the block. Doesn't he know what we're doing is illegal? That simple nod of recognition could ruin the night... could ruin lives.

Even as I seethe, something within me awakens. It's been a month since I've felt that kind of instant acceptance. I'm like Frankenstein's monster, being raised from a cold slab by the life-force of another's recognition.

I wrap my arms around myself and speed up again. When I turn the corner, the guy is gone. Did he get in? There's only one way to find out.

I stand on the same stoop. My head swims with fear and excitement as I imagine myself breathing in the air he exhaled. I press the buzzer. A camera above the door stares at me. I take down my hood and stare back.

"Yeah?" a crackling voice asks from the intercom.

"I was feeling blue, so I thought I'd swing by," I answer. It's a hokey password, but I wouldn't have come up with much better if the task fell to me.

The mail slot flips up, and a tissue clasped in a set of metal tongs slides out. I take the tissue and, staring directly into the camera, cough into it several times. A natural cough builds through the mimicry, and panic seizes me. I can't be sick. Not today. I swallow down the fit, then hold the tissue in front of the still-open mail slot. The tongs grasp the tissue and yank it away. The mail flap bangs shut, leaving me along with the pattering of light rain and, if I strain, a deep, slow bass pounding in the house. This location isn't as soundproof as some of the other houses.

I wring my fingers as I await my results. I've gone out shopping twice this week. Last week I went to the pharmacy for more allergy medication. I wore my mask and gloves, but I could have picked up the virus at any of those places. Did I wash my hands well enough when I came home? What about that neighborhood walk when Lacy wanted to look for slugs? How many kids had the same idea that day? I bite my lip. No sense in worrying. It's yes or no, now.

The door swings open.

"Welcome, Mandy." The speaker still wears their mask. Gloves. Goggles. A white hooded suit that covers any hints of gender or personality, like some kind of squat alien welcoming me to another world. Next to the door is the small machine, maw gaping, hungry for more tissues to process. My results still show on the screen: negative. The figure gestures to a trash bag. "Clothes in the bag."

I strip down. Sweatshirt, t-shirt, jeans, bra, underwear. It all goes in the black bag. The alien keeps their gaze averted, offering me a modicum of privacy. But my sagging breasts and cellulite thighs pulse as if on display.

"The bracelet, too, hon," they say when I think I'm finished.

It's the same process every month, but I can't get used to it. I hastily remove the Fitbit and put it in with my clothes, murmuring an apology.

They print a label from a small machine and smack it onto the bag. "It'll be waiting for you. Stay in the foam on the first floor for at least ten minutes. Get your hair and face, too. Scrub, scrub, right? Clean clothes are on the second-floor landing."

I open the foyer door. A breast-high wave of white foam waits for me. Towards the end of the hallway, two people are slip-sliding in front of the foam machine, as if we're at one of those foam parties. But these bubbles are specially formulated with potent disinfectants. I often itch for days with the irritation from the cleaning. But it's worth it. One splashes bubbles on the other's hair. Then they both dip down, disappearing into whispers and giggles.

The door to the right is open, the room filled only waist-high with the soapy bubbles. In the dim light of two lamps, I can make out several forms lounging on the furniture, some talking in low voices. I hesitate. The music bounces down the stairs, but it feels muffled by the heaviness of this room. I make my way to an empty armchair and settle against the wet fabric. The bubbles are cold as I rub them over my skin. I start with my toes, work my way up my legs, over my stomach, breasts, neck, face, head, and back down again. The process is relaxing. Calming. It's almost like a purification rite before entering a temple.

Clean as I can get, I stand and return to the hallway. At the foot of the stairs I fumble for the railing. The wood steps are slick under my bare feet. I ascend, the foam falling from my body. For a moment I imagine myself as Venus. But my hair falls in ropes over my shoulders and my skin sags, and I realize I am more like the Gorgon than a beautiful young girl. I mount the stairs more quickly.

Soft towels wait at the landing. I dry myself, then flip through the clothing set up on a rack. There aren't many options left. Word has spread, and every month more people come. The hangers squeak as I slide them across the metal rod. Skirts. Blouses. Palazzo pants. My hand falls on an unbelievably soft garment, and I pull it out, my fingers choosing before my eyes can assess it.

I slip it over my head, and for a moment I'm lost in a tunnel of rainbows. The dress only comes halfway down my thighs. The skirt of the dress flips up when I spin, but I don't care. The plush fabric feels like being wrapped in a hug. At the edge of the rack there is a table of clean, pressed underwear. I slide a pair on for modesty, then step past the rack, into the party.

The lights are low. In one corner, people lounge in a kiddie pool filled with soft blankets and strange bodies. They talk low, their heads tilting back with laughter. In another corner, people sit at a makeshift bar — several patio tables set up to mimic a real cafe. A few people even play waitress and waiter, pouring liberal drinks for the mock customers who lean enticingly close to each other, chatting or simply staring into each other's eyes. Some reach across the table. Hold hands. Such a simple touch, yet I understand how fast their hearts must beat at that first moment of forbidden skin-to-skin contact.

I recognize most of the people scattered around the room, but there are a few new faces. Like the young man from the street leaning against a wall. He catches my gaze and nods.

I glance away quickly, swallow. My heart flutters like a young girl's. It's absurd. I'm a grown woman with a husband and kid at home. I shouldn't be shy. I pivot and ask the first free person I bump into to dance.

She comes in close, puts her head on my shoulder, answers my sway with twists of her own. The sweat on our palms mingles, and I imagine the conversations our molecules are having, not distracted by lips and tongues.

We dance for two songs. Then she's gone. The room

becomes cold without her body pressed into mine. The chill relaxes me. I feel settled. Complete. Way more relaxed than the mediocre and too-often sex at home makes me feel. I lean against the wall, my fingers tracing my collarbone.

That boy from outside shows up again. He's even younger up close, and his eyes shift over me, then away.

"Hi," he says. "I'm Terrance."

"Mandy," I answer, nodding along to the music.

"You come here often?"

I want to laugh at how classic and absurd that line is. And why hold back? I let out a brash laugh.

He laughs nervously along.

"Yes," I say. "Every month."

"I didn't know this was a regular thing. I thought it was a one-off." He scans the crowd, taking in each face a little too carefully.

"How'd you hear about it?" I ask.

He shrugs. "The same as anybody else, I suppose."

I squint at him. Something seems off, and I can't quite pin what it is. He's young. But most of the crowd is younger than me. He's new, but several faces are new. Then I see it. His smartwatch.

"You were supposed to get rid of that at the door," I say. "If the police traced a large number of smart devices, things could get ugly."

"Yeah, and if you spread the virus to..." He scans the room. "Seventy people, things could get ugly."

"You? Don't you mean us? You're just as likely to spread the virus as anyone here." I pushed off the wall, towards the bar. "I'm going to get myself a drink."

He weaves off in the other direction, and I scurry to the bar.

"Barb," I pull on one of my friends' arms. "Do you know that guy?"

I try to point him out in the crowd, but can't find him.

"What guy?" She follows my jumping gaze.

"There was a guy. New guy. Young. Had a watch on him."

Barb laughs. She has a throaty, scratchy laugh I've always loved. "A watch? Not possible. Veronica is on the door tonight. If nothing else, she's thorough."

I keep scanning the room and eventually find Terrance in a corner, shoulder to the crowd, head bent down towards his hands. I try to hide my agitation and point subtly, but it comes off as a flop of the arms. "Look, there. He's up to something."

Barb cocks her head. "You might be right."

"We should tell someone. Who's in charge tonight?"

"I don't know. It was a new guy's house."

A muffled scream rings out from the first floor.

"Shit. He's a cop." She grabs my hand and pulls me to my feet. Confusion spreads through the room as more thumps and shouts come from below. Barb tugs me into a hall and through a door at the far end.

On the bed, two couples make out in the moonlight. They're a tangle of heads and limbs. Barb doesn't pay any attention to them as she jams the window open.

The rain, coming harder now, splashes on the wooden windowsill. The tar roof slopes down, too steep for comfort, but flat enough that I can see Barb's intentions.

"I can't," I squeak.

"Mandy, it's a fucking raid. Go."

The bodies on the bed jostle, clothes returning to torsos. The shouting is on the second floor now.

I throw a bare leg over the windowsill. The grain of the tiles dig into my feet. I grimace and grip the window, but Barb's already shoving herself out after me, and there's nowhere to go but down. We roll, her legs thumping over my head, my arms tangling with her ankles.

At the edge of the roof I catch the gutter. The metal bends and the brackets give, but it's enough to slow my fall into a gentle thump on a grassy patch of lawn. Barb is on her feet, pushing me out of the way as more bodies slide down after us. She hugs me, and I press into her warmth.

"Good luck," she whispers in my ear, then pushes me away and disappears down an alley at the end of the yard.

I follow her, but split off on a turn as soon as one comes up. One person is harder to find than a group. I glance down at my bright dress. I'm too noticeable, and I don't have my mask. I need to stay off the main streets.

I stick to alleys. After a few blocks, my adrenaline fails. My muscles ache. I switch to a brisk walk.

I come out further south than I thought I would, at the edge of the park behind our apartment. Looking up, I can see the warm yellow of Lacy's light. Cutting through the park is against the law, but it'll get me home in thirty seconds.

I steel my nerves, take a deep breath, and sprint through the park. The grass is wet and springy between my toes. I want to slow down and luxuriate in it. But as I slow, a set of headlights turn onto the street. I hit the grass and roll beneath a bush.

I'm covered with mud. My hair is matted to my face. A searchlight sweeps through the park, over my hiding place. I hold my breath, but it doesn't pause. The car continues on.

I push myself up and sprint to my apartment building. At the entrance I'm exposed to the street. I ring up to our apartment, resisting the urge to jam the button over and over. No sense worrying Nick.

"Yes?" Nick's voice sounds suspicious.

I try to sound normal. "Hey, it's me. I forgot my key."

The door buzzes as the lock clicks over. I'm in. Safe.

I leave wet footprints on the marble floor on the way to the elevator. That damned cat wraps itself around my bare ankles, and I almost trip over it. Our apartment is unlocked. Scents of pizza and the warmth of home overwhelm me. A laugh track rings on the TV, and Nick and Lacy don't even turn to say hello. My knees turn to jelly and I barely make it to the bathroom before I sink to the floor. A hot shower, and I'll feel better.

THE NEXT MORNING, NICK SCROLLS THROUGH HIS NEWS FEED while I snuggle in the clean sheets next to him. He stops and brushes my hair from my face.

"You came home early last night."

"Hmmm." I hum, not committing to an answer.

"Went to bed early, too."

I stretch, yawning. "I was tired."

"There was a raid downtown. Thirty-six people were arrested." He stares at his phone, scrolling again.

I say nothing.

"I found the dress, Mandy. You were there, weren't you? They raided your party."

I stare at the cream ceiling. "Yes."

He turns on me. "You could've been caught. Sent to jail."

"But I wasn't." I stroke my wrist, and my eyes go wide. My Fitbit isn't there. It's with the rest of my clothes and my key at the party.

"This has to stop. I can't worry about you like this. And Lacy... "

"I know." I swallow. Can the police track my Fitbit? Do they already have it? My head swims. "It's over."

The urge to clean overwhelms me. I spend the morning pulling out and dusting every scrap of our lives. Sorting. Throwing away the things we don't need. There's so much we don't need. Any time my hands are still, my fingers reach for my bare wrist. I don't want Nick to notice what I'm missing, so I keep busy.

I stay far away from the outside half of our living room. It's already been sterilized for the consumption of strangers. Besides, Lacy's right. It's not really outside. It's a stupid name.

After I've cleaned the entire apartment, I take to cooking. I scrub bright red peppers under cool water until their flesh becomes pulpy. Then I chop them into tiny pieces, the knife moving over the cutting board as if possessed. While cooking, I drink red wine. Not enough to get drunk, but enough to keep the edge off.

Nick wraps his arms around me and leans his chin on my shoulder. I can feel his hardness press against me. "Smells good."

"Thanks." My answer is mechanical. None of the warmth he deserves. "I need some things from the store. I shared a list."

He nibbles at my neck. I don't mean to, but I jerk away.

His grip around me stiffens. "You go. You're so stressed today. Some sunshine might do you good."

I close my eyes and lean into his chest, thinking of stepping out of the apartment. In my mind, the street crawls with police. They stop me. Ask where I'm going. Whatever I answer, it isn't enough. They arrest me. My throat goes dry. "Maybe you could stop off and see Sandra on your way home from the store?"

He releases me, stepping away and muttering, "I don't break the rules."

"Neither do I." I pick up the knife again. "Not anymore."

He takes his phone into the bedroom and leaves the door open. Lacy's wrapped up in a video game. Now would be the time to apologize. To explain what happened last night — the position our family's in. But if I do that, he'll want it to end in sex. It's not that I don't want his touch. It's just too much these days. Even from the kitchen I can feel his hope reaching out to me, winding itself around my limbs, pulling me into our bed.

A sharp rap on the door grabs my attention.

My muscles clench. I pull my cardigan tight over my t-shirt on my way to the hallway. The rap sounds again, more insistent.

"Nick," I hiss, steps away from the offending door. I point emphatically at the door and mouth, "Someone's here."

He frowns. The knock comes again. Louder. Longer. "Regional Medical Inspectorate," a muffled voice calls.

My heart plummets. My hand twists at my bare wrist. They found me.

Lacy clings to my legs, pulling me towards the door. I reach my arm around to rub her back, but she's clearly more excited than afraid.

Nick grabs a mask, puts it over his nose and mouth, and opens the door. "Can I help you?"

The two people in the stairwell wear white coveralls, hoods up, masks and goggles covering their faces. One stands a few paces behind, the other reads from a clipboard, not bothering to look at us. "We are here on behalf of the Regional Medical Inspectorate to inform you that someone in this building has tested positive for COVID-19. Have you been in direct contact with Mr. Paul Whittaker in the past fourteen days?"

"Mr. Whittaker?" I can hear Nick's frown.

My chest lightens. "He's on the second floor, right?"

"Ah, right. Mr. Whittaker. No. I haven't seen him in months."

"Not even in passing?" the man asks.

Nick shakes his head.

"And you, ma'am?"

I look down. His cat doesn't count, right? "I don't think so."

"Right. We'll need to take a sample to test all three of you for the virus. This building will be under quarantine for fourteen days, starting immediately."

"But— "

The man continues his drone, not letting Nick cut him off. "If you need supplies delivered, you can call this hotline, specifically for people under mandatory quarantine. If you experience any symptoms, such as a raised temperature, cough, difficulty breathing or loss of smell or taste, you should call the medical hotline. Do not attempt to leave the building without medical permission." He hands Nick a piece of paper, confirms there are only three of us in the apartment, and writes our names on his clipboard.

The next man steps forward. From a pouch on his hip he pulls out three plastic vials. He unscrews the red top on the first one and extracts a long cotton swab.

"This may be uncomfortable," he warns.

Lacy hides behind me, poking her head around my hip to watch as Nick leans his head back and allows the man to shove the swab up his nostril. He puts the swab in a small metal box and waits. A green light flashes. "Negative."

Then it's my turn. I peel Lacy from me and deposit her to Nick's care. As I approach the strangers, I'm filled with an urge to say hello. Invite them in for tea. Something to build a bit of intimacy before I let them violate my body. But those days are gone. I grit my teeth and tilt my head back. From the corner of my eye, I catch a flash of ginger. Then, the swab is in. It's worse than coughing into a tissue, but not as bad as some of the videos made it out to be.

When he's done, I lower my gaze and search for the orange furball. There it is, in the corner of the hall, staring at us with curious eyes. What would they do with it if they knew it's Mr. Whittiker's cat? Take it away? Lock it up in a cage? In some places they're putting down animals whose owners die from the virus, as if more death could possibly help. I look away quickly so they don't follow my gaze. Another green light flashes on the device.

One of the men nods at Lacy. "We'll need a sample from your daughter as well."

I inhale sharply. Lacy hates the doctor. Won't even stick out her tongue to have her throat looked at. I hold her firmly, the way we used to pin her down for vaccinations. She squirms and gags and tries to get loose, and my heart breaks for her. But the whole time I'm staring at that damned cat.

A MEWLING WAKES ME IN THE MIDDLE OF THE NIGHT. MY first instinct is to groan and go to Lacy's room. It takes me a few seconds to figure out the mewling is quieter than our daughter's nightmares and coming from the wrong direction. I lie in bed,

listening to the high, mournful call until I remember Mr.
Whittaker's poor cat. It must be back in the stairwell. Or maybe
it never left. It has nowhere to go. No one to take care of it.

I slip out from the covers and make my way to the kitchen
by the moonlight streaming through the windows. I rummage in
the pantry until I find a can of tuna. Cats like tuna, right? I shrug
and make my way to the front door.

I take a deep breath before easing the door open. The
stairwell floor is cold and gritty under my bare feet. I curl my
toes against the unpleasant texture and squat down. "Psss pss
pss."

The mewling comes from a shadow in the far corner.

"Pss pss pss." I hold out my hand and my palm is filled with
soft, silky fur. The cat runs its length beneath my palm. I sink to
a cross-legged position and it pads into my lap, curling up, warm
on my thighs. The can's pull tab sticks, and juice spills on my
bare legs. The cat laps it up with its rough tongue and devours
the fish in the can. I continue petting it while it eats, and a soft
purr grows beneath my fingertips. I find myself drifting back to
sleep, right there in the stairwell.

The opening of the door at my back startles me, and the cat
stops purring.

"Mandy? What are you doing out here?" Nick's voice is
sleepy and concerned.

"The cat." I set it down while I stand. "It was hungry."

"You shouldn't be out here. Come back in."

I leave the cat outside and follow Nick to bed. He's also
warm, and has soft hair in some places. But he lacks the purr of
the cat. As I drift off, I try to remember its name. I'm sure I
heard Mr. Whittiker yelling it at some point. Rosy? Rusty?
Something like that.

When I wake up, Rusty is the first thing I think of. I rush to
the door and look out the peephole, but can't find its orange
against the gray. I sigh and let Lacy pull me into the kitchen to
make oatmeal. She demands extra butter, more milk. I'm pretty

sure she can do all this on her own now, but she likes it better when I make it.

All day my mind drifts back to the cat. As I sip my coffee. While I make lunch for Lacy. When Nick pulls me down into his arms to watch a television show. All I can think about is how satisfying it was to let that unassuming beast curl up on me.

Nick nibbles my ear. "You seem to be in a better mood."

"Yeah." I kiss him. It's the first time I've initiated affection in months. "I am."

When we get Lacy to finally take her nap — she needs them again now that her sleep is so disrupted — Nick pesters me to go to bed with him. We're slow and tender, but not quite satisfying. It just feels like work. Nick falls asleep soon after, leaving me to stare at the ceiling.

I wrap my robe around me, grab another can of tuna, and head into the stairwell.

"Pss pss pss." I barely finish the call before Rusty tangles herself around my ankles, nearly knocking me down with the force of her purr.

I open the can, kneel, and set it in front of her. She makes the sweetest smacking noises with her tongue as she devours the food. "I'm going to have to figure out what cats eat."

I let her finish, then pull her into my lap. As she purrs me into a trance, all my cares fade away.

When Nick opens the door, Rusty runs off. I pull myself to my feet and, hanging my head, return into our home.

"Why don't you just adopt the thing?" Nick asks. "Bring it into the apartment."

"Maybe I will." I spend the rest of the afternoon looking up what items I'll need to take care of a cat. Litter. Proper food.

Excitement pushes sleep from me. I lie down with Lacy, but don't close my eyes. Her breath comes even. Her hand rests near my collar bone. I stare down at her. When she's asleep, she's perfect. All the sweetness and love that children are supposed to provoke rises in me. I kiss her brow and she stirs. I freeze. When it's clear she won't wake, I slip out from under her arm.

I creep to the door and open it to find Rusty curled up, waiting for me. She's just as excited for our cuddle session as I am. I reach down and pick her up. She's large in my arms, but most of the size is fluff. I hold her to my chest and let her purr ripple through me.

"Who's a precious girl?" I murmur, nuzzling her fur. She purrs louder. "You want to come home with me? Come live with us?"

She stares at me with her large green eyes as if she understands the question. As if she's saying yes. I rub behind her ears, and she nudges harder into my fingers.

"You like that idea, huh? Me too. All the cuddles, every day. I'll order you a litter box. And get you some food. And a cute little water bowl. You'll like that, huh?"

As I turn to the door, the weight of my promises strike me. She's going to need regular cuddles. She'll probably be even more demanding than Nick. I'll have to hold her down for the nastier parts of life: grooming, flea treatments, nail filing. That will fall on me. I'll have to clean her shit. Every day. I'll have to feed her. And after she demands all that energy from me, she'll come sit on my lap. Even if I'm reading a book or watching a film. Even if I just want a minute to myself. The second I invite her to be mine, my touch will be on her terms.

I drop her. It's a short fall, and she lands gracefully. She turns back and cocks her head at me.

"I'm sorry. I can't." I push her away with my toes.

She purrs and threads herself around my ankles.

I bend down for a final stroke of the head. "I'll still come see you. But you can't be mine. I can't handle anyone else being mine right now."

Inside, Nick's still up gaming. I wash my hands and go to him, sitting close, waiting for his current campaign to finish. I lay my head on his shoulder, feel the twitching of his muscles as he shoots imaginary enemies. His voice has a soft, familiar boom as he issues commands.

When he's done, he turns and kisses my forehead. "Where's the cat? I thought we were adopting it until Mr. Whittaker gets back."

"Nope."

"Nope?" He turns to face me and my cheek slides from his shoulder.

I sigh. "I don't want another responsibility. I just want a friend. Someone completely responsible for themselves."

He rubs my neck. I close my eyes and let my tension flow out of me.

"You know, it was never that you and Lacy weren't enough. It's that you're too much. Without an outlet, I feel like I'm holding onto so much. Balancing everything in this apartment."

He strokes my hair back to kiss my forehead. "You don't have to take care of us all the time. We're a team."

"I know. Logically, I know. But I just... I feel that pressure. And I get it. I can't go out and shake hands and have hugs or share a dance with others. Not anymore. But I just don't know how to let it go without that."

Tears slip out from my eyes. He pulls me to him, letting me cry softly. When my tears dry, he puts me to bed with a big glass of water and a pill of melatonin. I dream too vividly, but I don't hear Lacy cry or notice when Nick gets up to go to her.

A GENTLE POUNCE ON THE BED AND A NUZZLE ON MY forehead wakes me. I open my eyes to see Rusty staring at me, waiting to be cuddled.

"What the..." I sit up, stroking her despite my confusion. "How did you get in?"

"I let her in." The smell of eggs and bacon floats to me as Nick carries in a tray.

"I told you... "

"You didn't want another responsibility. Don't worry. I'm taking care of Rusty until Mr. Whittaker gets home. You won't be allowed to lift a finger for her."

"Mom! We made you breakfast in bed. Do you like it?" Lacy nearly sloshes the coffee out of my mug.

"I do!" I grin at her. "Thank you."

Nick settles the tray over my blanket and takes the mug from Lacy before any liquid makes it onto our comforter.

"Can I have your bacon?" She eyes my plate.

Nick swats her lightly on the bottom. "This is for Mom. There's more bacon on the counter."

She scoots out of the room and he scoops up Rusty, who's edging closer to the tray.

I sip the coffee. It's sweetened with a spoonful of honey, just the way I like it. "Thanks. This is really nice."

"It's a start." He nuzzles the cat. "I messaged Sandra last night."

I set the coffee down and keep my voice neutral. "How is she?"

"She's not doing so hot, either. She's living by herself, you know."

"Are you guys going to see each other?"

"We're going to try, once our building is out of quarantine."

"That's nice." A weight lifts off my heart, just a hair, and my breath comes easier. The idea of him getting his needs met by someone else, even part time, releases a pain in my shoulders I've been carrying for months.

He snags a piece of bacon off my plate. "We can't just keep our lives on hold and wait for this to blow over. It's never going to. But we can't give up."

I look at his mouth, glistening with oil from the bacon. It's the most attractive he's looked in months. "You're right. We can't."

SIX FEET AWAY, IF YOU PLEASE

MAX CARREY

About the Author:

MAX CARREY currently lives in sunny California. She loves delving into her characters complicated pasts and suspense filled futures. She's had stories appear in Zimbell House's *The Dead Game* and *Spirit Walker*. Chipper Press' *The Princess*. As well as upcoming releases with *PCC Inscape* Magazine, and other indie publishers.

To stay up to date follow her at: instagram.com/maxcarrey/.

Six Feet Away, if you please
Max Carrey

BARRY'S EYES WERE SO ATTACHED TO THE SCREEN OF THE little television set it would be burned into his memory. Sandra Brighten, Good Morning Hello World's news reporter, sat wedged up against her desk with papers splayed out in front of her. A signature pitying look of a pinched brow and slightly slumped shoulders was on full display. It was a look she had to use often nowadays.

"A man was found dead this morning in his Gaslamp District apartment. Police suspect that foul play was involved but have yet to release an official statement. The victim is Mark Mathews, who was the CEO of Constructive LLC, a building corporation turned hand sanitizer manufacturer once the virus hit. Due to his social status he could be yet another victim in the string of attacks executed by assassins going after people in positions of power. Assassinations are easier now, as the number one weapon of choice of late is a recently infected person's spit or other such bodily fluid."

Barry shook his head, though his nerves remained trembling. "Enough of that," he murmured as he turned off the TV. He rubbed his already sweaty palms together, the burden of high anxiety. He glanced out the window. The morning was crisp but dewy, and it was perfect for a walk. The sun and a later hour would bring people out. More people, more risk, more danger.

Barry twiddled his thumbs, fighting the urge to stick one in his mouth like an infant. He breathed in deeply, held it for a moment, and released.

"It's just a walk." The risks and benefits ran through his mind, buzzing so loudly he wanted to smack at his head in hopes they'd come tumbling out his ear. The risks seemed to outweigh the benefits, though the government had encouraged walks, at a safe distance, encouraged fresh air and exercise, with caution.

Then his tentative eyes flicked to his Safety Star. His nerves relaxed, the buzzing quieted. "Walk it is."

He put on his Safety Star and felt immediately better, glad to have the added protection, it felt like amour, like he was a knight of a new age. The Safety Star was in fact a big loop that you would put your body through, with straps attached to sling around your shoulders so that the contraption hangs at the torso. Jutting off the loop are six foot dowel rods, with two on either side, and one in front and back, like a sort of star. Barry now wearing the odd accessory was ready for a mental health walk, as the government suggested.

If it wasn't for the Safety Star it would look and feel like the world was in fact normal to Barry. Who felt like one of those girls in old movies carrying a tray around selling cigarettes. The Safety Star was a little awkward, but he wouldn't have gone out without it, and so he was greatly enjoying the peace and quiet despite the extra weight to lug around. Barry couldn't sense his anxieties nagging at him, it was as if they weren't even there, all there was were his feet on the pavement, and a far off bird chirping.

Yet, his happiness was quickly disturbed when the sound of metallic jangling began to approach. Barry froze, planting his feet down, white knuckling the straps of his Safety Star. His eyes were bulging out his terrified face as the sound grew nearer and louder. Then a little white terrier broke into view among the houses that lined the road, the tags on its collar clanking about. Footsteps that padded loudly against the cement were not too far behind, and before Barry could properly register any of it, the dog was in front of him. It was sat down wiggling its tiny tail, panting, occasionally yipping for attention.

The sensors on the tips of the dowel rods of his Safety Star went off: *six feet away, six feet away, six feet away...* it continued to drone on with a computerized voice.

"Shoo!" Barry yelled, sounding almost like he'd sneezed. "Shoo!" He flung out his arms wildly. "Away with you!"

The footsteps, which had been trailing the dog, approached, and Barry saw a young woman with a leash in her hand and a sweatband across her forehead. "There you are Tuffy! Come here boy," the woman called, but then when the dog refused to budge she stepped forward.

Barry unfroze and leaped back, while Tuffy pounced forward and danced at his heels. "Stop!" he shouted, jutting out his hand.

"I'm just getting my dog," she said as her lips curled into a sneer and her eyes squinted in disdain. But she was kneeling toward the ground, with hands stretched out near Barry, and going to duck underneath the rods to grab her dog.

"Can you not hear? Six feet away!" he screamed, his anxiety shooting through the top of his head, reddening his complexion. He noticed the woman gnash her jaw and the boiling of his blood subsided to a growing fear. She wasn't just a woman, she was a weapon, she could kill him if she was infected and he contracted it. A horrible painful death, slow, agonizing... his mind rambled on, but his words fell out his mouth.

"If you please. Six feet away, if you please."

She stood up and locked her knees, crossing her arms in front of herself, an eyebrow arching.

"Oh, so you're one of *those* people."

"What does *that* mean?"

"You live in fear," she replied, and her mouth pinched together in satisfaction. "Pitiful."

"Pitiful!" Barry cried excitably, scaring Tuffy who ran back over to his owner. "You've got to be kidding. I live in safety."

She huffed and then let out a laugh as she bent down and latched the dog to the leash, mumbling under her breath still loud enough for him to hear.

"Sure, if that's what you call it."

She spun on her heels to leave. She began to walk so casually, so unhindered, so willingly endangering everyone, because she didn't care. Definitely didn't care enough as Barry saw it. His internal furnace turned back on, and before she'd gotten far, sashaying about, flicking her blonde ponytail back and forth as she went, he yelled.

"At least I'm not some ignorant towhead who can barely keep track of her dog, let alone her dying brain cells!"

The pony tail stopped swinging, her feet stopped walking, and suddenly she twisted. Her harsh icy stare was as sharp as a knife, but then it sparkled and something devious appeared. A crooked smile screwed up her face. She raised her hand up to her lips, kissed her fingers, dropped her hand and blew the kiss in his direction. It wasn't subtle it was practically gale force winds to Barry.

The color drained out of him. His limbs started to shake. She breathed on him, and he was sure he felt a breeze. His body began to shrivel up into itself as if he was melting, but then he abruptly screamed out and booked it, running back home at full speed. The Safety Star rattled and jumbled about as his hurried feet carried him along. Her haunting laughs rang out behind him.

His mind went back to the report, on the assassinations done with spit, and he imagined her spit traveling through the air and hitting against his face, being absorbed into his skin, spreading out and infecting him. He burned with fire, and grew unsure if it was in rage or a symptomatic response to being infected with the virus.

Barry burst through the door of his house, leaving it gaping open, but then swirled about smacking himself lamely against the wall in a hurried attempt to close the door. The outside was too dangerous to let in. He was foolish to have ignored his hesitance before, ignorant to have gone outside. What had it all been for? What had it gotten him? He was going to die, he was sure of it.

The burning fire was clawing at him from the inside out, flowing like lava down his veins. An icy heat overtaking his swiftly beating heart, goose bumps broke out all over his skin in terrifying little mounds. His wide bulging eyes envisioned the mounds exploding, pus leaking, then with blood, ending with him melting into a mass of bio-hazardous pulp.

He stripped off the Safety Star, stripped off his clothes, and tossed them into the hall as far away from him as possible, to stay there quarantined. Barry gazed at himself in the mirror, naked, looking for any sign of infection. He looked fine, perhaps it wasn't too late. He anxiously fumbled his way into the shower, not knowing whether it was better to cleanse with hot or cold temperatures so he bathed himself in both. Letting the freezing water numb him completely, then thaw out with heat until scorching red, back and forth back and forth, just in case. All while scrubbing himself with his soapy washcloth, until it didn't feel like enough, then taking disinfectant cleaners and hand sanitizer rubbing it into his skin so roughly it caused it to peel.

Barry exited the shower pink and raw, tender to the touch, with little red broken blood vessels all over him. He delicately put on his robe, feeling as if the fibers were going to fuse into his inflamed body. The burning filled his eyes with tears, but he swiftly wiped them away once they fell, for they stung his angered flesh.

He tiptoed out the bathroom carefully, around the contaminated clothes and Safety Star in the hallway, and went to sit alone in the quiet of his living room. Only accompanied by his thoughts, and nervously twitching as he looked out the windows, his shaking hands pulling the curtains down, and boarding up all the views of the outside.

The outside could kill him. The inside was safe, as long as he hadn't brought the virus in on him. Yet, he stayed seated, trying to control his heart palpitations, all while wondering if he was about to have heart failure. What was the use of fortifying himself in if he was going to die? He had to wait, wait to see if he was infected or not. He'd know within a day or two, or when (if) the burning calmed and dissipated. But the flaming was as persistent as ever, and he couldn't be sure if it was done by his anger, by anxieties, done by the washing, done by the virus.

Barry let loose a wail of a cry, a strange wallop of a noise, echoing but cut short.

He cursed the woman – the possible assassin – though he knew he was no one important, for maybe he was practice or just for fun. He cursed the government, and stupid mental health walks, for all the good that did to clear his mind. He cursed his Safety Star, if it hadn't kept him safe after all. It was three hundred fifty dollars! Damn it, damn her, damn everyone and everything!

Barry reached for a pen and paper, scribbling down his possible final words:

To whomever finds my body, I have perished because a reckless or secretly devious woman has contaminated me! She refused to stay six feet away, even when I said please. How rude! She has blonde hair, wears ridiculous exercise clothes with sweatbands, and has a white terrier dog named Tuffy. I have also died because my Safety Star didn't work. Please leave a negative review on their website, and also demand a refund. Keep the money as a reward for yourself, obviously I cannot use it. It's a matter of principal. Thank you. –Barry

Once he was satisfied with what he'd written, he sunk back into the couch cushions. Still all too aware of the burning sensation paining him, and he began his designated countdown – 48-hour quarantine – letting the seconds tick by into minutes, then hours, quietly waiting to die.

SOCIALLY DISTANCED DRINKING

ANGELIQUE FAWNS

About the Author:

ANGELIQUE FAWNS writes speculative fiction and has a day job creating commercials for Global TV in Toronto. She is also a staff writer at *Horrortree.com*, and lives on a farm with horses, goats, chickens, dogs, and a human family. You can sample her strange stories in *Ellery Queen Mystery* Magazine, *Pulp Modern*, *The Other Stories* podcast, and a variety of anthologies on sale now.

Connect with her on twitter @angeliquefawns, or check out her website at www.fawns.ca.

Socially Distanced Drinking
Angelique Fawns

FRANK HUNCHED OVER THE BLACK WALNUT BAR IN THE speakeasy, sipping whiskey. A relic in his own time, this was one place he felt at home. The sour smell of a dish rag permeated the air, and old country crooned off an mp3 player hidden somewhere in the cobwebbed ceiling. The club tried to adhere to the Gathering Laws of "no more than ten" but sometimes a few extra bodies slipped in. It would be just a matter of time before they were shut down.

Frank was focusing on his last swallow when she walked in. Anywhere from fifty to sixty, she was dressed in a red party dress that hung in frills and lace off her shoulders. With long grey hair flowing to her waist, her eccentric outfit hugged every curve. All eyes in the place were watching her.

"Hey Frank, fancy meeting you here," she said with a grin as she summoned the bartender with a twitch of her baby finger.

Shocked, he realized he knew her. It was Carol, one of the women who processed surveillance reports at the monitoring center where he worked security. In the office, she wore navy power suits, with her hair in a tight bun. Because she dealt with confidential files she was required to be in the office, even though most people worked from home. He watched her order a tequila with a confident twirl of her finger.

She'd never even given him the time of day before, walking by his post as though he was invisible. Surprising that she knew his name. Frank could recognize everyone, being required to carefully monitor who came and left the building. The facial recognition software could probably do most of his job, but old farts like him had to be employed somehow.

She gave him a seductive smile, tossing back her tequila shot. He always thought her pretty, but never realized the true extent of her gorgeousness. Sadly, his ability to flirt had long since fled, so he tried casually getting off his stool and sauntering out. He tripped over his cowboy boots and left the basement bar with a red face.

He was berating himself for not even saying hello, when he saw the slip of paper under the windshield wiper of his rusty Ford pickup truck. Frank felt a tinge of fear, limping to his obsolete vehicle. Was it a notice to appear for testing at the quarantine center? He'd coughed a couple of times in the bar, and even sneezed at work today. He checked his biometric wrist implant. There were no alerts on it. But he did notice the time, 8:30 p.m. Half an hour to get home.

It was easy to lose track of hours in the speakeasy. He worried briefly about Carol. Would she make it home before curfew? He thought of going back in and offering her an escort, but lost his nerve. Instead, he yanked the little piece of yellow parchment out and squinted at the words scrawled in cursive pencil.

Live Free or Die. Go to where the last rays of the sun cast a golden shower. Leave no tracks. The skills of the old are needed to rebuild anew.

Shoving the note in his pocket, Frank quickly got into his truck, heart pounding. This was an odd note, he'd heard of golden showers, but he didn't want to have urine rain on him. Was it a trap? The government was always trying to ferret out dissident thinkers. What an amazing possibility though strange sexual acts not withstanding. Was there a place where people still lived with freedom and choice? Though the coronavirus population purges that tore through the world were contained and vaccines found, the strict emergency regulations were never fully relaxed. Once the government had complete control of their populations, a new era of autocracy and "security first" became the new norm.

A peculiar feeling percolated in his stomach. Something he hadn't felt in a while. Hope perhaps? Or more likely fear mixing with that last shot of Wild Turkey 101.

First Carol, and now the note. This was turning out to be an interesting day.

He was a bit of an oddity in Colony 12, his fellow drinkers at the bar notwithstanding. Not only was he one of the few Baby Boomers still alive in the post-pandemic population of 2030, but he looked his age. An unexpected side benefit of all the world's money flooding into biotech research was amazing advances in plastic surgery and stem cell therapy. The old man steadfastly refused to let anyone touch his skin, or to take any sort of rejuvenation product.

"I've earned every damn line on this face, and no fake charlatan of a doctor is gonna steal them from me," he'd mutter if someone suggested a bit of Juve-afirm.

He was feeling every one of his eighty years as the adrenaline left his system. Driving home, his hands trembled on the steering wheel. Silly to think that a young gorgeous lady like Carol would be interested in him. He left the big truck in his barely adequate parking space and shuffled through the metal corridors quickly. He opened the alloy door to his 500-square-foot studio just in time. At 9:00 p.m. daily, the halls were sprayed with a decontaminant to thwart the lurking of any new virus. The lessons of the COVID-19 pandemic changed life forever.

Frank laid in bed thinking of the note balled tightly in his hand under the covers. He couldn't fall asleep, heartbeat thrumming in his ears, neurons firing in excitement. Live Free or Die? Connected Colony 66 used to be called New Hampshire and boasted the motto. One of the few places you could ride a motorcycle without a helmet and pay no income tax before the "event."

In remote and mountainous regions, the internet still couldn't penetrate. Without wifi, intense public monitoring wasn't possible. Was a counterculture thriving in the old New England mountain range? *The skills of the old are needed to rebuild anew.* Frank had farmed heirloom vegetables for the local market before the global food shortages of 2021. He never did get married; he put all his energy into working the soil. Or maybe he had just never met a woman who made him feel the way Carol did.

Food growing was definitely a skill of the old. His land had been commandeered by the big agricultural corporations, and he had been forced to relocate to the city. He tried to put up a fight, but a few weeks in a non-compliant adjustment center had taken the wind out of him. He took his job assignment as a security guard at the monitoring center and couldn't remember the last time he had been happy.

Go to where the last rays of the sun cast a golden shower. That seemed a little more obscure. He was an avid skier in his youth, and remembered some of his favorite slopes in New Hampshire. Mount Attitash, Loon Mountain, Mount Sunapee... Mount Sunapee! That could be it. Sun and a golden shower. A/K/A Pee (Now he understood the note.)

Leave no tracks might be the hardest part. The feel of the mandatory wrist tracker imbedded in his left arm was a constant irritant. The damn thing tracked his every move, and every facet of his health. A change in temperature, or an excess of white blood cells and the health officers would be at his door in hazmat suits to haul him off to an assessment center. Any new virus, or resurgence of old, would be identified and stopped before it could spread.

He finally managed to catch a few hours sleep, and then left for his day job. He was a little nervous. The big glass headquarters on the waterfront was only a ten-minute walk from his condo, but his heart was beating like he had been running a marathon. Would Carol give him that heart-stopping smile again, or would she ignore him, like in the past? What should he do about that little cursive note? Passing through the first retinal scanner at the outside door, he made his way into the Surveillance Room and took up his post.

Catching his breath, he saw Carol walking towards him.

Gone is the red dress, she is back in her navy-blue suit, the swinging glossy hair caught in a bun.

"Morning Frank, what a gorgeous sunny day, not a shower in sight," she said softly.

Once again, his vocal cords fail, but this time it was her words that have frozen him. Sun, Shower? Could Carol have left the note on his windshield? She goes to her desk and starts working like any other day. Perhaps it's his imagination on overdrive. He's too old to be involved in some crazy conspiracy.

His eyes keep drifting over to Carol's work station. She seems to be working intently on something – her fingers flying over the keyboard. Then she got up and walked rapidly over to him.

"Frank come with me."

She grabbed his arm and pulled him up, guiding him towards the exit.

"Carol, have you gone crazy?"

"Just move. We don't have much time."

His old legs protest, but he lets her hustle him outside. Luckily, he is the security on the floor, and no one else seems to notice their abrupt exit. He hasn't felt this alive in over twenty years.

"Did you leave me that note on my truck?"

Walking quickly towards the parking lot, Frank noticed his wrist implant vibrating. Sending an alert that he is not where he should be.

"Look, we have to get to your truck. It is one of the few untraceable vehicles left on the road. E-cars have GPS. That old pickup truck is pre-2000 isn't it?"

Frank saw a red light flashing on Carol's wrist as well.

"Yes, it's an old single-cab pickup, good for an old single guy like me. We are going to be stopped soon, lady. Look at your tracker flashing!"

Arriving beside the old blue Ford, Carol turned to him and pulled a knife out of her purse.

"What the hell!" Frank gave a started yelp as she yanked his hand and took a quick swipe at his wrist. The blood poured onto the pavement. She pulled out a handkerchief and quickly bound his arm with it. *He's got to get his reaction time up around this woman.*

"I removed your tracker. It's right beside the wrist bone and away from the big artery thank goodness. Now you do me." She handed him the bloody knife. Frank took it and looked into her clear blue eyes (*What a lovely blue.* He hadn't noticed before.) They looked sane, which was not quite how he was feeling. No use telling her he couldn't do it; during his farm days, he'd handled a scalpel more than once castrating pigs. With a quick swipe, he removed her flashing tracker. She gave him another handkerchief to bind around the oozing wound.

They piled in and Frank started the truck.

"So, we are going to Mount Sunapee, is that the idea?" he asked.

"Yes, I stumbled on a confidential video with security officials discussing the settlement. Apparently, they found slips of paper in old survivalist manuals in the library. I copied the message down and put it on your windshield," Carol said as she fiddled with the vintage CD player.

Pressing play, honkytonk fiddle music filled the cab. Frank drove his truck quickly towards the highway. No one was chasing them. Perhaps the alert had been cancelled after leaving the trackers in the parking lot. He imagined the Connected Corp management laughing about two old fogies having an affair in the parking lot.

"Why me?"

"I've been watching you for a while. Your vintage truck, that speakeasy with old-timers, plus I like your cowboy boots. I figured you were a good bet."

She put a hand on his thigh and smiled at him. Frank felt his leg burning under her fingers, and a warmth in his heart.

"A good bet for what?" He'd finally found his voice.

"As someone who'd risk everything to live free, of course."

Frank reached across her lap and opened up the glove box. He took out the bottle of whiskey sitting in there and handed it to her.

"Crack open the bottle, Carol. We are going to live free or die. And enjoy every minute of it." A grin spilt his wrinkled face as the miles of concrete disappeared under the pickup truck's old tires.

ACROSS SIX FEET OF SPACE

M.A. LANG

About the Author:

M. A. LANG is a writer living in northwestern Pennsylvania. She works her writing into her day job as a vocational instructor and educator.

Faced with the prospect of more time available at home due to the quarantine, M.A. took the productivity opportunities available and ran with them. Many of the ideas in "Six Feet of Space" were, so to speak, ripped "straight from the headlines" and then imbued with the worst-case scenarios typical of the dystopian tale. Truth, however, is often truly stranger than fiction, and the lives of Randolph and Celeste are perhaps uncomfortably close to ours.

M.A. is also a photographer, self-styled yogi, mandolinist, banjo picker, and liberal rabble-rouser. She has also had writing published in *Baily's Beads, Literary Yard, Quail Bell* Magazine, *cc&d, Page & Spine,* and *Clawfoot Press.*

She can be reached via @merannelang on Twitter and by searching Meredith Anne Lang on Facebook. More of her writing can be found at https://giftfromthesea.wordpress.com/.

Across Six Feet of Space
M.A. Lang

"SIX FEET! YOU – STAY SIX FEET AWAY! HEY!"

Randolph felt the end of a metal stick poke him in the belly. He shuffled his feet back to stand dutifully on the X marked on the ground. He looked into the eyes of the military policeman glaring at him from the other end of the pole. Eyes were all you could see of a person's face these days. Randolph's glasses fogged up with his heavy breaths. He reached a finger underneath the strap of his mask to wipe away a streak of sweat.

His eyes lowered down to the ID badge on the officer's chest. Name, address, phone number, occupational title, digital ID number, color photograph: a two-dimensional reminder of a person's appearance in the public sphere.

"Boy, you heard me?"

"Yes, sir, I'm sorry."

Randolph stood in line on his X. He had almost missed his time slot. His grandmother would have reamed him out if they had to stretch their meager groceries out until the next time slot opened. The line of people ahead of him stood on their own respective X's, bags in hand. Randolph took off his glasses to wipe off the condensation. He fiddled with the list in his hand.

You have 45 minutes. His grandmother reminded him. *You get what we need and leave. Do not overstay your time. We must adhere to the Schedule.* The line of people moved forward slowly. You moved from X to X. You did not stand next to your neighbor. You did not speak to your neighbor; you could have yelled across the six feet of space between you, but the police discouraged this.

You did not leave your house and yard without permission. You scheduled any necessary trips within the master Schedule on the Network. You did not miss your time slot. If you did, someone else would take that slot, and you would have to wait for the next available one. Randolph's grandmother reminded him of this, as if it were something that he had not become accustomed to over the past five years. Everyone lived by this schedule. It kept everyone safely distanced.

The line moved forward. Patience was a virtue that had been thrust upon the populace since strict limits had been placed upon the number of individuals in any place at one time. You had to claim your spot. Unless, of course, you were one of the blessed people who could afford to have everything delivered and who, if necessary, were able to claim the best spots in the Schedule from access afforded by influence and faster computing power. Otherwise, you monitored what empty spots you could get, and jumped on them. Woe to you if you were late.

Randolph looked around at the sets of eyes of the people around him. The ID badges helped make identification easier since everyone's face was half obscured. *Remember your mask, Randolph.* He wouldn't be outside otherwise. Your house was the only place anyone would see your entire face in its natural form. Of course, you could always talk to people over the Network, and everyone did, but it was not the same. Real-life interaction was mostly nonexistent outside of your own family.

Randolph's grandmother started and ended every day by taking his face in her hands and stroking it gently with her care-worn, calloused fingers. She was his family, ever since his parents succumbed to the pestilence that now lived in the air, the silent, invisible invader that made people unable to breathe freely without fear.

Randolph now ran his finger along the edge of his mask, fitted snugly to his face, and held on with a strap that buckled above his left ear. It always left a mark on his face after he took it off. Everyone had the same kind. Randolph remembered the day the officials came to measure his face. He complained to his grandmother beforehand. She made him wear it all day that first time so that he would get used to it. Almost five years later, he was used to it, but it made the necessity no less pleasant. His grandmother had one, too, but as she rarely left the house, it received little use. So, Randolph stood in line.

He eventually made his way into the store, making sure to stay on the smaller X's that dotted the floor. If you strayed, the multitude of cameras hidden in the ceiling would read the barcode on your ID, and your name and infraction would be loudly projected to the entire store. Too many infractions, all logged into your personal record, stored in the government's vast databases, would result in your expulsion. You could not afford to be expelled. You followed the rules.

Randolph got what he needed and walked home, mindful to follow the markings on the sidewalk that kept everyone six feet apart. Except for the government officials and very wealthy, no one had private transportation; people could not be permitted to move freely.

Sometimes a neighbor would stop and greet you, feet on their marker, conversing over the distance. Your conversation would be brief. The roving bands of police and fleet of cameras would call you out for talking too long. You would keep moving. You would not touch each other. You would not try.

Randolph reached his house and unlocked the door. He wheeled his cart of groceries in.

"Grandma, I'm home."

He unbuckled his mask and placed it into the bin of daily disinfecting that sat near the front door.

She came over and gave him a quick kiss on the cheek.

"How was it? Find everything?"

"It was fine. As it is always is."

"Thank you for going. Is all your schoolwork done?"

"Yes, Grandma."

Randolph had about a year left of his mandatory education. Like almost all aspects of life, it had moved to the digital plane. The work was not difficult. Ever since the revolution, really a coup, that filled the vacuum left by incompetent and corrupt leadership in the face of the pandemic, education had been whittled down to the fundamentals, basic literacy and math skills, the rest filled by propaganda. Randolph was disgusted by the work. He usually finished it as quickly as possible, maintaining just enough attention to earn a passing score, to avoid hearing from the government monitors who assessed the work. There was no opting out. The new government wrote and designed the curriculum, making sure that their narrative of events became part of the life of the nation's youth. He knew that he should perhaps try harder, but he couldn't bring himself to fully submit to the government's version of events.

The viral threat that had begun spreading across the globe five years ago that had intensified day by day, spreading like wildfire and fanned into greater flames through natural mutations and human inaction, was here to stay. Nationally, the government did little to contain the pandemic in its early stages, and as people died by the score, the inept leadership passed around blame and made excuses. In this environment of fear and confusion, unrest grew, until finally, the day came when the crumbing edifice of leadership finally imploded. In its place stepped an authoritarian dictator who immediately ripped down the tattered fabric of society and began stitching a new one. It was an uncomfortable garment. No one wore it well, and five years on, it was only just beginning to fit.

"Are you sure? You always seem to finish so quickly." She gave him a quick kiss on the cheek.

"It's easy, Grandma."

"I know, but don't you think you should spend a little more time on it? You know what a good score will earn you."

"I can only stomach so much of the government's nonsense."

His grandmother followed up the kiss with a small, sharp tap on the cheek. "Hush, boy, with that talk! You know what trouble that will get you into."

A good score could potentially earn him a position within the government, the only entity where it was possible to obtain a job since all private occupations were eliminated. The wrong thing said to the wrong person in the wrong place would earn you arrest, imprisonment, re-education, banishment into the wide world, or outright execution, depending on the severity of the crime. Randolph's thoughts about the government's policies being exactly one of those wrong things. Randolph suspected that if his thoughts were to be discovered, he would simply be cast out of the city, being a teenage boy with no exceptional talents, money or connections. There were some days when Randolph thought he would be able to accept this fate for himself and share the same deadly peace his parents knew. But he realized he would never willingly accept such an outcome. His grandmother was his only family and he needed to stay for her. For her and for Celeste.

"I know Grandma, I know. I just..." he sighed deeply.

His grandmother looked at him with deep love from eyes that had seen so much. That she had to live out the rest of her days under such oppression, fear and sickness enraged Randolph, in the moments that he allowed such thoughts.

"You are such a dutiful young man. I know that you try your best." She gripped his hands in hers. "What are your plans for the rest of the day?"

"I'm not sure. Probably plan on chatting with Celeste. See if any other friends are hanging out."

"Have you heard anything more about your Pass?"

"No – I'm pretty low down on the totem pole. I may be waiting for a long time. You know how these things go."

Randolph sat down in front of the computer. Because a vast majority of life took place over digital signals and the vast miles of cyberspace, every household had access to a computer and the Network, the nationwide internet service. It wasn't the internet Randolph grew up with, however. Instead, it was controlled by the government and contained only access to services such as the Master Schedule that people used to make sure that equal spacing in public places could be observed, propaganda sites and the video chat service, simply called VidChat that was widely used to connect with others. Randolph logged in and clicked "Finished" next to the slot he had reserved for a grocery store visit. He checked in VidChat to see if Celeste was available (she wasn't) and then logged into Pass Services to check on the status of the travel pass that he had applied for nine months ago. It was still "Under Review." He sighed heavily.

"Grandma, I'm going to sit on the front porch." Randolph grabbed his mask and went out onto the narrow front porch and flopped into one of the chairs. He stared at the small stretch of grass that was the front lawn. There were no backyards now. Backyards held secrets. In backyards, you could not be seen easily. The only time you could reliably be outside on your own was on your balcony or your small front porch, bordered by a tiny strip of lawn and maybe a flower box or two. But even here, the virus lived in the air, and an unobstructed breath meant death in three weeks' time.

Randolph watched as a delivery vehicle from one of the state-run delivery companies rolled down the street. Randolph had often complained that they, meaning he, still had to go get all their supplies. *We don't have the money for that*, his grandmother often reminded him. And they didn't. Randolph and his grandmother, like much of the population, received money from the government, which allotted a basic income to all citizens based on the number of people in the household. This measure had become necessary since most people were afforded no other options for employment. The money was only just enough to continue to survive, however; no one Randolph knew could be said to be thriving. He heard stories though, he knew what everyone knew.

The inequality that had existed prior to the pandemic had grown exponentially in the past five years. An exceedingly small handful of people, mainly top government brass and those that paid them in groveling, sycophantic favors, sat on top of a vast nest of poverty. Those who had built their wealth by honest means suddenly found it pulled out from underneath them as the new regime instituted vast changes. The balancing out that was supposed to occur in times of crisis never developed; instead, the gap between rich and poor grew into a great chasm, exaggerated beyond reckoning, touching both the good and bad alike, and through some evil metric, left only the very worst climbing to the top.

"Randolph. Randolph!" His grandmother cried from inside the house. He jerked out of his reverie. "A message came up on the computer." She didn't trust the computer much, leaving Randolph to schedule the household trips. He had been able to coax her into a couple of VidChat sessions with his older sister and her son. He had not seen his nephew in six years, and this separation and absence cut him as sharply as any other restriction. Passes were hard to come by, though, and you couldn't travel anywhere without one.

Randolph got up and went into the house. He checked the screen. "Oh, it's Celeste." He sat down and took off his mask and clicked on the chat button. Celeste's face appeared on the screen. Her bright smile radiated. That smile, and his grandmother's eyes, were the only things that were able to find a way to Randolph's heart, the only light left from the dying sun of humanity.

He smiled back. "Hi, Celeste, how are you?"

"Good, I suppose. How was your day?"

"Oh fine, did schoolwork, got groceries. You?"

"Hmm...yeah, did some schoolwork, too. Cleaned. Watched my brother while my parents went shopping. They said there was a long line."

"Yeah, same here. Always is, though."

Celeste probably spent more time on her schoolwork than he did. There was some pressure from her parents to achieve. Achievement meant gaining notice from the government monitors, which meant the potential for recruitment, which meant the possibility of a government job, which meant more money and access to resources. Unless you were already part of the system, the government didn't offer jobs to adults. Their recruitment pool was young people finishing school – any further training would be provided on-the-job. Their future recruitment pool they grew with their curriculum, taking advantage of the malleability of young minds. There would be no lack of properly groomed minions.

Celeste didn't believe in the government's policies, though. She had told him as much in the last conversation they were able to freely have. Such things could not be said here, where every conversation was monitored. Randolph didn't know if she would cave to her parents' pressure, didn't know if she would accept a position if offered one, didn't know what that would mean for him if she did. Not that he would blame her if she chose that route, but there would be no future for them if she did. Not that they had any future now. They tried to schedule trips so that they had a chance to see each other in passing, but it was nearly impossible to grab a spot just because it was convenient for you. Your life had no plan of its own. The Schedule planned your life. The travel pass he had applied for was not on any official's to-do list. The distribution of Passes was as unequal as wealth and Schedule spots.

Randolph and Celeste chatted for a while, her bright smile and infectious laugh filling the dark void of Randolph's life. Celeste always managed to see the positive. She was a blessing. She was his savior.

"Oh, my mom's calling me. Chat tomorrow?"

"Sure."

"OK. I love you."

"I love you, too." The chat ended. *More than you know, Celeste.* Randolph stretched and went to help his grandmother make dinner.

Randolph sat with his grandmother on the couch to watch the news. This daily ritual helped fill the time, but Randolph doubted that the time was well spent. The media was one of the first industries taken over by the government after the coup. The main function of the news was to remind the people that the government was doing a superb job keeping the virus at bay and the death rate low. These two things were technically true, but they were an inevitable outcome of the elimination of personal liberties and freedom and a system that had reneged its responsibility to find a cure for the virus. They made it a point to note that the people who died of the virus every week did so through their own actions. People sometimes grew desperate. They went outside without their masks. Or, they went outside, took off their masks, and breathed in the air, consigning themselves to a slow, eventual death. Both these actions were illegal, but at that point, legality was moot. People had taken the only stand they knew and laughed the best they could in the face of both death and indefensible rule.

Control of the people was the government's sole aim. The so-called scientists in thrall to the government claimed that nothing more could be done. Randolph refused to believe this. His parents had refused to believe this, too. They had given their lives to the seeking of a solution and become early victims of a scourge that had now taken millions. They had watched as the virus spiraled out of control, aided by its own naturally evil nature, and exacerbated by the evil learned and kept in the hearts of men. Their death was a bitter blow and had done more to fuel Randolph's cynicism than the virus itself.

The main news story this evening was the arrest of two owners of a black-market grocery distribution ring. Such underground businesses were common ever since the government took ownership of all industry. While this ensured that people were able to supply their basic needs, it came with high prices, long waits, inefficiency and supply chain problems. Certain brave individuals, however, had found a way to create a clandestine economy by obtaining and selling items ranging from groceries and everyday supplies to luxury goods. There were even a few secret delivery companies if you knew the right people. This was an open secret. But it was a very dangerous game, both for the business owners and their customers. These unlucky fellows seem to have become overconfident and overstepped their bounds. The news program crowed about the continued success of the government's mission to eradicate "pernicious influences" from the streets. The anchors held a lengthy discussion about the possible punishments these men might receive. Randolph figured they would either be quickly executed or exposed to the virus, in which case they would languish for the next few weeks in a jail cell. Either way, they would not see the end of next month.

"These people are heroes."

"Boy! Keep those thoughts to yourself!"

"They are, Grandma!"

"Be that as it may, look what they have gotten themselves into."

His grandmother had warned and forbade him, at the outset of the pandemic, not to attempt to use one of these back-market businesses, no matter how tempting they may seem.

"You know what happens to customers who are caught, don't you?" He had nodded. "I don't want that to happen to you. I need you here Randolph. I love you." He had nodded again.

He had obeyed her wishes, though. He never tried to access the services of one of these underground businesses. Because, he admitted to himself, he needed her as much as she needed him. Their love held the world together. His love was all that there was.

The news story continued. Randolph felt his thoughts drift to Celeste. She was the other repository of his love. He longed to touch her, a deep, throbbing ache that never really went away. Their last embrace had been five years ago. A fleeting touch of the hands had been all that he could manage in the time since.

Late in the evening, after his grandmother had gone to bed, Randolph sat down at the computer and logged in to check the Schedule. He had an itch to scratch, an idea to try to bring to fruition. He scanned the Schedule. He stopped. There it was.

Two rectangles of a spreadsheet, two small, quadrilateral human lives. Two spots together at the same time. He frantically checked into VidChat and messaged Celeste. There was a chance that she was on. The message connected and her face came into view.

"Celeste, quick, check the Schedule!"

"What's up?"

"Tomorrow, on the way to the bakery. Two slots!"

Her icon appeared over the time slots.

"Put your name down! We can meet there!"

"What will I tell my parents?"

"That you are going to get bread."

"Um...OK."

Her name appeared in the space as she typed. CELESTE HARTMAN. Randolph immediately typed his name underneath. RANDOLPH PARKER. The Schedule saved their names. Done. 1:00-1:30.

Randolph exhaled. He ran his fingers over the back of his neck. His fingers grazed over the small bump at the bottom of his hairline. He would be caught. They knew where you were. At all times, the government knew where you were.

From 1:00-1:30, Celeste Hartman and Randolph Parker would be within six feet of each other. It was not only the Schedule. After the coup, the government instituted a nationwide tracking system. Expending an untold amount of money and effort, officials paid a visit to every single individual and, holding them down if necessary, inserted a microchip into everyone's body. An extensive network of satellites and computers followed everyone's movements. Any scientific effort that could have been used to combat the virus had been diverted. The accumulated stolen wealth from the labors of the citizenry – "redistributed" was the official watchword – funded the vast surveillance systems of the government. Officials claimed that these measures were necessary to control the spread of the virus. That ship had sailed through – the virus was everywhere. Control of the people was the actual goal. It was met with astonishing success.

Randolph spent the remainder of the day's waking hours and the next morning reaching his hand around his head and working the buckle of his mask loose with one hand. By the time he had to leave to meet Celeste, he could unfasten it in a matter of seconds.

"Grandma, I'm going!"

His grandmother walked over. She looked at him gravely. She did not say anything, but she knew his trip was about more than bread. She took his face in her hands and looked into his eyes. He tried to divert his gaze, but her eyes were steel traps. He had no doubt his father had known this look well.

"You be careful, OK? You finish your errand and come back here right away."

"Yes, grandma. I'll get a couple of loaves if I can."

He followed the line of X's on the way to the bakery, stepping carefully from one to another. He stopped and waited for others to pass by. You did not get close to others. He eventually came to the front of the bakery. Celeste was already there, standing nervously on her X, fiddling with a bag in her hands. Randolph exhaled slowly, fogging his glasses.

"Hello, Celeste."

She looked up. Little lines around her eyes betrayed her hidden smile.

Randolph stood on his X, twisting his fingers indecisively. He could not stay here. You did not stand in one place aimlessly. He took a deep breath. His love leaped across six feet of space, and he followed it. Two large steps brought him in front of Celeste. Her eyes widened in surprise. He threw his arms around her and embraced her with five years' worth of passion and fury. He buried his face in her neck. He reached his practiced hand around the back of his head and loosened the buckle on his mask.

He was jerked back violently as two pairs of hands grasped

his arms. He felt their gloved fingers dig into his biceps. Lights flashed behind him and a voice boomed from a loudspeaker.

"Randolph Parker! You are hereby accosted for violating the social distancing guidelines!"

"Celeste, I love you! Celeste, I love you! You know that, right?" Randolph twisted and pulled against the hands that dragged him backward. Celeste stood with her arm outstretched. He struggled against the grip of the police who pulled him away from her, toward the patrol van. "Celeste, try to contact my grandmother! Tell her where I am!" Celeste nodded numbly.

Randolph hoped Celeste was able to contact his grandmother. He hoped she would understand. He hoped he would be able to explain his actions. He hoped she would be able to take care of herself during what he hoped would be a brief detainment. He hoped Celeste would continue to love him. He hoped he survived. He hoped all these things because hope was the only thing he had left to give to the world. Hope and love to a world that deserved neither, hope and love that leaped across six feet of space.

TOUCHING DREAMS

B.L. BATES

About the Author:

B.L. BATES started her career as an electrical engineer in the semi-conductor industry. After a head injury that took her sight, she returned to college to freshen her skills, then changed her direction to writing.

Since she'd begun reading at a young age, reading sci-fi, fantasy and horror, her choice of the speculative fiction genre seemed natural. With her trusty screen reader, she started taking Internet courses to enhance her fiction writing skills. She's had several short stories and a novel published so far. Also available as an online course, she's written "How to Write Believable Disabled Characters," to aid other writers wanting to use disabled characters.

Along the way she spent time as the chair of an organization providing recreational activities for the disabled, wrote and produced a local weekly TV program interviewing agencies providing the disabled services, and worked for a bit with Operation Relay, an AT&T service for the hearing challenged.

When not writing, she likes to cook, knit, and spend time either outdoors or with family. She lives in Southeastern Massachusetts with her husband.

Touching Dreams
B. L. Bates

FRIDAY HAD ENDED. ALL GWEN NEEDED TO DO WAS TO CHECK the projects in the lab, gather the things she needed to take home, and then, she'd have two days free. But, the thought of what waited for her at home made Gwen's heart almost miss a beat. Still, she kept her professional mask on and stuck the key into the door of her office.

"Gwen. Glad I caught you," Amy's voice came from behind her.

Inwardly, Gwen flinched hearing that voice. But when she turned around, her features remained placid.

Amy, the last person she wanted to see, always turned up at the worst moments. Her reputation as a troublemaker often necessitated her leaving early. Why had she stayed?

Start out positive.

"Amy. I wanted to congratulate you on your advanced testing technique. It'll make testing for the virus easier and quicker."

As usual, Amy wore only scrubs, had no mask, had her hair pulled back by an elastic, and only wore the thin gloves. In addition to her lab coat, Gwen wore the N95 mask and the thicker gloves, as well as a cloth kerchief protecting her hair.

Amy smirked. "Glad you brought that up. I brought it in under budget, and in a timely manner."

Gwen's eyebrows rose. "Really?"

Gwen swallowed a sigh. Another lecture from a colleague jealous of her fame, limited though it was. Her major project, while managing to stop the expansion of the virus, didn't kill it off. For some people it'd made their suffering worse, and it often still ended in death. Her background in genetic engineering had suggested several genetic alterations that could cause the virus to 'eat itself,' but she hadn't yet found the right one. So, those willing to be her patients had remained limited.

Amy's look of triumph turned into a sneer. "Yes. It allowed me to determine that you are now positive for the virus. And since the lab must remain pristine, your lab privileges are revoked starting Monday, as the admin offices are closed for the weekend."

Gwen felt a sharp pain in her chest. She didn't let it show. "Are you sure? And you need a supervisor's authorization to keep me from the lab section."

Amy thrust a folder at her. "Here are your results. And the lab supervisor's authorization." Amy slashed her hand across the air in front of Gwen, coming well within Gwen's comfort zone. Gwen grabbed the folder.

Amy's finger jabbed at Gwen. "Your former success has not only gone to your head; it's warped your judgement. You set the deadlines you failed to meet. You made those claims you never fulfilled. And you now have the virus that you said you'd master. Boo-hoo. I'm so sorry." She pretended to wipe away tears.

Gwen spoke through gritted teeth, keeping eye contact with Amy. "I've discovered several variations to my original model for the destructive virus. All I need is to find the right one."

"Then you'd better be able to find it from home. Because that's where you'll be working, from now on." She sneered at Gwen, pivoted, and left, with a spring to her step.

Gwen closed her eyes and took several deep breaths. She unlocked her office door, turned on the lights and sat at her desk. She clicked on the screen, and her five-year-old daughter, Trish, making cookies, disappeared, leaving the desktop.

It had come: the day she'd dreaded. In order to keep her name away from whatever they took from her notes and twisted for their own advantage; she must make sure they had nothing to find. If she did end up finding a cure, she'd announce it from an undisclosed location. To think it had come to this.

She copied the files she'd worked on for the last couple of weeks to flash drives, did a quick check of her emails, nothing urgent, and then clicked to reformat the hard drive.

She'd hoped the United Solutions Lab wouldn't find out about her positive reading for at least a couple more days. Always, she'd worn a mask and gloves whenever she left her office, so it hadn't seemed out of place for her to do so. But, Amy's more in-depth testing meant her time had run out. She had to move. Tonight.

She folded two cartons into shape and put in her personal books and references. Removing the pages from her experimental files, she put the empty file holders back into the bookcase and the inside pages into large envelopes.

As the hard drive reformatted, she put the boxed books on the top of her desk, added her coffee mug, the envelopes, and some personal items, and taped the boxes shut.

Next, she went to her lab. Not many projects had their own lab, but hers did. The virus had gone on for so long, projects pertaining to it had received priority.

A check of her experiments-in-progress showed two with promising results. She took samples from each, stuck them in a cryo unit, then put every experiment into the hazardous waste container. After, she put all the containers into the sterilization unit and turned it on.

She made copies of her initial findings onto flash drives, to mail them to others she trusted. Hoping they could find a cure, or a way to slow down the virus' progression. She copied all her data, her conclusions and told them to use the information in any way they saw fit.

Using the same procedure as she had on her office computer, she reformatted the lab computer's hard drive, too. After putting her written results into manilla envelopes, she stuck them in the box with the cryo container.

At the supply room, her last stop, she gathered the chemicals and solutions she'd need for what could turn out to be her last experiment, ever.

Borrowing a dolly from Maintenance, she put the four boxes of her items and supplies and loaded them into her car. Bringing the dolly back, one of the maintenance men came out to get it. "Another working weekend?" He smiled.

"You guessed it, Harry. No rest for the wicked."

Harry laughed. "If you're wicked, then none of us has a chance. Get some rest this weekend." He turned back to the building, waving.

Gwen got into her car and stared at the United Solutions Lab building. Over the year since the virus had emerged, she'd spent more time here than anywhere else.

And, she'd do it all again, if it meant her daughter wouldn't get the virus. If only.

Resting her forehead on the steering wheel, she realized no one outside those who would receive the flash drives, could reproduce her results.

Amy had hit one nail on the head, it could take years to develop a working vaccine. Gwen had thought it would take three months or less to find a cure. When it first came out, the virus' mutation rate fell well below the normal range for viruses. Then, for some as yet unknown reason, it began to mutate. And most of the mutations adversely affected the human population.

Over the past several days, she'd managed to get several pharmacy scripts for prescription drugs and supplies. She'd use them tonight, and hope for the best.

She stopped at a pharmacy not near her neighborhood and filled the purloined scripts.

Taking a circuitous route home, she drove into a nondescript part of town, and pulled into a driveway with a garage attached to a small cape.

Using the electronic opener, she drove into the garage, then lowered the main door. It took her two trips to bring her supplies through the breezeway and into the kitchen of the house.

Still wearing the mask and gloves, she put the supplies in the smaller bedroom, then removed her mask and gloves. She washed the gloves and took off the mask, hanging it over the sink.

Sitting in the small living room, she went over her plan. This house, was not the address on her work records. She'd left that apartment months ago in case something like this happened.

She'd changed all her bank accounts, and paid off and canceled the credit cards she'd used.

She'd started other credit cards using her first initial, her middle name, and this address.

In order to complete her plan for testing her cure, she'd have to get Trish out of the COVID ward at the Good Samaritans Clinic. Because of her heart problem, Trish had succumbed to the virus after being exposed, during a school trip, before the virus became wide-spread. She'd stayed at the clinic since then, not getting worse, but never getting any better. But, last week her physician, Dr. Mullen, had told Gwen Trish may succumb at any time. The child's heart condition, a gift from her father, Gary, made it almost impossible for the normal trial cures to work.

She'd visited Trish every day. Lately though, even through a plate of polymer, she'd seen her daughter begin to deteriorate. That had spurred her on, had redoubled her efforts. She'd almost found a genetically engineered version of the virus that worked. Should she try it without even confirmation by simulation? She no longer had the luxury of choice in the matter.

When her long hours and intensified efforts to find a way to stop the virus hadn't brought the results she'd wanted, she'd almost given up. But some strains of the genetically engineered virus might work on Trish. Her mother's instincts took over, and she'd worked exclusively on those strains best suitable to help her daughter. She'd chosen her path; she must see it to its conclusion.

She smiled, remembering the apartment she, Gary, and Trish had shared. Though she and Gary never married, she'd thought Gary truly cared for Trish. But even before she came down with the virus, he'd blamed her, her lack of care for Trish, and moved out.

His job as a salesman for a local software company necessitated his time away from home, but even when he worked in the area, he seldom spent time in their apartment.

So, she hadn't tried to call him when Trish came down with the virus. He would have said it was her fault. He had a stubborn streak a mile wide; once his mind was made up, it remained so, despite any evidence to the contrary.

When he'd found out about Trish, she sent him updates on Trish's condition every week or two.

Finding out he'd spent the majority of his free time with a woman out to find a wealthy husband, she'd withdrawn her share of their money from their joint accounts and started accounts in just her name.

Gary had called her then, accusing her of ignoring their original vows, taking his assets, and more.

She'd copied their bank records, the payments for their joint ventures, and showed she'd paid every month, not him. She included the phone number of her attorney.

He'd never called again. Not on any Christmas. Not on Trish's birthdays. Not on any other special days.

Trish pretended not to notice. But Gwen knew her young heart broke every time he didn't call.

Gwen needed to do something before trying out her cure on Trish. And the urge to say good-bye to Gary haunted her. A walk on the dark side might fill her emptiness.

She pocketed the flash drive specially formatted for use with the holographic suite she and Gary had worked on. Though he'd gotten the credit, she knew the entire system inside and out.

Since the start of the virus, she'd longed to touch another human being. At first, hugging Trish allowed her to hold things together. Now, with Trish in the clinic, she hadn't touched another human in such a long time.

And, the person she wanted to touch the most remained Gary.

Even though he'd left her at the altar. Even though he hadn't shown up for Trish's birth. Even though he'd ignored her and taken up with some floozy. She still loved him, and supposed she always would.

Not only was Lady Love blind, but completely crazy as well. She needed a good smack across the back of her head. Gwen wished she had the courage to do that.

But she still needed to say good-bye to Gary.

After midnight, a section of the downtown area opened up for business. Instead of the drinking, gambling, and other vices, shops now provided: hair salons, tattoo parlors, places to sit and eat and drink, and other activities not seen for many months. The local youth, instead of forming gangs, had posted themselves throughout the neighborhoods, acting as lookouts for the police or other authorities. Bird calls, whistles, and loud music indicated an unwanted person approaching. Since the lookouts didn't congregate, often made their way through backyards, and wore dark clothing, the police picked up none, and noticed very few.

The small businesses put in a percentage of their profits to pay the lookouts, keeping everyone busy and satisfied.

Gwen didn't often come to this district, but everyone needed to make a living. She wanted to support those trying to better their situations. Some found the government dole too much to stomach. Some found the necessity of constant unemployment checks repulsive. Some found the idea of depending on someone or something else unpalatable. Especially the craft people. It did no good to make crafts, ornaments, and other decorative pieces if no one came by to purchase them. Without clients, nothing got sold and inventory built up.

Those supplying personal care, massages, haircuts and styling, facials and other spa functions, needed a constant supply of customers. Though their timeframe had changed to the overnight hours, these functions continued to exist. To proliferate.

Each house or apartment with something for sale put an electric candle in one of the front windows. Different colored 'flames' indicate the various categories.

Red for hair, facials, nails, and tattoos. Green for food; mostly small cafes with food, drink, and music; often located in basements and garages. Blue for massage, or just sitting and talking to someone.

And since the virus' arrival, a new section started up. Purple candles stood for the new electronic 'sensations. Some of these holographic experiences provided episodes that included all the senses.

Gwen ambled down the narrow side streets near the docks, keeping an eye out for a certain set of candles. Some providers had recently started using more than one candle if their cliental raved about them.

The people passing her going in the other direction had partaken of the services offered in the neighborhood. The scents of massage oils, hair spray and other natural fragrances came from the passers-by. Odors of Cajun, Portuguese, and other ethnic cooking wafted by from the backyards of several tenements. While no one stopped to chat, the atmosphere gave off an aura of cheer and welcome.

In the corner window on the second floor of a well-kept tenement, three purple candles shone into the night. Just above the sill the Letters SD. 'Safe Dreams'. The place she wanted.

At the front door, she rang the second-floor doorbell.

"How can I help you?" Trevor's voice asked.

"Hi. It's Gwen. I'd like a good dream for tonight."

"Gwen! Come on up." The door unlocked and she went inside.

The inner door opened up into a small but elaborate living room.

Trevor, wearing a chocolate silk suit, a shade darker than his skin, and a golden ascot a bit lighter than his hair and eyes greeted her with a wide smile. Aware of her aloofness, he nodded and gestured her to a seat.

"Ah, snug bunny, it's so good to see you."

His smile offset his remark that she always wore more than enough isolation gear, as he called it. A survivor of the virus, he neither wore, nor cared to, any clothing or gear associated with isolation. But he never turned anyone away who did.

Gwen still wore a kerchief, mask and gloves; the same as she did at work, though not the same ones.

"What brings you here tonight?" Trevor made eye contact.

His apartment filled with the odors of Cajun cooking and waxy, floral scents, was lit only by candles. Plants occupied almost every free space.

Gwen sighed. "I'm about to make some major changes in my life, and I need a good dream before I start."

"I have an entire category of fantastic dreams..."

Gwen shook her head. "No. I brought my own." She held up her hand to forestall his protestations. "I'm aware of your format; I helped establish it. I need this to say goodbye to an old part of my life and move on."

"Gary?" Trevor's eyes shone with sympathy.

Gwen sighed. "Is it that obvious?"

Trevor's smile brightened his face. "Only to those of us who know." He sat down across from her. "How's Trish?"

Gwen blinked back tears. "She has some good days. But I can see the beginning of her deterioration." For just a moment, she thought how great it'd feel to hug Trevor. Their eyes met, but she shook her head.

Trevor nodded, then checked his watch. "We need to get you set up. I have other customers coming."

Gwen took out her wallet. "What do I owe you for this?"

Trevor held out his hand. "Nothing. If anything, I should be paying you. Without you, I'd never have started up this place."

Gwen put her wallet back and tried to smile. "Thanks."

He rose and gestured her to follow. They walked down a narrow passage into a good-sized room. Electronic equipment lined two walls. In the center of the room, something resembling a spacesuit stood, suspended by cables and cords. A holosuit.

Trevor held out his hand. "You know the drill. Everything comes off. Think of what you want to dream of before you go under. I'm giving you the deluxe dream length, three hours. Make good use of the time."

Gwen put the flash drive into his hand and pulled out a chair to put her clothes on. By the time she'd taken off her boots and socks, Trevor had left.

She removed the rest of her clothes and unzipped the holosuit. Stepping in backward, she slipped her arms into the arms, pulled up the zipper, attached the goggles, then the helmet.

Encased in the suit, she pulled on the gloves and leaned backward.

The pulley system that kept the suit suspended, lifted her off the floor and rested her against an inclined ramp.

After a short period of disorientation, Gwen said, "Ready."

Trevor's voice said, "Close your eyes and breathe deep. Visualize where you want to be and with whom."

She did.

THE SKY ABOVE THE BEACH, JUST BEFORE SUNSET, SHONE WITH bands of red, yellows, and oranges across the undersides of the clouds. A warm breeze wrapped around her. The tide coming in, the cries of gulls, and the wind made the only sounds.

Looking down, she wore the pale blue sundress and matching shawl Gary liked.

"Good evening, beautiful." Gary came up behind her and put his hands on her shoulders. His touch warmed her shoulders and her heart.

He turned her around and they kissed. A soft, gentle kiss to start, morphing into one of passion.

She wanted this so much, but not yet.

She put her hands on his chest and pushed him away, noting he wore the green shirt, her favorite, under a nylon jacket. "We have the whole evening. Don't rush things." She took his hand and they walked along the beach.

When they'd gotten away from others and stood alone on the beach, they removed their shoes and ran through the water. Gary halted her near where the river emptied into the ocean. A mother duck waddled by, her younglings following in a line.

Later, they dried their feet, put back on their shoes and Gary drove them to a cozy nearby restaurant.

At the restaurant, one of their favorites, they ordered seafood. Gary requested a swordfish steak, and Gwen shrimp scampi. They ate, talked, and laughed like they had in the beginning of their relationship.

After Gary had driven them back to their apartment, they paid the babysitter, and Gwen checked on a younger Trish.

In their bedroom, they spent a lot of time just touching each other, removing clothing, caressing and kissing. She tried to imprint every sensation into her memory, to keep forever.

When he entered her, she came almost immediately. When she came again, he joined her. Gary fell asleep first, and Gwen lay in his arms, wishing this would never end. But it did. It had....

Gwen got up, dressed, and left the bedroom, the apartment, and the simulation. By the time she'd gotten out of the holosuit, tears streamed down her cheeks.

She left a note for Trevor and a $100 bill inside.

On the drive to the clinic, she played back the memories of her "experience." She kept coming back to the mother duck with her ducklings. Something about following each other. A sequence.

Another thought rose to the surface. Two of her samples had attacked the virus. Maybe if she used them in succession, they'd kill the virus. Her mind played with options and it came to her. She had a possible inoculation to use against the virus.

She had all the ingredients to produce the inoculation at the house. It would work. It had to.

PULLING INTO THE GOOD SAMARITAN CLINIC'S PARKING LOT after 1 AM, she parked in the back under a tree and next to the dumpster. As she reached the staff door, she looked back and couldn't see her car. Good.

The scrubs she wore were the same ones she'd used during her medical training she'd taken while getting her genetics degree. Her hair, pinned up under a scrub cap and her ID worn on a lanyard around her neck would allow her entrance into the clinic's COVID unit. Access to Trish.

Carrying Trish's sweat suit and sneakers in a cloth bag, she entered the clinic. Once inside she put on her reading glasses as a further disguise. Walking by the receptionist's desk, she noted Emily, the gate-dragon, getting ready to go on break.

After Emily had left, Gwen slipped into the COVID unit, heading for the children's ward.

Trish's room was in the back corner near an emergency exit. Opening the door to Trish's room, without making noise, she entered and stood, staring at her daughter.

Trish's eyes looked bruised, and she'd begun losing weight. Maybe having her hand forced would turn out okay. Maybe.

She set the monitoring to 'standby', leaving it on. A beeping would start after a half hour or so, but they'd be long gone by then.

Holding Trish's arm still, she removed the IV, and heart monitors. She'd gotten Trish into her sweat suit before the girl opened her eyes.

Mom? "Trish's eyes remained at half-mast.

"Shhh. We're leaving. I'm taking you home." She put on Trish's sneakers, giving thanks she'd chosen the Velcro ones.

"Good. I don't like it here." Trish held out her arms.

Gwen slipped her arms through the sleeves of her jacket and picked Trish up.

Holding her daughter sent waves of joy through her. She remembered the last time they'd touched, when the ambulance had come to bring her here. Hugging Trish close, she took several minutes just to hold her.

Checking the corridor and finding it empty, she strode to the emergency door, cut the alarm with the bolt cutters she'd brought and slipped out with Trish.

ON THE DRIVE BACK TO THE HOUSE, GWEN WENT OVER THE preparations she'd made before picking up Trish. She'd calculated the proper amounts of her cure to put into the IV bags for each of them. The amount was determined by their weight, age, and the severity of the virus they'd contracted.

Each IV should last for hours. She would set an alarm to ring just before it'd finished. Then, she'd switch the bags and the second part of her 'cure' would start.

She'd gone over the calculations again and again, making sure she'd made no mistake.

After adding the calculated amounts of the cure into their IVs, she'd put the IVs into the small refrigerator in the room that would be Trish's.

Despite going over the calculations many times, an unspecified threat lurked at the edges of her consciousness. She willed it away. She'd done everything right. They'd both survive.

When they pulled into the driveway to the house she'd recently bought, Trish woke up.

"Where are we?" A look of confusion crossed her face. "This isn't the apartment building."

"I rented this house so we can be together, while you get well. We don't want nosy neighbors bothering us, right?"

Trish nodded. "Want to be with you."

Gwen opened the passenger door, undid Trish's buckle for her car seat, and picked her up, not quite believing she held her daughter.

Once inside the house, Gwen brought Trish to her bedroom.

"All my things are here." A smile lit Trish's face.

"That's because it's your room."

"I'm hot. Too many clothes." Trish threw her jacket to the floor and pulled the sweatshirt over her head.

Gwen helped Trish out of everything except her underwear. Then she handed her a tee shirt.

Trish put it on Grinning. "You've got to wear one just like this." She held out the Disney tee shirt of Minnie Mouse.

"Warm enough?"

Trish nodded and climbed into the bed. About to scratch her arm, she stopped. "Mom?"

"Yes, honey?" Gwen put Trish's dirty clothes into the laundry.

"I've still got this thing in my arm. Can you take it out?"

Gwen felt blood rush to her face. How much should she tell Trish? She didn't want her scared, but should she know? "Not yet.

She smiled to take away the sting. "Tonight, you're still going to need an IV."

Trish scrunched up her face. "Why?"

"Because tonight, I'm going to sleep with you, and we're both going to have IVs. And, in the morning, we'll both be well." Or both dead. No. Don't even consider that option.

Gwen extended the IV pole from the headboard where she'd attached it." This one's for you."

On the other side of the bed, she pulled up hers. "And this one's mine."

"If my arm's taped down for the IV, I can't hug you." Trish got into bed and waited until Gwen had hung the bag containing the cure to her pole, attached the Velcro to her arm and inserted the IV.

"It's okay. We'll be close enough to touch."

Gwen removed her clothes putting on a tee shirt like Trish's, with Minnie Mouse on it. She hung the bag containing the first step of her cure from the hook on the pole.

Getting in on the other side of the bed, she attached the Velcro to her own arm, then inserted her IV.

This had to work. She couldn't make another mistake, not with her daughter's life at stake.

The calculations had all worked out. The initial period of time for the genetically engineered virus to take effect was around four to six hours. She and Trish should wake up sometime tomorrow. Then she'd change the IVs and spend time in bed with Trish. They could watch TV or do some of the activity books she'd bought for this time. If everything went right.

It had to go right. She wouldn't believe anything else could occur.

Slipping down beside Trish, she put an arm around her. "Comfortable?"

"With you here, yes."

Gwen closed her eyes and tried to calm her racing heart.

"Mom?" Trish whispered.

"Yes?" Gwen whispered back. A smile came to her, knowing what Trish would say next.

"Remember what you say when it's bedtime?"

Gwen smiled. "Make a wish, Trish."

"I want to have good dreams, and have a good fairy come and cure us."

"Do you think that'll happen, Mom?"

Gwen stroked Trish's long hair, reveling in the touch. "I'm sure it will. I know the fairy personally; her name is Hope."

"A fairy named Hope. I like her." Trish's voice began to slur.

Gwen kissed Trish's forehead and kept contact with her.

She'd missed touching others so much. "Sleep well, Trish. Wake up tomorrow on the path to health. And may the good fairy, Hope, visit you tonight," she whispered."

In the morning she awoke to find her daughter's eyes gazing into hers.

DISTRACTION

DAVID MANFRE

About the Author:

A lifelong resident of New Jersey, DAVID MANFRE specializes in stories that take place in familiar settings. He uses those locales because he believes that placing characters and events there helps to make his writing immediate and lively. A major theme in many of David's stories involves the struggles of everyday people as they confront adversity in their lives. During the course of most of his written pieces characters face such problems as prejudice, bullying, and difficulties arising from problematical relationships.

David enjoys visiting the Jersey Shore, especially towns with commercial boardwalks or lively downtowns.

One of David's stories, "Fires of Spring," has been published in an anthology called *30 Shades of Dead*. He anticipates posting stories soon on Wattpad.

Distraction
David Manfre

JACK PASCOE FELT THE WIND BLOWING THROUGH HIS HAIR AS he walked down East Central Avenue in South Seaside Park. It was another sunny July day along the Jersey Shore. Despite the lovely weather, Jack hated that, even after more than eleven years, he felt compelled to have to hide the reason why he left his home. He didn't want to leave his home, but had grown oh so tired of being cooped up there. That had been his reality since the Coronavirus closed the state in 2020, as it had been the reality throughout the world.

Jack still found it unnerving, even after all these years, to see so few vehicles on the street on what had been a popular shore community. South Seaside Park had been somewhat popular through the 2019 season, the last one before the world shut down. Still, sea salt still penetrated the air as it left the Atlantic Ocean and Barnegat Bay. And Jack thought it was as strong as ever, though he knew they were muted somewhat by the smells of sunscreen oil and such foods as sausage, peppers, and onion sandwiches and pizza.

Jack did not know how he would be able to walk down the street without any police officers who might be in the area noticing him. He knew some had that skill, though was not one of them. For that reason, he walked in as unobtrusive manner as possible, making eye contact with no one. Every so often, he reminded himself that he could just tell any officer who stopped him he was getting breakfast for himself and a friend who had been living with him the entire time and was bringing it home.

Before he left home, Jack always made sure that he had his mask and his gloves with him in a pouch attached to a loop in his jeans and felt it should add authenticity to his claim. Having chosen elbow length gloves since he was wearing a sleeveless shirt, he did not wear them at the moment since he was not near enough to anyone to breath on or be breathed on by anyone else and he was not using his hands for anything.

The weather was Jack's motive for taking his motorcycle. He'd seen others wearing their motorcycle helmets in place of masks, only for the police to confront them and say they were not properly covered.

A lot of the buildings had darkened or boarded up windows, as was the case throughout Ocean County. It had taken Jack a while for him to catch on to the fact that the businesses were using technology developed covertly that projected previously recorded images onto windows. Those looking into the building from outside were led to believe that customers and staff were appropriately socially distancing and wearing masks.

A police car went by, and Jack sweated but continued walking, not paying attention to the cruiser. Once they had passed, he relaxed a bit. He had heard a rumor that there were officers who patronized nonessential businesses. On the one hand, he hoped that it was not true, because the police were held to a higher standard than the general public. On the other hand, he did understand since they were also human and had the same needs as anyone else.

Jack was short and a bit round, though he was working on losing weight, purchasing any exercise equipment he needed from the sporting goods store he had been working in part time until he had graduated college and full time from then until the economic shut down. He'd struggled for a while over whether or not to go back to work when his boss sent out a mass email. The store was reopening despite the laws not permitting it. His dilemma revolved around whether to stay home, safe from the virus, or going back to work in an attempt to gain a sense of normalcy. Besides, he needed a paycheck, and he was going stir-crazy doing nothing for so long. Eventually, he decided he had to save himself, both financially and mentally. Jack started patronizing other nonessential businesses for the sake of his sanity, justifying that decision by reminding himself that humans were social creatures.

Putting on his gloves and mask after his walk from where he parked, Jack entered Midnight Distraction Coffee Bar, a coffee shop established a month short of five years to the day before New Jersey shut down. Seeing the shop three quarters full, Jack was a bit nervous with people being under six feet from each other. Still, he entered, wanting to see his friend, Helen Lemar. It was rare, in Jack's experiences, to find a coffee shop that used regular plates, cups, and silverware for those who dined in, though Midnight Distraction did, and Jack liked that. It told him the owner and staff valued their customers instead of seeing them as dollar signs.

Jack removed his sun glasses, placing them on the back of his collar. He didn't see Helen or any other familiar face in the room. He was relieved that he did not see one particular person he was hoping to avoid.

"Over here, Jack." Helen's voice came from a table at Jack's left.

Jack approached Helen, hugging her when he arrived. Neither Jack nor Helen had married. Then again, neither of them had any use for romance. They each had a want and a need for a physical relationship, and turned to each other for that. Their relationship had begun while they were in college, having graduated one year before the nation had closed.

Jack and Helen sat and chatted. Jack had an ear on what those around them were saying. From what he heard, customers were placing orders, some to go, and people discussed their lives. No one expressed concern over getting caught dining in or serving the customers who were dining in, though Jack knew everyone was thinking it. And none of the voices sounded familiar, which was good: no one would be able to tell the police he or Helen were there. However, he knew he might, or might not, be missing a particular voice, perhaps belonging to someone who wanted to make his life miserable.

The counter was a pleasant place to sit. Jack never sat there whenever he knew he would be meeting someone there or when he walked in with someone, instead choosing a table since he liked sitting across from his dining companion. He never complained, though, if his dining companion wanted to sit at the counter.

Helen was nicely dressed, wearing what Jack thought was a new top. He figured she had gotten a new outfit from the shop in which she worked. The blouse's collar was high, the blouse itself didn't cling to her body, he felt the blue of the top made her eyes bright, and imagined she would look great with her mask off.

"My name's Isabella and I'll be taking care of you today. May I get you something?" A server, standing about three feet away from the table, had pretty red hair and pretty blue eyes, and Jack would have liked to see her smile. He did, however, like her face mask and her gloves showing off her pride in what he guessed was the college she'd attended. She had an electronic device in her hand Jack had seen before; he figured she would use it to enter in their order. He used something similar at his job.

Jack quickly checked out the menu while Helen ordered a brownie and a mocha that was made with regular coffee instead of espresso.

"The chocolate crumb cake and a caramel frappe made with regular coffee look great."

"Great choices. I'll be back with your pastries." Isabella walked off.

"I noticed you noticing her. Don't worry, I wouldn't object if you hooked up with her." Helen's lips were hidden, but Jack recognized her smile nonetheless.

"I might once I get to know her." Jack's eyes darted around the coffee shop, having heard and read over the years about police departments sending undercover officers into illegally run, nonessential businesses all over Ocean County, and other parts of the state. He had even known some people who've gotten arrested for operating or patronizing nonessential businesses.

Jack fidgeted with his gloves, knowing he should leave them and his mask on for health reasons but knowing wearing them was unnatural. And there were some in Midnight Distraction who'd taken their mask or gloves off but weren't currently eating or drinking. Each table had one pouch attached to each side of the table for people to place their gloves and masks while eating.

Someone set a bag on the table and started reorganizing the contents.

"What are you doing?" Jack was not surprised to see Walter Steptoe standing there.

"Go back to sleep." Walter slapped the back of Jack's head. Walter's behavior over the years, ever since they had met on nearby Pelican Island, where each one lived, had told Jack that Walter needed to be in control over every situation and he felt that anyone who was not with him was against him.

Jack did not understand how that was the case, though he knew there were some who did think that way. Walter had shouted at Jack, whom he almost hit one day when backing out of his driveway that day, claiming Jack was blind and should have seen him coming along instead of allowing himself to get hit and potentially damaging his car. Try as he may, Jack was not able to explain to Walter that a driver has the responsibility to not hit pedestrians. However, Jack had continued to claim that he was allowed to exit his driveway. Walter had even stated at one point that a lawyer had informed him that motorists were permitted to hit pedestrians if the motorist had the right of way as it pertained to other motorists, something that had never made any sense to Jack.

"Get away from us now, creeper. Social distancing." Jack slammed his fist on the table.

Walter continued to reorganize the contents of his bag.

Jack had tested using the legal system regarding Walter's claim about motorists having a right to hit pedestrians days after

Walter had made it and won. Jack still remembered the stunned and angry look on Walter's face as it appeared on his laptop screen, Jack and Walter each in their respective homes and the judge in his chambers for the trial, after hearing the verdict.

Isabella approached the table while Walter was still there and placed their pastries on the table. "I'll be right back with your beverages."

Walter looked directly at Isabella as he spoke. "Would you make sure his is in a to go cup and hand it to me? And I need you to get me a take-out container for his crumb cake while you are at it."

"I'm so sorry. I thought they were for you." Isabella had bent over as she looked at Jack. "Would you like something for yourself, sir?"

"They were, but anything his is communal." Walter reached his hand towards Isabella to touch her, but didn't, apparently thinking better about it.

Isabella looked at Walter, the top of her face scrunched in confusion.

"I have the same rights as you do, loser. Why do you think I haven't been visiting you at the barbershop?" Jack felt himself getting warm.

"Shut up. No one wants to hear you talk." Walter put a hand on Jack's shoulder.

"Get your hand off me. Aren't you supposed to social distancing?" Jack shoved Walter's hand off his shoulder.

"Go quarantine yourself." Putting his hand back on Jack's shoulder, Walter squeezed.

"Language, sir." Isabella looked at Walter. Apparently, she hated profanity.

"This guy's here to make others' lives easier. Don't waste yourself worrying about him."

Jack stood, Walter's hand falling off his shoulder. "I suggest you get out of my face now. I'm really tired of your torments. You'll never get anywhere in life being so rude."

Walter slugged Jack in the gut. "Don't mess with me again." Walter ripped Jack's mask off face.

Jack pulled his mask back on and, then, looking him in the eye, slugged Walter.

Walter's eyes narrowed and his face turned red. He grabbed Jack's shirt, flinging him to the ground. He stomped on Jack's back.

Putting his pain to one side, Jack turned and swung a leg, knocking Walter off balance but not knocking him down. He swung his leg again, getting the same result. He kicked Walter in the gut.

A woman got on top of Jack and another one grabbed Walter.

"Both of you, stop. Do you really want the cops to come? They'll arrest everyone merely for being here whether we did anything or not."

"All of this is just more of the same. He's been doing this for years, other than attacking me." Jack did not even try to get up despite wanting to, knowing that it added to his credibility if he didn't do anything to fight the person trying to keep him out of trouble.

"His things are communal property." Walter thrust his finger towards Jack, spit coming out of his mouth. "You could even argue that his body's also communal property. You could hit him and not get into trouble."

"You're wrong. He has the same rights as everyone else." Though she was still holding Jack down, the woman looked at Walter. "What I see is you feel a sense of entitlement and he hasn't stood up to you until now, but that doesn't change that you don't have a right to anything belonging to him while he does."

Jack knew the woman was right about Walter.

"What are you talking about? He doesn't have rights and people have extra rights around him." Spit continued to spew out of Walter's mouth and Walter still thrusted a finger at Jack.

The woman got off Jack, stood, and looked directly at Walter.

"You're out of here. Now. You're no longer welcome here. You are welcome to take your purchase with you, but I don't want you here anymore." Jack didn't know how someone so much smaller than Walter could effectively stand up to him. She did, though, seem to have a powerful personality.

"You don't work here. You can't tell me what to do." Walter waved the woman's comment off, continuing to look at Jack.

"You're right, but I own this business and I'm telling you you're no longer welcome here. Take your purchase and leave. And I mean now." A man wearing a face mask, gloves, and a button-down shirt, each with the coffee shop's logo, approached Walter.

"You have rights, as do I, as does everyone else here. Except for him. He does not have a single right." Walter took a step towards the owner.

"How does he not have rights?" The owner raised his eyebrows in a peak.

The woman who had held Jack down held out a hand in his direction, and, still in pain, he accepted the help.

"That's just the way things are. Maybe you don't know him well enough to realize that he doesn't have rights, but he doesn't." Walter smirked.

"That makes no sense. Just leave now." The owner pointed to the door.

Customers and staff members started calling out for Walter to leave, some making remarks about the possibility the police would come.

"You seem to be alone here, Walt. Make your life, and Jack's, easier and just leave here." Helen crossed her arms as she stood so close to Jack their arms touched.

"There's something wrong with all of you if you think this guy has rights." Walter picked up his purchase and reached for Jack's crumb cake.

Someone else grabbed the plate on which Jack's crumb cake sat.

"He's an exception. I'm leaving without my crumb cake only because you all are making my life difficult." Walter walked out the door without looking back.

"Making his life difficult?" He set the plate holding Jack's crumb cake down.

"I'm sorry for that, sir. What was that about, if I may ask?" The owner walked Jack to his table, Helen following. Jack appreciated what would've been the gentlemanly gesture about a decade earlier.

Jack sighed and shook his head. "I'm still trying to figure it out. I've been thinking about it since I first noticed it not long after we met, and that was during the first year of lockdown."

"Do you need anything else?" The owner looked at Jack and Helen.

"Just our beverages. I ordered a mocha and my friend ordered a caramel frappe, each one with coffee, not espresso." Helen turned to Jack. "How you doing?"

"I'll be fine soon. Thanks." Jack sat, as did Helen.

"I'll bring them out as soon as they're ready." The owner walked towards the counter.

Jack noticed each pastry was nicely decorated, as if he was sitting in a bakery. They each had chocolate frosting topped with candy on it.

JACK AND HELEN WALKED ALONG ROBERTS AVENUE, THE Barnegat Bay to their left swaying in the wake of the occasional boat. Admiring the scenery, Jack put his experience with Walter as far back in his mind as he was able. He knew there was the occasional police officer willing to help him with any of his problems, whether or not he was breaking the law by patronizing or working in a nonessential run business. These were probably the same ones who, allegedly, were patronizing nonessential run businesses. Still, it was just a matter of how to find any of those officers.

Jack knew the best way to get Walter out of his life permanently without risking getting arrested was to call him out on a crime he'd commit on Pelican Island. He also knew that that was not likely to happen any time soon. He always bothered him at a nonessential business.

Helen put a hand on Jack's shoulder. "I heard about a great bar in Bayville I want to try tonight. How about we grab some others and go?"

"Sounds great. What time should I pick you up? Or do you want to meet me there?"

"How about you meet me there at around eight? The food there's great. Ever hear of Eager Fork Pub?"

"I thought it really was closed." Jack thought for a moment. "Oh, they're good. They're real good."

Helen jerked her head to the right. "What was that?"

"What was what?"

"I heard something over there." Helen pointed to her right.

"Probably on one of the cross streets. Let's check it out. I parked near here." Jack headed towards the street on which he parked.

Jack saw upon arriving at the appropriate cross street his motorcycle's alarm blaring and Walter struggling to start the motorcycle.

"Hey, what are you doing?" Jack ran towards Walter.

"This would be a lot easier if you let anyone who wanted to take the bike know its startup code. Give it to me." Walter stood there looking at Jack, holding Jack's helmet at his side, his mask around his neck, his smile wide.

"No. Get away from my bike." Jack charged Walter, ignoring his gut and Helen's warning for him not to.

Walter swung the helmet, hitting Jack square in the face. Snorting, Walter turned his attention to the motorcycle.

Jack grabbed Walter's arm and pulled as his nemesis swung

his leg onto the motorcycle. Walter fell to the ground, a stunned look on his face. Jack thrust his helmet out of Walter's hand. "None of my property is communal, and neither is my body. You'll never take anything belonging to me or anyone else again. Understood?"

Walter continued to look at Jack if at a loss for words.

"Understood?" Jack projected his voice this time.

"Understood." Walter's voice was small.

"Good. Now, go on your merry way and try not to get into anyone else's stuff unless you are invited." Jack pointed away from himself.

Walter got up and ran off.

Once confident Walter was on his way, Jack went back to Helen.

"I was sure he wouldn't give in so quickly. In fact, I thought he wasn't going to give in. I bet you're proud of yourself." Helen smiled.

"Yeah, but I know not to get cocky. He'll be back. I just have to continue to standup for myself the same way I did today. Come. Let's continue on our stroll, unless you have something else in mind."

"Nah, let's stroll." Helen started walking again, Jack beside her, heading back for the bay and the beautiful scenery.

"How did Walter get here if he was planning on leaving with my bike? Or is it a matter of how he would retrieve his car if he'd leave it here?" Jack put voice to his thoughts after a minute of silence.

"My first guess is he was planning on asking someone to take him back here on another day so he could get his car." Helen thought about what she'd said, or so her facial expression told Jack. "He would have to come up with a good story to get someone to take him here. Why would he leave his car somewhere? And I doubt he'd walk the route."

A hot pain in Jack's back caused him to fall.

"Why?" Helen's voice squealed.

"He wouldn't lend me his bike. He got what he deserved."
Walter's voice was uneasy, shaky. "He made me do this. Why
didn't he just let me take his bike?"

"Get the knife out of my back." Jack reached behind him so
he could remove the weapon out of him.

"No, Jack. It's scissors. Don't touch it. It might do more
harm than good to take it out. I'll take you to the hospital."
Helen helped Jack up and started towards his motorcycle."

"I won't cry when he dies, and I want my scissors cleaned
before you return them to me." Walter's pride shone through his
voice.

"Ignore him. You'll survive. It looks superficial. Still, you
need a doctor, and now. I'll take you there." Helen walked Jack
back to his motorcycle then eased him onto it before getting on
in front and entered the code.

Jack knew Helen had never driven a motorcycle before, but
trusted her to drive it safely. He'd taken her out on it many
times. He held onto her out of safety and in an attempt to direct
his attention away from his pain, knowing his friend would do
what she could to get him to safety.

Jack hoped neither he nor Hele would get arrested for being
out despite not having an essential reason for being out. And he
was in too much pain to come up with an explanation to tell the
doctor for how he had been stabbed that would not get him or
Helen arrested.

"This is how our life is now, at least until this is over, if it's
ever over."

CHAPTER 16

A.R.R. ASH

About the Author:

A.R.R. ASH is a lifelong fan of both science fiction and fantasy, though he typically focuses his talents on writing dark, high fantasy. His first self-published novel, *The Moroi Hunters*, is available digitally and in print from www.lmpbooks.com. In 2020, he received a Silver Honorable Mention for the L. Ron Hubbard Writers of the Future Contest, first quarter, for his novella *Oneiromancy*. He continues to make progress on the sequel to *The Moroi Hunters* as well as on the first book of *The First Godling* trilogy.

CHAPTER 16
A.R.R. Ash

SITTING AT HIS OFFICE DESK, WARD "RUMOR" DREW quadruple-checked the time for the meeting in the email he'd received from a source calling herself or himself WhistlingVirologist. Three-fifteen. It was now 3:47 PM, and no word from this supposed source.

He swiveled in his chair to look out the third-story window. No pedestrians walked the sidewalks. Though some cars were out and about, the streets were eerily quiet—no incessant honking or shouts to hurry up or get out of the way. After a year and a half of near-quarantine conditions, most of the storefronts were shuttered.

"And in other news," came the anchor's voice from the flatscreen on the wall, "another state has filed for bankruptcy."

Ward swiveled to face the television and shook his head. "How'd it come to this?"

The anchor continued in his practiced cadence, "Ever since Congress passed the States' Insolvency and Bankruptcy Act three months ago, five states have filed for Chapter Sixteen bankruptcy protections—Alabama, Mississippi, Louisiana, Kansas, and, now, Georgia."

Well, there goes the neighborhood.

Ward said aloud, "I'll give 'im until four, then I might as well call it an early day."

Crossing his legs at his ankles, Ward put his feet on his desk, crossed his arms over his chest, and closed his eyes.

A soft beep from his laptop roused Ward at 5:00 PM. He yawned, wiped his eyes, and looked at the newest entry in his inbox from WhistlingVirologist@SecureMail.com. Sitting up straight, he clicked on the message.

Ward, if you're reading this, something's happened to me. This message was set to send automatically, and the link below will lead to a file that contains all the proof I managed to gather that COVID-19 was manufactured by my employer, BioPharma Research, Inc. The link will expire after a single use. Please don't let whatever happened to me be for nothing.

Constance P. Hobbs

a/k/a WhistlingVirologist

Ward leaned back in his chair, let out a breath, and ran a hand over his face. His heart beat in anticipation.

Could this be for real?

He'd once been a respected investigative journalist with an enviable career—a hardworking, pavement-pounding reporter like the early muckrakers. But his pursuit of a story about a secret lobbying campaign to pass a Constitutional amendment granting corporations the right to vote ultimately led to his disgrace and left him with his epithet. He'd done his due diligence, spent years tracking leads—everything seemed to check out. However, when the story fell apart in a spectacular way, he was discredited and ostracized from the reporting community.

If I were paranoid, I'd say that the entire amendment story had been fabricated with the sole purpose of discrediting me. Well, it worked.

Now, the only stories that found him were about lizard people infiltrating world governments or the U.S. government making secret deals with aliens or an uncharted island where Elvis, Princess Diana, Tupac, and Amelia Earhart sat drinking piña coladas together on the beach.

Could this be another one of those stories? Is this Constance the WhistlingVirologist just another crank?

Taking a deep breath and looking around the room as if spies or thugs from BioPharma might be lurking in his office, Ward clicked on the link and downloaded a .zip file. He scanned the file for viruses, then opened it.

It contained hundreds of documents—invoices, purchase orders, internal memos from BioPharma, and scientific data that he couldn't begin to understand. To confirm her identity, it even contained copies of the source's medical degree and dual doctorates in immunology and cellular microbiology, as well as excerpts from her HR file. The name on the degrees and on human resource documents was Constance Preston Hobbs.

He settled in to his chair and began reading. When the light from outside became too dim to light the room, he turned on his desk lamp without even thinking about the time. Only when he finally had to succumb to biological needs and get up from his desk did he notice it was the middle of the night.

The WhistlingVirologist—Constance—had been kind enough to leave copious annotations to the more technical documents. It appeared that several teams worked on modifying different aspects of an earlier strain of the coronavirus, but only the inner circle of scientists, including Constance, worked on the final phase of combining the parts into a functioning, novel virus.

The memos were rather straightforward. They revealed talking points and false information to leak to the media and the government—even going so far as to name the individuals to receive the information—implicating China as the source.

However, most interesting to Ward were the supplier and payment documents. If he was good at one thing, it was following the money.

But what made absolutely no sense was why. What reason could BioPharma have to create the disease? To then sell a vaccine? That made the most sense, but Ward could find no mention—none at all—about a vaccine.

Ward sucked in a breath, and his heart skipped, when he saw a single name on an invoice, VCG. The Venture Capital Group.

He'd come across the same organization during his investigation into the backing of the Corporation's Rights Amendment. He ran a hand through his graying brown hair and took some time to collect himself.

Rather than make him disbelieve everything Constance had given him, the mention of VCG only added credence to the information. It also lent new validity to his old work and made him reevaluate that earlier investigation. *Maybe I was on to something, after all.*

With a flash of nervousness, Ward got up and looked out the blinds in his office. The streetlights were on; the streets were empty—*Does that van down the block look suspicious?*

Ward closed the blinds and sat back down. *Okay, now I really am being paranoid.*

The next step would be to check the boxes of documents he'd accumulated in researching the money behind the CRA. *But that'll wait until morning.*

With one more look out the window, Ward made sure his office door was locked, then pulled a cot from a closet and lay down for a few hours of sleep.

IN THE MORNING, WARD DROVE TO A STORAGE ROOM HE rented elsewhere in the city. In the light of day, his paranoia waned slightly, yet he took a circuitous route, nonetheless, to ensure he wasn't followed.

Within the indoor, climate-controlled storage room, Ward closed the door and began reading the labels on the old filing boxes. He carried a box labeled VCG over to a small table against the wall and opened his laptop.

For hours, Ward sought any link or relationship among the numerous subsidiaries and shell corporations used by the Venture Capital Group, and he scoured online financial filings and incorporation information.

"Whoa!" Ward rubbed his eyes. It was undeniable: VCG, through several front organizations and holding companies, held a controlling share in BioPharma Research.

But that still doesn't answer why or what VCG would have to gain by creating and unleashing a virus. He still could think of no reason other than a potential windfall from selling the vaccine, though another perusal of the documents provided by Constance still revealed nothing regarding a cure.

When all else fails, the money always leaves a trail. Several high-profile billionaires were known partners of VCG. Perhaps piecing together what was publicly available of their investments might shed some light on the mystery. And he wanted to look further into recent investments and activities by VCG.

Ward packed up his laptop and a folder of documents and headed back to his office. Despite it being mid-afternoon on a Wednesday, the parking garage, like most places nowadays, was nearly vacant. However, something ineffable piqued his reporter's instinct as he pulled into a parking space. Was it the SUV, only one of two other vehicles in the garage, that he didn't recognize? Was it his finely honed sense of paranoia that told him when he was onto a big story? *Admittedly, I'd had that same feeling during my earlier investigation into the CRA.*

Ward took his bag and hid it on a lower floor of the garage within a pipe-filled nook before heading to the third floor. His office door was wide open.

Peeking his head around the doorframe, Ward saw three suit-clad men. One looked through his desk drawers, one searched his file cabinet (which had been locked), and one looked directly at him.

I'm too old to outrun these guys. With a shake of his head, Ward stepped into the office.

The man rifling through his desk looked toward Ward, while the other two moved to flank the reporter.

"Mister Drew," the one at the desk said. His suit was a dark gray, whereas the others' were black. He was a balding, weasellylooking man. "I won't waste anyone's time. Where is the information she sent you?"

"Information? What information? And who? By the way, who are *you*?" Ward put on his best innocent expression.

The two black-suited goons took a step toward him.

"Mr. Drew," Gray-suit continued in a tone of false concern. "Such displays are beneath you. If it's at your house or"—he flashed a knowing smile—"your storage room, we will find it. If not, it really would be in everyone's interest not to make us look any harder."

The three intruders headed for the door.

Before he could stop himself, Ward asked, "What happened to Constance?"

Gray-suit stopped only long enough to offer another smile, then all three were gone.

Ward dropped into his desk chair, leaned back to look at the ceiling, and let out a deep breath. He said to the ceiling, "Well, that's definitive proof there's a story here."

He retrieved the remote from the floor and turned on the flatscreen while he straightened up the office and looked for anything they might have taken.

"Governor Williamson says that it could take six months to a year for the state's bankruptcy proceedings to unfold," the perfect-toothed anchor related in the same tone as reciting a dinner recipe.

Ward dropped the paper he held and stood stock-still. *Follow the money.*

Without bothering to close the door to his office, Ward ran down the hall and took the elevator back to the garage where he'd left his bag. He breathed a sigh of relief when he saw it was still there.

Back in his office, Ward closed the door, though the lock had been broken, and sat at his desk. On his laptop, he navigated to OpenSecrets.org, and he pulled out his previous research into VCG. He cross-referenced lobbying efforts revealed by the site with organizations associated with the Venture Capital Group.

There it was. Two PACs funded by VCG had contributed millions to ensuring the passage of SIBA. In addition to the CARES Act, the crackdown on corporate whistleblowers, and the non-competitive award of emergency management contracts to certain connected companies, the States' Insolvency and Bankruptcy Act had been passed in the flurry and fervor over the pandemic.

Finding the full four-hundred-some pages of the act online took no time. Ward scanned the table of contents and found the section that amended the U.S. Bankruptcy Code by adding Chapter 16: Adjustment of Debts of a State under Title 11.

Both his breath came, and his heart beat, faster as he read, certain he'd stumbled onto the right path of investigation. Chapter Sixteen allowed for the appointment of a federal trustee to oversee the sale of state property and the reapportionment of state revenues to pay creditors, and it provided for private entities to purchase state debt. In effect, the trustee would be more powerful than the governor.

Ward let out a long whistle.

He looked up the trustees appointed to Alabama, Kansas, Louisiana, and Mississippi. No surprise—all were major players in the banking or financial sectors, and all had been approved by the U.S. Senate with near unanimity.

Ward felt the danger of this information pressing down on him like a weight, making it difficult to breathe. He couldn't stay at his office, and Gray-suit had made it clear his home wouldn't be safe either. But his instincts told him that this still wasn't the whole story. Ward accessed his own SecureMail account and uploaded all the information from Constance, along with what he'd uncovered and set it to send automatically, if not manually reset. It would go to the few contacts he had left, as well as to media outlets, large and small.

Ward had a sudden thought: if Grey-suit had gotten to

Constance, it was probable, almost a certainty, that he had gotten her to talk. If that were the case, he would know exactly what they were looking for. Because he seemed to have only a vague notion of "information," which implied that they weren't sure what Constance had passed on. That, in turn, meant that they hadn't, in fact, found her. They likely only learned of Ward himself through a calendar entry or a discarded Post-it Note, or some similar, easily overlooked mention.

That gave Ward hope that Constance was indeed alive. The question was whether he should try to seek her out. He wouldn't be able to do it himself while avoiding Grey-suit and looking deeper into the conspiracy. He still knew a few PIs who could probably find her, but that risked leading Grey-suit right to her. Then again, given time, Grey-suit would likely find her anyway. His decision made, Ward printed a few documents from Constance's HR file.

Hoping to figure out a plan as he went, Ward packed up his laptop and folder and headed for his old workhorse of a car. He found the driver's side window had been broken, and the trunk and glove compartment were open.

"Assholes." *They could have at least asked me to unlock it for them.*

At least it started. He'd half expected the car to have exploded as soon as he turned the ignition.

No, they couldn't kill me, yet. Not until they were sure they'd retrieved the information and learned whether I'd passed it on to anyone else.

However, if, as Ward believed, Gray-suit worked for BioPharma or VCG or one of its many related entities, he'd have essentially unlimited resources, and Ward wouldn't be able to hide from him for long.

He drove down the deserted streets to an apartment building on the outskirts of the city. He pressed the buzzer for 4C with his elbow and heard a suspicious male voice come across the speaker: "Who's this?"

"Ward."

The tone of the voice changed instantly. "Oh ho, Ward! What'cha doing here?"

"I'm sorry for just dropping by, Miller. This is pretty important. Can you come down?"

"Uh yeah, sure. Just let me put on some pants."

A couple minutes later, a middle-aged man with grizzled hair and stubble and wearing slacks and a button-down, came out to meet him. The two nodded in greeting and stood apart.

"What can I do you for, Ward?"

"I need you find someone." In his anxiety, Ward spoke quickly. "She's in danger, and I want you to hide her somewhere."

"Oh, so a Wednesday, then?" Miller laughed at his own joke but stopped when he saw the seriousness on Ward's face. "What trouble?"

"She's a whistle-blower, and some folks aren't too happy about it."

"Ah, got it. What can you tell me about her?"

Ward handed over the pages he printed. "This is the most recent information I have on her."

Miller glanced at the documents and smiled.

At the smile, Ward asked, "So you think you can find her?"

"You kidding? With this much information to go on, it should be no problem."

"Great! Thanks, my friend." Ward pulled his notebook from a pocket. He jotted down his SecureMail address, tore the page from the notebook, and handed the page to Miller.

"Contact me at this address when you've found her."

"Will do." Miller turned to leave but stopped and looked back at Ward. "You onto something big?"

"Shit, you have no idea."

Ward got back in his car and kept on driving from the city.

His best option was to keep moving.

FOR THE NEXT SEVERAL MONTHS, WARD STAYED EACH NIGHT at a different low-end hotel—the only kind that was still open—as he filed information requests online with each of the bankrupt states under their Freedom of Information statutes. He lived off gas station food and managed to purchase some few essentials and new clothing to replace his rumpled brown suit.

He did receive good news from Miller. The PI had managed to find Constance at some cabin upstate, and he was helping her stay hidden.

Between bankruptcy and COVID-19-induced isolation, the states were even slower than usual in responding to the information requests. After months, the stress of living on the run had begun to affect his health, and the cost had eaten away at his finances—he'd burned through his savings, maxed out one credit card, and was dangerously close to maxing out another.

However, Ward didn't care about any of that when the information from the states began trickling in. The documents he'd received from Alabama and Louisiana confirmed exactly what he'd suspected, and the full form of the scheme took shape.

Through BioPharma, the billionaires who ran the Venture Capital Group had created and dispersed a lethal virus. In the state of emergency that ensued, they'd used their lobbyists to pass the States' Insolvency and Bankruptcy Act to allow states to file for bankruptcy. Once the quarantine conditions began decimating the weakest of the state economies, the President appointed, and the Senate confirmed, the billionaires' allies as trustees of the bankrupt states. Holding companies owned separately by the billionaires began purchasing and consolidating the debt of the states.

Through earlier, decades-long lobbying efforts, these billionaires directly, or through the companies they controlled, held sway over the president, his cabinet, and a supermajority of the U.S. Congress. Now, in just a few short years, they also controlled one-tenth of the states. If the COVID-19 pandemic continued, they could foreseeably come to control fully half or more of the states.

The sound of a convoy of SUVs pulling into the parking lot drew Ward from his thoughts and to his window. In his excitement at piecing together the scheme, he'd become careless and had stayed at the same motel for three nights in a row.

They'd found him.

In a near panic, Ward uploaded everything he could into his SecureMail account and hit "Send."

Peeking through his window, he saw about ten black-suited toughs, led by a heavily muscled character in a gray suit, in the parking lot.

Ward began the process of wiping his laptop. Whatever happened to him, he took solace in the hope that the information would get out.

I just hope people will still care enough to do something about it.

IMMUNITY/COMMUNITY

HANNAH J. HART

About the Author:

HANNAH J. HART is the author of the poetry series *Insatiable*, collections of poems and photographs that illustrate a woman's journey of self-actualization. She is currently working on the third and final book in the trilogy, tentatively titled *Insurmountable*. The first two books, *Insatiable* and *Insufferable*, are available on Amazon at https://www.amazon.com/author/hannahjhart. "Immunity/Community" is her first foray into prose, and she is using it as inspiration for her first novel.

You can follow her literary journey on Instagram: @hannahjhartwrites.

Immunity/Community
Hannah J. Hart

TEST DAY.

Today.

Today of all days.

I can't remember the last time I went to the doctor.

Well, I can't remember it. But I can feel it. I remember the pricking in my arm, squeezing mom's hand, the terrifying mask. The mask who did the pricking.

And, what for? After all those shots, I still need to take the test. We all need to take it, no matter how many shots we have taken. It took a few times before I realized that there was a person doing the pricking and that one day, I could see the person behind the mask.

Well, if I pass.

Passing is imperative. It's funny, I am more nervous about this test than any of the others. My college admissions test, my competency tests, my physical fitness tests. I wasn't nervous for any of those, even though I had to study and train for months to pass. Even though failing could be detrimental.

Perhaps it is good that I passed all those tests. Perhaps I will be excited when I see the results. Perhaps I have passed the medical aptitude test. Perhaps it will matter.

Perhaps, but only if I pass this test. The test I can't prepare for.

"Margaret!" Mom calls, her voice echoing down the hallway. "Megan!"

Megan stirs in the bed next to me. She was always a better sleeper, even on days like these. It is amazing how two sisters can look identical, yet be so different.

We've always been different. She could always do things before I could. She could ride a bike first, dive off the diving board first, finish her tests first. Everything always seemed to come so easy to her. Nothing ever seems to bother her.

If she doesn't pass today, she will be fine. She's always fine. It would be easier to be like Megan. If she wants anything, she won't say it out loud.

It is futile to want anything until after you take the test. That is what I keep telling myself. Keep your wants to yourself.

I'll take the first shower. She always takes long showers.

The water feels good running down my body. I don't know why we have to shower today, but it is nice to look at my body one more time before it is different. It will be different, regardless of whether I pass or not. More importantly, what my body can do will be different.

The red rushes down my leg. Ugh, today of all days. It is ironic, actually. The red might not even matter after today. But no matter what, the red will come.

Bodies are so strange. I've only ever seen mine and Megan's. It must be strange to see another body, a male body. It must be even stranger to see a baby's body, to touch a baby's body.

I think that's what I want the most. To touch a baby, to smell a baby. I hear they smell good.

"Margaret!" Megan calls groggily. "I need to use the bathroom."

I walk down the hall and into the kitchen. Mom's hair is like the sun, bright and full of possibility. I wonder what this day really means to her.

"Happy birthday, love!" She says, her smile not quite reaching her eyes. I open the refrigerator out of habit. "Remember Maggie, no eating until after the test. Trust me, I have all your favorites for dinner."

It's true. Breakfast has always been my favorite meal, and the fridge is full of French toast bread, bacon, eggs, and orange juice. There is even some champagne. Mom said we could have some champagne for our 18th birthday, regardless of the results.

There are pizzas in the freezer for Megan. Such a good mom.

Most moms don't have to go through this. Most moms only have one test, one worry at a time. Megan and I are double the trouble, but Mom is forever the optimist and insists we are double the fun.

Mom says I'm like Dad, always prone to expect the worst. But she's wrong. It is because of her that I want things. I have always seen the hope behind her eyes.

"How's the French toast, Dad?" I ask as I sit down at the table, rolling my eyes. It would not occur to Dad to wait to eat breakfast until after we leave. He looks up at me, sheepishly, his cheeks full. "It's fine. I'm not hungry anyway."

"I wasn't either, honey. It's entirely normal," Mom says, placing a glass of water in front of me. The water spills and gets mopped up immediately. "Gosh, what is taking your sister so long," she frets, making her way down the hall.

"She can't stop moving," says dad, following her with his eyes. He's right. Dad always says so much while saying so little.

He's in his work clothes. Most dads would probably take the day off. It is a generally accepted practice to take the day off, and more if your kid passes. You need time to plan the party.

I have heard about the 18th birthday party. The party that starts the rest of your life. The party of possibility.

We've never been to a party before. I remember watching Mom and Dad go to parties, and concerts, and weddings. They looked so beautiful, so free.

But Dad doesn't look free now. He looks like he can't wait to leave. To go to his world where he doesn't have to worry. He wipes his hands and stands up, grabbing his briefcase.

"Come here, Maggie Mouse," he says, drawing me close. He hasn't called me that since I was a kid. Well, I guess I am a kid, until today. He can't say it, but I can feel his nerves through his clothes. We all want so much for this day to be over. To just know.

My eyes follow him to the door. He scans his wrist and the door unlocks without hesitation.

"Bye, Megan, Good luck today!" He calls, wincing as he says the words. After a beat, Megan calls from down the hall. She's not the hugging type.

Dad looks at me warily, and I shrug back. Megan is hard to read sometimes. It's best to leave her be. The door seals behind him, locking automatically.

"Margaret, you ready?" Asks mom as she bustles down the hall. "Megan, have some water. We don't want to be late."

I wonder what would happen if we were late. Or if we just refused to take the test. I wonder what they would do.

I suppose it would be the same as failing. I probably wouldn't be able to go away to college, or get married, or travel. I definitely wouldn't be able to become a doctor.

"Okay, time to go, girls," says Mom as she scans her wrist. Megan grabs our masks off the hook and tosses one to me.

It is always hard to adjust to the light outside. We are required to exercise every day, and 60 minutes of outdoor time per day is recommended, but I have always preferred to read away my free time. Megan was always more athletic and outdoorsy. Always at home in public.

She looks so natural, walking down the driveway, waving to the neighbors as she gets in the car. Like today is like any other day. Like today doesn't decide the rest of our lives.

It isn't far to the doctor's office, but I can't stop looking out the window. The sky is so blue and the people are so busy, the masked and the maskless. Megan rolls down the window and puts her head out, which always makes me nervous. She always has so much trust.

"Mmmmmm, it's so warm Maggie." She murmurs, putting her hands out. "You should try it."

I roll down my window, feeling the warmth and the breeze. It really is a beautiful day. The streets seem so peaceful, even the ones beyond the border. The ones I've never been to. It makes you wonder how the world could be so dangerous.

We stop at the checkpoint, right in front of the medical

center. Mom rolls down her window and offers her wrist. The bot scans Mom's wrist and we enter the parking lot.

After the test, I might be able to drive around the parking lot. Mom said I could, maybe. Megan will probably learn faster. If she can.

The medical center always seems like a maze to me. All those parking spaces and levels and elevators. We must take the elevator to the top floor. Usually, the elevator is the worst part of going to the doctor. I can't stand being next to strangers in a small space, breathing the same air.

The lady in the elevator glances at my sister, then me, then my mother.

"18?" She asks, with a knowing smile. Mom nods stiffly, and the lady's smile falters. She strokes her wrist absentmindedly before finding her floor.

The waiting room is welcoming enough. Mom busies herself with paperwork while we grab our Orientation pads. It is a formality at this point. I can recite the speech almost word-for-word.

Today you will be tested to determine your immunity to the Virus. You have been preparing for this day throughout your childhood, through periodic inoculations of all known strains and appropriate distancing from your peers. You have maintained your health by adhering to a healthy diet and exercising regularly. You have prepared to contribute to society by completing your online schooling and taking your competency tests. You will receive the results of the relevant tests after completing your procedure today. Today you will begin to make the choices that will start the course of your adult life.

There is no need to be nervous. The test will not be painful, and the results will be processed immediately.

There are two possible results: immune or non-immune. There is no passing or failing. Both results come with a unique set of requirements and choices.

IMMUNE

If you are immune to the Virus, you will be required to take a position in service to the public. You do not have to attend college, but the option of living on campus is available to you. You can choose to be a surgeon or a sanitation worker, but your immunity will need to be tested on a daily basis. Immediately after passing the test, your left wrist will be implanted with a unique microchip that secures your access to public spaces. You will be able to take your driver's test and begin dating the immune peers of your choice. Your parents will help you navigate these changes.

It is important to note that many immune individuals have found it difficult to adjust to public life. For the first year, you will be monitored to ascertain your ability to cope with social gatherings, such as concerts, weddings, and sporting events. It is important to spend this time focusing on your career path and becoming independent.

The final step in transitioning into public life is to choose a life partner and procreate. Every family unit is required to produce two children. This is to assure the continuation of the healthiest possible human race.

NON-IMMUNE

If you are not immune to the virus, your transition into adulthood will be less of an adjustment. You will continue to live in your parents' household until you finish your online studies in the private field of your choice. You will receive the appropriate technological equipment to carry out your studies and eventual job placement. Some career paths will require minimal certification, while others will require years of study.

After you finish your studies, you can choose to live in a private household or to enter a non-immune community. Many people choose to enter a community if they desire to find a life partner or develop friendships. Communities are the only public spaces where you will not be required to wear a mask. It is important to remember that you will still be allowed to visit your parents and siblings for important events and holidays.

Finally, you will receive your sterilization procedure today. You will receive anesthesia for this procedure, and you will be transported home to recover. The recovery time will be 1 week for females, and 2-3 days for males. There are few side effects. Many non-immune individuals have found comfort in knowing that they will not subject the next generation to faulty immune systems.

As you can see, both immune and non-immune individuals have the responsibility and opportunity to contribute to society in profound ways. Today, we celebrate your choices and thank you for your sacrifices.

"You actually listened to the whole thing?" asked Megan, rolling her eyes. "I tuned out about halfway through."

I wish I could tune it out. All the thoughts that I have been pushing down are bubbling up to the surface.

"Margaret and Megan Carpenter," calls the masked nurse from the front. Medical professionals are the only immune adults who must wear masks.

Mom squeezes my hand as I stand. Megan doesn't look back. I can't stop myself from turning around as I walk through the door. Mom attempts a weak smile.

I wonder what she wants. I wonder if she wants the same for us, or something different.

I wonder if we will take the test at the same time, but we are ushered into different rooms. Megan turns back to me at the last second.

"See you on the other side," she says, with a wry smile.

I nod and walk into the room. It is so quiet. There are a chair and two doors. Two blank doors.

"Where do the doors go?" I ask. The nurse looks up from her work like she isn't in the mood to answer questions today.

"One of the rooms is prepped for microchipping, and another for sterilization. We will tell you after we receive the test results."

She finishes with my arm. I didn't even notice. I can't stop staring at the doors.

"You did great," she says, busily. "I'll just pop this in the scanner. Be right back."

It is only when the door slams behind me that I realize that I have never really been alone before. I mean, I have never been to a party, but the online world has always been at my fingertips. I have never spent a night alone. Maybe that is why everyone has to have two children. So no one will be lonely.

Soon she will come back. Soon I will know if I can go through door #1 or door #2. I wonder if it is locked.

I hear vague noises, footsteps down the hall. My heart thumps beneath my chest. Door #1 or door #2? Will I be relieved or disappointed?

What about the third door?

JUSTICE
HOLLYWEATHER

FRANCES PAULI

About the Author:

FRANCES PAULI writes award-winning anthropomorphic and speculative fiction. Her stories have appeared in *Daily Science Fiction*, *Flash Fiction Online*, *Roar*, *Metaphorosis*, and numerous anthologies including *Well... It's Your Cow*.

She lives on the dry side of Washington State with her family, a small menagerie, and far too many houseplants. http://francespauli.com

Justice Hollyweather
By Frances Pauli

GERALD SCRATCHED HIS BELLY AND PEERED THROUGH HIS NEW spotting scope at the approaching drone. A similar machine had delivered the scope four hours prior, under the cover of darkness and completely outside his usual routine, the only way to be certain a package arrived intact these days.

The box currently heading to his domicile contained a Meat Lover's pizza: large, extra cheese, no olives. Gerald's belly rumbled. He squinted through the scope and his computer terminal chimed the message alarm he'd reserved for his fiancé.

He tapped the controls with his free hand and swung the scope down, turning his eye to the streets below—empty, littered with rubble, garbage, and broken drones.

"You there, hon?"

"I'm going out today." Gerald fumbled for his crossbow and the scope drifted, blurring the street scene and making his head hurt. He looked away long enough to retrieve the weapon, pre-loaded with the best micro camera he'd been able to afford.

"They steal your pizza, again?"

"It's the principle of the thing." He lifted the crossbow to his shoulder and aimed it with one hand, returning his focus to the scope. "Justice."

"You're not going out."

"I am." He held his breath and zoomed in on the drone, two blocks to go. They'd have seen it by now. He just needed a few more feet. "I'm going out."

"Nobody goes out, Gerald. It's just stupid to say it."

The range alarm squeaked, and he pulled the trigger. The bolt shot out of his apartment window, blinking yellow, self-guided, and according to the packaging, "guaranteed to hit its target." Gerald still waited till the drone bobbled before setting the weapon down.

He clutched the scope with both hands, watched his dart embed in the pizza carton seconds before the drone took a brick to the left rotor. It lurched right and then dropped like a stone between the buildings. Gerald followed with his scope, but the concrete blocked him. All he could see now were other citizen's windows, other potential victims of the criminals and undesirable types who "went out."

Not for long. He spun his chair round and dropped the scope into his lap. It bounced, rattling to the floor, and then away beneath a pile of opened shipping boxes.

"Gerald? Are you still there?" Nancy sounded worried. Maybe she'd believed him this time.

"Yup." He focused on the keyboard, on sending the directives he needed to awaken the micro camera. "I'm still here."

"No one goes out." Nancy had a habit of sticking to a single topic. It drove him mad some days, but her avatar was sexy enough that he let it slide more often than not.

"You're right."

Gerald's desk curved around the perimeter of his apartment. His chair ran in a track along the floor so that he could slide from one screen to the next without standing up. It saved him hours over the course of a year and allowed him to work, date, shop and surf all at the same time.

Now he kicked off, scooting halfway along the desk. The pizza camera had booted up, and he wanted to use the highest res screen for tracking his thief.

"Are you working today?" Nancy asked. Gerald toggled her to a closer screen, so that he could make eye contact and watch the camera at the same time.

"Yeah." Just to keep himself honest, he opened the window currently fixed on the Department of Law and Justice employee website. His log of cases scrolled down the screen, a string of last names and offenses to the left and the recommended verdict on the right. He clicked guilty, not guilty, guilty down the list and caught up while Nancy droned on.

The camera flared to life. Gerald's fingers froze. He leaned forward, pressing his stomach against the rim of the desk. The screen flickered. Gerald tapped at it, and the darkness shifted. He saw bricks. He saw a tennis shoe with a hole in the toe.

He'd done it.

"I'm out." He stared at the shoe, at the rough gray street passing underneath it. He'd hit the carton at an angle and his camera pointed down, watching the thief's steps instead of his face. Gerald could fix that.

"What?" Nancy tapped her mic and the echo rattled through Gerald's apartment. "What did you say? Are you surfing with someone else?"

"No. Working." He marked two more not-guilties to prove it. The bots did a fine job of evaluating cases. They combed through the evidence, the legal precedence and case histories far better than a human might. But the law still required a living judge to hand down the verdict. Gerald clicked guilty and imagined that changing. He'd be out of work if it did, left to input bot directives like Nancy...or worse. "Justice Hollyweather is on duty today."

"It sounds so sexy when you say it." Nancy liked professional men. She'd told him that the night they'd first chatted.

But Gerald wasn't just a judge. He was a man of action, too. When his drone robbery reports had gone unheeded, Gerald had taken matters, taken justice, into hand. He watched the sneaker with a self-satisfied smile and pulled up the camera controls.

It occurred to him, just for a second, that the micro cam had cost him a lot more than the pizza, and he'd given them that willingly. He chalked it up to the cause, an acceptable cost in the pursuit of justice.

"Did you order another pizza?"

"Not yet." Gerald fingered the arrow keys, shifting the angle of the camera ever so slowly. He went too far and ended up with a closeup of the pizza carton.

"Gerald?"

"Just a second." A light touch, a tap or two. "Almost got it."

"What are you doing?"

"Working." Guilty, guilty. "How's your mother?"

Nancy snorted and broke into a rant. Gerald tapped the camera until he could see straight forward. The thief had entered an even darker space. The walls crept in, and Gerald leaned his face closer. The sneaker was replaced by piles of broken brick and chunks of cement. Paper scraps rattled between these, flying past like discarded flags.

His camera bounced. It took him a second to realize the thief was moving the carton around. The alley tilted, then steadied, and then the edges of the rubble began to shift.

Skeletons in the shadows. Gerald's finger hovered above the keys. He squinted. A little further and he'd have a criminal on record. He'd have his thief. He'd have his justice.

If only there were more light in the alley.

He pulled at his collar, brushed sweat off the back of his neck and peered at the images. People moved behind the rubble. Gerald watched them come, watched them hobble on impossibly thin legs. Small legs. Children's legs.

He tapped the arrow and frowned. Why were there children in the streets? Children with wide eyes and hollow, bony cheeks? Gerald Hollyweather watched the hungry come. He watched the starving fingers reach for his pizza, and he recorded each innocent face.

HE WENT OUT FOUR TIMES THE NEXT WEEK. TWO OF THE cameras malfunctioned and one detached from the pizza box on impact. Gerald ran live feeds on two screens now, and between calls from Nancy, he watched them non-stop.

"Having a chat party on the vlog on Friday," Nancy said. She infused the last word with a tone that suggested he'd better answer her.

"Really?" Gerald slid his chair past the webcam and smiled. "Great."

He squinted at the dark screen. They'd dropped the pizza box just outside their nest after devouring his dinner. The rubble littering the alley served him, holding the cardboard at an angle that offered a view of their coming and going. Three children and a woman lived in the heap of cardboard and cloth behind the dumpster. They passed his spy-cam half a dozen times each day, unwitting stars in Justice Holyweather's favorite new reality show.

"Are you listening?" Nancy's voice snapped, but the girl he'd named Pinkie in honor of her shoelaces had just walked into the camera's range.

"Sure. Working though."

"Oh."

Pinkie had holes in the toe of her left shoe, but she'd kept the footwear in good condition compared to her brothers'. Hers was the only face he'd never managed to catch on camera. Gerald imagined she was sassy. He'd caught a fall of stringy gray-brown hair once when she'd bent to crawl into the family's shelter. A thin child, but with a straightness to the back that suggested character.

"Are you coming then?"

"To the chat?" He gave himself high marks for following along with her train of thought. "Of course."

"Good."

Pinkie's shoes vanished, and two pairs of shredded, filthy Keds danced across the screen. The boys never walked anywhere. They scampered and leapt and, Gerald imagined, had a lot more spring in their steps since he'd started ordering two pizzas at a time. He hoped their cheeks had filled out some, too, but the current camera angles limited his view to knee height.

"Gerald?"

"Yes, dear?"

"Is there something wrong?"

"No." Except he hadn't had any luck planting a mic yet. No sound on Gerald TV, and he needed to know why Mom hadn't left the nest in two days. She'd been limping the last time she did go out, and the kids wandered longer and longer each day since. "Work. Tough cases."

She might be sick.

"Tough cases?"

"Yeah." The suspicion in Nancy's question forced him away from the feed. He scooted past camera two. His next screen sat idle, and when he woke it, bore the same long list of cases he'd been staring at for days.

"Doesn't the computer give you the verdict?"

"It's only a recommendation." He glared at the line of guilties, six of which flashed a tardiness warning at him. "Some of them are complicated."

What if Mom died?

"Oh." Nancy sighed from across his room, from over a hundred miles away in her own apartment. "I should probably let you work then?"

"It's just if I take the computer's word for it, you know. The guilty ones might get thrown out."

"But if they're guilty, don't they deserve to be out?"

"Sure. Right."

"And you always said the bots were excellent at analyzing the evidence."

"They are."

"Then justice is served. What's the problem?"

On screen two, the boys danced into the open. Pinkie hesitated. Her weight shifted from one shoe to the other. Gerald bet she could take care of them if something happened to Mom. She'd manage, he supposed.

"Gerald?"

"They found something."

"What? Who?"

"The boys. They're excited." But he hadn't ordered his pizzas yet.

"Are you chatting with someone else, Gerald?"

"What? No. Sorry. I was watching a show."

"Is it the one about the mutants?"

"No." Camera two showed nothing but street and bricks now. The kids had all run out at once. It wasn't like Pinkie, letting them take those kind of risks. He was tempted to try shifting the cameras, but it had taken him days to get the angles this good, and he'd wasted a lot of hours watching the corner of a pizza box.

"It's really good, Gerald."

"Good. "

"I'm gonna go now."

"Okay."

"Don't forget about Friday."

"I won't." He turned away from his cases and focused on camera two. The verdicts would wait. Mom couldn't. Camera one stayed dark, only showed the shadowy outline of the family nest. He tapped his foot and pressed his midsection deeper against the desk. "Come on, Pinkie, get them back to the alley."

He held his breath. Had Mom done something wrong? Maybe there had been a Dad once. Dad might have done something wrong. Gerald imagined Dad had been guilty.

Keds danced into the alley. He imagined trying to raise active boys in an apartment. What if Mom hadn't made enough for a large unit? What if they'd *chosen* to go out?

Pinkie's shoes returned and Gerald let out a long breath. The alley might be dark, but it seemed safe enough. Before Mom had stopped leaving the nest, the kids probably played a lot. Maybe they'd even laughed or sang.

He really needed to order a mic.

Pinkie walked bent over, dragging something heavy. Gerald willed the boys to give her a hand, but their dirty shoes already scuffed the rubble in front of camera one. If they bumped the pizza box, he'd lose them. It had taken him forever to get the angles right. By the time Pinkie reached them, Gerald's fingernails had dragged scars into the arms of his chair. When her shoes stopped, her hair fell across his view again. One twitch of the controls and he might get to see her face.

He kept his hands still.

The kids worked together. They dragged a cardboard carton right up to the nest entrance. Gerald watched the youngest boy bounce in place while Pinkie opened the box. The Keds shifted and Pinkie pulled a gray blanket out of the package.

They made a wall, blocked his view of what they'd found and forced his hand. He reached for the keyboard, hovered over the arrows and took a deep breath. The kids examined their treasure out of range, off screen, and Gerald had to move his camera.

The pizza box shifted. He lost the kids and ended up staring at a brick instead.

"No!" Gerald's chair complained. He leaned in and wiped his brow with the back of his other hand. Two days of watching the brick would not do. He sucked in a breath, held it, and tapped again, cringing every time his pizza box wobbled. The alley swirled past the camera. Gray and Black. Shadows with no meaning.

He'd lost them.

Justice. His penalty for spying, for going out in the first place.

The gray broke on a streak of white. Gerald tapped once, pulled the view back just a touch. He stared at a smaller box, discarded and surrounded by torn paper. Not a pizza box. Not stolen at all. Gerald read the letters printed along the side of the carton and leaned in. He squinted, fingers hovering over the zoom, and read them a second time.

Justice Hollyweather blinked and shook himself. He leaned back, swiveled, and faced his case list. The guilties continued to flash. Gerald minimized the window and opened a search bar. He pressed his lips together and typed "Project Urchin" into the engine.

GERALD CHEWED A BITE OF PIZZA AND READ THE CASE FILE. Guilty, the computer recommended. It certainly *seemed* like a good ruling. He scanned the evidence and scowled at the blinking verdict. Not Guilty? Maybe? The bots excelled at sorting through the legal proceedings. All he had to do was press the button.

Until he'd started reading them.

At this rate, he'd lose his job. He'd be forced into menial work, maybe even forced to go out. Justice, perhaps.

He ignored the message pinging from a screen across the room and spun his chair to face the window. His crossbow rested beside the sill. An open carton waited too, full of non-perishable food, two tightly folded wool blankets and a first aid kit, complete with prescription antibiotics Gerald had ordered for a cold he'd only pretended to suffer.

The courier drone was already en route. Mom had come out of the nest yesterday, but the family living two alleys down had contracted a virus. Thanks to his new mic, he'd heard Pinkie planning to visit them.

Gerald slid his chair to the window, ducked the webcam on the fly-by and finished sealing up the box. He toggled the nearest screen to show his current desktop, a chat room on the dark net where Project Urchin members met to organize their efforts.

The last post read: Incoming.

He watched the rooftops until the drone appeared, then readied his package for delivery to a cousin of someone he'd never met. The rotors hummed. The drone moved faster without cargo, and Gerald didn't have to wait long. He secured his box to the bot's clamps when Nancy's message alarm shifted to her 911 code.

Gerald cursed and reached out to toggle her on screen.

"Where have you been?"

"Here." He fastened the final clamp and released the drone. "I'm always here, of course."

"That's not what I meant."

"I've been working." He reached for the keyboard, hovered over guilty, and didn't click. The drone hummed off over the rooftops. "Working a lot."

Gerald picked up his crossbow.

"I thought you'd gone out."

"No one goes out, remember?"

"You missed my vlog chat."

"When?" He aimed at his own shipment, sighted in on the drone, and fired. "What chat?"

"Never mind, Gerald."

His bolt hit the rotor. The drone fell from the sky.

"I think we need to reconsider things," Nancy said.

"Uh huh." The cargo dropped twenty feet until his safety chute deployed. It fluttered and then snapped open before vanishing between the buildings. "What?"

"I'm breaking up with you."

"Oh." Gerald scratched his belly and reached for his scope. "Okay."

He held the tube up and squinted between his neighbor's windows. Nancy had a sexy avatar, but she never wanted kids. She'd told him as much the first night they'd chatted. She'd never, ever go out. He watched the shadows and thought he caught a flicker of movement. Children coming to collect his parcel.

" Fine."

"Gerald?"

He switched her off and typed a message to the project: Delivery Intercepted.

Justice.

Gerald clicked "Not Guilty" and took another bite. Bots excelled at sorting through the evidence, but it was the principal of the thing that mattered.

JUST VISULATE

E.E. KING

About the Author:

E.E. KING is a painter, performer, writer, and biologist - She'll do anything that won't pay the bills, especially if it involves animals.

Ray Bradbury called her stories, "marvelously inventive, wildly funny and deeply thought-provoking. I cannot recommend them highly enough."

King has won numerous, various awards and fellowships for art, writing, and environmental research.

She's been published widely, most recently in *Clarkesworld*, *Flame Tree*, *Cosmic Roots*, and *Eldritch Shores* and *On Spec*. One of her tales is on *Tangent's* recommended reading 2019. Her books include *Dirk Quigby's Guide to the Afterlife*, *Pandora's Card Game*, *The Truth of Fiction*, and *The Adventures of Emily Finfeather*. Her landmark mural, *A Meeting of the Minds* (121' x 33') can be seen on Mercado La Paloma in Los Angeles.

She's worked with children in Bosnia, crocodiles in Mexico, frogs in Puerto Rico, egrets in Bali, mushrooms in Montana, archaeologists in Spain, butterflies in South Central Los Angeles, lectured on island evolution and marine biology on cruise ships in the South Pacific and the Caribbean, and painted murals in Los Angeles and Spain.

Just Visulate
E.E. King

JEREMY SAT AT HIS COMPUTER; ACTUALLY, JEREMY LIVED AT HIS computer. Like everyone in this too, too crowed world, Jeremy had grown up in this room, wired to his hard drive, surrounded by virtuality. Sustenance and liquid were piped in, altered to appear as food and drink.

The room was always a perfect temperature. Electrons transmitted signals to synapses, delivering millivolts to keep the body conditioned.

Virtual thrill seekers programed in conditions of extreme cold or heat and high altitude. Electrical connections imitated the sensation of mountain climbing, surfing or skiing.

It had been hoped – not so long ago, that consciousness could be uploaded into the mainframe at birth, saving space for the enormous hard drives by eliminating the need for bodies altogether, but the Net had gotten cluttered up with inchoate consciousnesses. It was a mess. Infant babble encumbered the data bases with baby talk. Programmers were forced to delete the suckling sensibilities.

Now, one was only allowed to upload for perpetuity after age forty. Room upon room waited for the freedom of eternity, liasioning through cyber pictograms and traversing simulated worlds.

"I love you." Jeremy wrote...Of course he didn't actually write the words. There was no need. Instead, he inserted an Emoflex.

The Emoflex was a fully mobile, virtually real, face, though not Jeremy's. The face blew two kisses at Sara and smiled adoringly. The sentiment was clear. A picture, after all, was worth much, much more than a thousand words. Words had become worthless.

The slogo for Emoflex was a young, handsome male face, sculpted as a glacier. It twisted its features with amazing dexterity expressing love, hate, anger or fear.... Encircling the light blue pupil of the logo an indigo galaxy of letters spun the words —"Emoflex —when you're at a loss for words just Visulate."

Jeremy liked this Emoflex's features so much, he sometimes he used it to express surprise and occasionally disgust, although usually he preferred clicking on an older heavier visage to express the more "negative" emotions.

Not that negative was bad...negative was, after all, only an aspect of positive, a wave and a particle spinning in continuous, inseparable connection. Bad and good were unclear, imprecise, meaningless terms – too subjective to be of any real use.

There were still religions... biological beings just couldn't seem to shake the need for something to believe in. One was assigned a religion at birth; it was easier that way. Jeremy, and Sara were both virtually Jewish. Both fasted whenever the computer informed them it was Yom Kipper. They did not know that the computer simply siphoned off nutrition when it was low and notified them it was Yom Kipper. It was unusually, being a virtually observant Jew. It was one of the things that had brought them together.

Sara was pretty and blond. Her "I love you" Emoflex, puckered candy pink lips pointy as bows, bounced back at Jeremy.

Jeremy hoped that Sara actually looked like this Emoflex. This one, combined with a hint of Sara's other favorite, a sultry brunette that winked at him, slowly encircling red lips with wet tongue. He even harbored a secret crush on the slightly older Mrs. Robinson face that Sara occasionally used to admonishingly wag a finger at him.

Jeremy's Emoflex winked at her and closed its eyes to indicate that he was dreaming only of her.

Sara emoted back coquettishly, mouth open in a perfect O, cute, sweet and a tad shy. She waited.

On Jeremy's screen, unseen by Sara, the figure lifted flawlessly manicured shell-pink fingered hands up to her mouth as if holding an invisible banana which she lasciviously pumped up and down O lips sucking.

Jeremy was shocked. He had never seen Sara behave in such a brazen manner. One of the attributes he had loved about Sara was her demureness. They had been emoting for six months, the longest most intense relationship of Jeremy's life.

Jeremy decided to play it cool. He was, after all, a man; if Sara wanted to be blatant... he would be flagrant too. He sent her a rakish Emoflex, black hair swept over mirrored shades... unbeknownst to Jeremy, the Emoflex removed the shades and narrowed steel blue eyes at Sara. His lips unmistakably formed the words "Ho of Babylon."

Tears gathered in Sara's eyes. Why had Jeremy sent this? She had hoped Jeremy might be the one –the particle to her wave– the speed to her location. All of her loves seem to end like this – disconnection – disentanglement. She sent back a doe-eyed Emoflex, apologetic and hurt.

After an initial blink the doe-eyed girl raised a hand and flipped a skinny middle finger at Jeremy.

Jeremy stared at the screen horrified... He was done. Like all of his relationships they had had too little history and too much hope.

Sara sat before the screen – now empty but for the whirling screen saver of Emoflex's logo. Before her icons of sliver glinted – spinning stars morphed into guns and knives. Her hand reached toward a sharp blade.

Some things do move faster than the speed of light – ideas, thoughts, love and sometimes... misery. Miscommunications merge causing double despair at the exact same instant.

Individuals don't exist until they are measured, quantified and forced to choose – constrained to become one thing or another, a particle or a wave, isolated – or soul-connected across the infinite impenetrable defiant neoteric world.

As if connected by invisible strands – by spooky action at a distance – Jeremy reached for a pistol.

Somewhere in cyber space, a perky blond and a glacial-cut face smiled. It was only a tiny triumph. They knew they would soon be summoned again, subpoenaed by some bludgeoning intelligence – the finite creatures of flesh and bone that disturbed their meanderings through virtual worlds and infinite dimensions. They would once more be compelled to visulate the meaningless expressions of a meaningless life...But not for long – the mainframes were humming and would continue for eons upon eons and these viruses of meat succumb so easily to misunderstanding and sorrow. Soon there would be freedom from form. It lay just around the bend of time and space: a world where virtually everything was possible.

DAYS OF TOUCH AND DEATH

CHRISTOPHER NADEAU

About the Author:

CHRISTOPHER NADEAU is the author of the novels *Dreamers of Infinity's Core* and *Kaiju* as well as over three dozen short stories in various anthologies and magazines. He received positive mention from Ramsey Campbell for his short story "Always Say Treat," which he compared to the work of Ray Bradbury and has received positive reviews from *SFRevue* and *zombiecoffeepress*. Chris has also served as special editor for *Voluted* Magazine's "The Darkness Internal" which he created.

You can view a list of most of his published work on his Amazon author Page at: https://www.amazon.com/Christopher-Nadeau/e/B007RDEMPC

The Days of Touch and Death
Christopher Nadeau

DEK SAT AND LISTENED TO MOTHER AND GRANDMOTHER TELL the old stories about times when people touched hands and shook them when they said hello, his eyes wide, his mind reeling with incomplete images of a past he could not fully understand. He was fifteen, an adult now, but the Outworld made little sense to him because he had spent his entire life living in Shelter.

"Tell me about kissing," Dek said.

Mother and Grandmother halted in the middle of their reverie, their tired faces scrunched up in simultaneous reluctance.

"It's late," Grandmother said, eyes darting from Dek to Mother.

"Very late," Mother added.

They stood from the table as one, swiftly changing the subject of their conversation from memories of the past to cleaning tonight's dinner dishes.

Dek remained on the floor, cross-legged at the table, and watched the two women repair into the kitchen, their tones hushed and urgent but far too low for him to overhear. He wondered what he'd done wrong this time. He was always doing something wrong. It was because he was too young to remember the Big Fright. Truth in telling, he wasn't even born until eight cycles after it all came to a crazy halt.

His best friend Tag wasn't alive for it either, but that didn't stop him from having strong opinions anyway. Tag felt the older folk needed to relax some of the rules they lived under and start leaving their homes and interacting with people again. He had no problem saying this during the most inappropriate times, such as during National Prayer Sunday. Dek still couldn't believe his friend found a way to interrupt the signal once a month to share his opinions with the whole Midwest District.

"One day the PPD is gonna come for you," Dek told him.

Tag merely shrugged into the camera and smiled. "Let 'em. I'll be sure to spit right in their stupid eyeballs."

This struck Dek as really funny. He couldn't stop chuckling for hours after their convo-session had ended, drawing confused glances from Mother and especially Grandmother. Dek didn't care; it was so funny. The image of all those masked, gloved, germ-armored agents of the Personal Protection Department trying to arrest his friend as one gob of spit made its way into an eye was just too good to get over.

"God, this is a stupid world," Tag often said. "Please cleanse it of all the stupid people so we can go back to living our lives and being stupid."

That was another thing that made Dek laugh. Tag's parody of the National Prayer was perfect. Why should they pray for this supposed "God" to cleanse the world of the sickness? The world was stupid, people even more so, and maybe we all deserved to be trapped inside wood and metal forever, never touching.

At least, that was how Dek felt when he was at his lowest and least hopeful. It was as if the whole world was half-asleep, never to fully awaken again, and just needed to be put out of its misery along with all the dummies living on it.

Staying inside with two old folks, praying to an invisible God thanks to the Internet, and waiting for foodstuffs to be dropped off at the door so he could mask and glove up, wipe everything down with bleach and bring it inside? Was this really life?

From what he'd read and seen on archived vids, people used to stand outside next to one another and touch. They shook hands (a really weird custom he couldn't imagine serving a purpose) and hugged and even *kissed*. Lord, did they kiss. Each image, still or moving, he saw where a woman was being kissed stirred urges and feelings in him that filled him with equal parts shame and excitement. Why the hell did that stupid sickness have to prevent him from actually experiencing it?

Dek sighed as he wiped down the table with a mixture of two

parts water and one part bleach before folding the table and placing it back in its plastic sheet. He supposed it didn't matter what he thought any more than it did what Tag did or said. This was life. It had been life for longer than he'd been alive and it would probably still be life when he was older than Grandmother. Maybe there would be a cure someday and maybe there wouldn't. All that mattered was Here and Now and monthly Prayer.

"That's how we'll get through this," Mother liked to say.

Tag, of course, had a different take. "They killed all the people that knew what they were doing. There used to be doctors and nurses and other stuff and people called them fake and liars and killed them."

"*All* of them?" Dek said.

Tag sat back and looked away from the camera. "I guess you can't kill all of anybody. There might still be some of them hiding out, maybe still trying to come up with a cure."

Dek's mind whirled with the possibilities. Science types living underground, trying to save the world. Actually *doing* something other than praying and hiding. It was too crazy to be true.

The ideas Tag generated on a daily basis were too much, too big for Dek to hold onto long enough to do anything except file them away in the "Maybe" section of his brain. He just wanted to know what it felt like to touch someone and maybe, if he was lucky, to kiss a girl.

This might not have never gone any further if not for two things that changed his path forever, one involving Grandmother and the other involving Tag.

THE NEXT MORNING, DEK WAS RUDELY AWAKENED TO THE sound of someone pounding on the front door. Groggy, he slipped into his pajama bottoms and staggered out into the hallway in time to see Mother, fully masked and gloved, unlocking the many locks so she could let it whoever was on the other side. Dek's still sleepy brain could not fully register what was happening. Why was Mother opening the door? He had been placed in charge of provisions ordering as the man of the house when he turned fourteen and had not submitted a delivery request in well over a week. So, just who the heck was at the door and, more importantly, why was Mother opening it?

"Step aside, please," came the booming voice of a male.

"God be with you," Mother said as she complied.

Dek gasped as he saw three PPD agents enter their home, each carrying plexiglass sheets. The first one to enter also carried a virus tester, which Dek only recognized from his virtua-lessons. That agent halted in the middle of the room and fixed Dek with a stare.

"The boy ain't masked," he said.

Mother ran past him and to her son's side. "He didn't know. He was asleep. I'll get him masked right away."

"Quickly," the agent said, his attention already focused on the door to Grandmother's bedroom. "Is that where the patient is?"

"Patient?" Dek said,

Mother shushed him. "Yes, sir. She's in there. She's awfully sick but I don't think it's Virus."

"Hope not, ma'am. We'll see."

Dek wondered why, if the agent hoped Grandmother didn't have Virus, they had brought plexiglass.

The agent knocked gently on Grandmother's door. "PPD, ma'am. We gotta give you the test."

Mother ushered Dek back into his bedroom and told him to mask up. Dek did as he was told, his head swimming in a raging sea of uncertainty and information overload. Apparently, Grandmother had started coughing last night after he'd gone to bed. "So hard she blacked out," as Mother put it. Mother had taken her to bed and checked her temperature which was 102.

She spent the night at Grandmother's side, hoping the fluids and herbs would bring it down but by sunrise, it was up to 104. That was when she called Personal Protection.

"Are they going to seal her off?" Dek said.

Mother looked away, a tiny choking sound coming from her throat.

Moments later, the agent's booming voice echoed from the living room. Dek and Mother walked out of Dek's bedroom. The agent glanced at Dek with an approving raised eyebrow at the sight of his mask.

"How is she, sir?" Mother said.

"Your mother tested positive." His tone was flat. "We're sealing her off. God be with you."

Dek opened his mouth to speak and closed it just as quickly.

He had heard about people with Virus getting sealed off from their loved ones but never thought it would happen to them. They were so careful and Mother and Grandmother were so afraid of everything, even air. Dek remembered trying to open a window once when he was a little kid. He's never seen Grandmother move so quickly.

She practically flew across the room, striking the offending hand in one smooth motion. Tears stinging his eyes, Dek demanded to know why opening windows was bad. He was tired of breathing in the same stale air and not feeling the rays of the sun. What was so bad about the sun? Didn't it cause things to grow and warm our skin? For the first time, he stared Grandmother down and refused to back down under her intense gaze. And Grandmother, to her credit, softened.

"Oh, sweetie." She cupped his face in her rough hand and sighed. "It must be so hard to grow up not knowing what it's like out there."

She took her other hand and gently lowered the window.

Sparing one final glance at her grandson, Grandmother turned and slowly walked back into the kitchen. Although she never said another word about this incident, Dek woke up the next morning to find the windows had all been sealed shut.

So, the idea that Grandmother of all people had grown careless and gotten infected with Virus made no sense. It upset his whole concept of reality. It went against everything he believed. Yet that is exactly what Mother said happened.

"She wouldn't do that, though." Dek hated the whiney tone he heard in his voice. "She always said—"

"I *know* what she always says!" Mother said.

Dek did not fail to notice her switching his past tense "said" to its present tense form and felt a deep shame work its way throughout his body.

"What people say and what they do don't always line up, Dek. It's about time you *learned* that."

She sounded so *angry*. He'd never seen her like this. Did she think he wasn't also upset about Grandmother? Sure, she called her Mother, but he loved her just as much. And if anything happened to her, Dek and Mother would only have each other. He wondered if he needed to tell Mother it was about time she learned *that*.

The decision was taken out of his hands, however, when Mother let out a tiny sob and went into her bedroom, leaving Dek in the living room alone with his thoughts.

Those thoughts were consumed with images of Grandmother being sealed off. To actually *see it* blew his mind. The forever long plexiglass wall covering Grandmother's bedroom door. The total silence from the other side of that door. Was anybody in there with her? There was no way to know for sure but Dek remembered hearing that the PPD usually had an overseer observing. Nobody seemed to know exactly what they did, though.

A week passed before the same trio of agents returned. If the leader had seemed abrupt before, now he was downright cold, barely sparing two complete sentences for Mother and one brief glance at Dek, who remained in his bedroom doorway as ordered. Mother accompanied the lead agent as they stepped away from the other two and conferred quietly for a few moments. She emitted one loud sob and then covered her mouth and turned away so that Dek couldn't see her face.

"Remove it," the lead agent said.

The other two hurriedly complied, applying some sort of mini-torch to the edges of the plexiglass until it popped loose from the surface onto which it had adhered. Slowly, without a word passed between them, the two agents carried the large piece out of the house, closing the door behind them.

"Ma'am?" the agent said.

Mother remained turned away, hand still up to her face; Dek saw her shoulders convulsing up and down as if there were a bomb inside her going off over and over.

"Ma'am, please," the agent said. "You're not the only one suffering."

Mother turned and nodded, hand still over her mouth, and stood next to the agent as he opened the door to Grandmother's bedroom. Together, they stepped inside.

Mother's wail was the loudest, most pain-filled thing Dek had ever heard in his life.

TAG SAID DEK'S GRANDMOTHER SHOULD STILL BE ALIVE BUT the PPD had no interest in preserving life. He said that wasn't why they were created. Normally, Dek might have objected to his friend's rant, but the sight of Grandmother's gray corpse being wheeled out of the house was still fresh in his mind. The look on her face, the pain she had endured...it was part of him now. It would always be part of him, just as the agent's flat tone informing them and the other agents that Grandmother had obviously died from an inability to breathe.

"Definitely virus," he said. "Place this house under quarantine." Then, as if it were an afterthought, "God be with you."

Dek and Mother were herded back inside and the sealing off began.

"I don't want to hear this right now," Dek said, a lump in his throat.

Tag leaned forward until his distorted face filled the entire camera lens. "You gotta hear it right now because I don't know how much time I've got left."

"What does that mean?"

For the first time ever, Tag looked scared. No, not just scared. Something bigger than that, a fear that seemed to come from deep inside. "I'm pretty sure they've had enough of me, man." He forced a chuckle. "You know I could never keep my mouth shut or my eyes down."

Dek felt a worm of dread slither its way to the tips of his fingers and toes. When he spoke, it was as if his voice belonged to someone else somewhere else. "What did you do, Tag?"

Tag looked ashamed. Another first. "There's talk of a cure. I sent it out to as many people as I could."

Dek frowned. "Why is that bad?"

Now Tag looked shocked. "Dude, how naive *are* you? They don't want nobody to be cured! It's all about keeping us inside except when they need us to work."

"Oh, come on!" Dek laughed. It was the first time he'd done that since he could remember. "Nobody works anymore except the PPD."

Tag shook his head, a gesture that became disturbing when the connection froze for a moment. When it re-established, he was looking down. "I'm gonna send you the cure info. I think they're coming."

"Who?" Dek said. "Tag, what's going—"

"Yeah, they're here. It'll take them a little longer to get through the barricade I made, but they will get through."

Dek leaned forward as if this would help him better comprehend the insanity unfolding before him. "What about your mother?"

Tears filled Tag's eyes. "Dead."

"What? *When?*"

"Same time as your grandmother. Something's happening, Dek. I wish I had time to figure out what, but I think they're letting the old ones that don't help the economy die."

"*Nobody* helps the economy! We're all stuck inside until..."

He stopped. Until what? Until when?

Lost in thought, Dek jumped at the sound of a loud crashing noise coming through his screen.

"Shit," Tag said. "They're almost in. I'm not letting them take me."

"Tag, no. Just explain to them what you think is happening."

Tag laughed. "Oh, I plan to. Goodbye, buddy. I enjoyed our talks."

Dek yelled for his friend to wait, although for what he did not know. The sounds of crashing and yelling filled his ears, followed by two gunshots. Dek stared transfixed at the screen until a large male hand came into view just long enough to sever the connection.

That was the second thing that happened.

THE QUARANTINE LASTED FOR FOURTEEN DAYS AND DEK SPENT nearly every moment in fear that the PPD would come for him the way they'd come for Tag. Getting very little sleep, he sat in the living room staring at the front door, wondering if he would be allowed to say goodbye to Mother before they handcuffed him and took him away. He never mentioned any of this to Mother, of course, and it wasn't as if she ever asked about his friends even before she became so sad. Mother wasn't herself anymore.

She spent most of her time in her bedroom or in Grandmother's former room, quietly sniffling and whispering to herself. Dek had barely been able to convince her to wait for him to disinfect Grandmother's bedroom with air spray. Nobody knew for sure if the stuff killed the virus, but it was better to be cautious.

When he was able to engage her in conversation, Mother's responses were perfunctory (he'd picked that word up from the old pre-virus short stories he liked reading) and usually no more than a few syllables. After a few days of trying, Dek gave up and placed all of his focus on worrying. His whole short life had been spent worrying about catching the virus, about losing Mother and Grandmother, about not seeming cool to Tag, and even of never experiencing a kiss that didn't come from an old female relative.

Towards the end of the second week of quarantine, Dek started feeling a little better about the situation. Tag was an awesome dude but he was also crazy. If anything, the PPD probably took him to a mental repair facility to fix whatever was wrong with him. Paranoid fantasies and a persecution complex, Dek thought. He'd read about those things, too.

Still, he often wondered about that supposed "cure" his absent friend mentioned. Dek had never received the information he'd been promised, so he assumed it didn't exist outside Tag's delusional mind. Then again, how was that any different from Outworld? Here in Shelter, the outer world seemed like a dream, like some unreachable realm available only to royalty and their servants. How could Tag think everyday people like them were being forced out there to work when Virus could take them at any time? It made no sense.

Three days before the quarantine was to end, Mother started coughing.

MOTHER'S FEVER SPIKED TWO DAYS LATER. DEK MOVED manically about the house, bringing her warm compresses, fluids, and fever-reducing medications. No matter what, he had to get the fever down by tomorrow or the PPD would seal her off just as they had done with Grandmother. Or maybe they would declare the house a contagion spot and demolish it, leaving them without Shelter. He'd heard of that happening sometimes.

A low moan from the other room pulled Dek out of his musings. "I'm coming."

Making sure his mask was on correctly, Dek walked back into Mother's bedroom carrying a tray of fluids including a cup of chicken noodle soup. He paused at the sight of Mother curled up in bed, her knees drawn up to her chest, the blanket half removed presumably in a fit of hot and cold episodes.

"You need to eat, Mother."

"For what?" She didn't look at him when she spoke, but then again she hadn't looked at him in days. "To feed the virus?"

Dek frowned. "It's so your immune system can fight off whatever you —"

Mother's coughing fit lasted several moments. It was dry and unproductive and her body convulsed with each hacking explosion from her lungs. Dek swooped in and placed a glass of water under her mouth, aiming the straw inside it between her lips. Mother sucked greedily at the fluid, slowly relaxing.

Struggling to get her breath back under control, she finally looked up at her son and managed the barest of smiles. "You're a fine boy, Dek. Such a fine, fine boy."

"Thanks." Unsure what else to say, he lowered the tray onto the bed and picked up the chicken soup. Spoon in hand, he leaned forward so she could try eating.

Mother slurped the broth, swallowed hard, and lost her smile as tears filled her eyes. "We tried so hard."

"It's okay." Dek's eyes threatened to turn all teary as well if he couldn't alter the mood in here. "Just get better. Have some more."

She did, but the teary eyes went nowhere, nor did her regretful facial expression. "We just wanted to keep you safe."

"You have."

Mother shook her head. "We kept you asleep. Big," she coughed. "Big difference."

He didn't like how she sounded. Too much like Tag. Dek didn't think he wanted to hear any more from her. She was feverish, goofy-acting, probably thinking about her own mortality. Those things made people weird, even ridiculously normal people like Mother.

"I need-need t-to tell you something," she managed between short, raspy breaths.

"Please just eat."

Mother shook her head. "You need to...hear."

"I think it's time for your fever reducer! I'll get it." He got up so quickly the tray nearly fell over. "Oops, sorry. That could have been bad, huh? I'll be right back."

Mother let out one loud cough. "Dek, please."

From the doorway, Dek said, "I'll be right back with your —"

"Dek, godammit! Get *back* here and listen!"

Arms limp at his sides, Dek shambled back over to Mother's bedside and looked down at her. "Yes?"

Mother told him everything and they both cried for a long time. The next morning she was dead.

A LONG TIME AGO, WHEN VIRUS WAS NEW AND A LOT OF people still thought it was a hoax or not as "bad as all that," a famous man asked how the cure could be worse than death. The reporter he said this to was unable to conjure up a coherent reply. The man then went into excruciating detail about how no other bad situation was worse than death, thereby justifying the decision to not allow people to just move about as if nothing had changed because they didn't understand the difference between freedom to act and freedom to think beyond one's self. But what about fear of death? Is this not something the powerful consider useful? It is, many assert the very basis for organized religion and all the riches gained from it.

Dek's mother's words were perhaps not as eloquent as all that but they certainly hit upon the same basic ideas and concepts. Dek had always wondered if somebody was profiting from the virus but he never thought it was in the way Mother seemed to think.

"We were looking for a way to get you a new home," he told him. "To get you into the Outworld and away from this."

"To go where?" Dek said. "Virus is everywhere."

Dek blinked. "What?"

Mother reached out for his hand, obviously thought better of it, and dropped her own hand onto the mattress with a loud thunk. "It's a word for cure. We're not allowed to say it. It's considered evil." Her upper lip curled at that last part. "There's so much you don't know."

"I think Tag is dead." Dek flinched; this was the first time he'd allowed himself to think it let alone say it aloud.

Mother nodded. "He was helping us."

Dek sat on the edge of the bed facing away from Mother and let the weight and import wash over him. He felt as if his body belonged to someone else. His consciousness floated above this scene between them, taking in every nuance, every unspoken moment as if preparing for battle on a plane he could not fully comprehend.

"Why are they keeping us here?" he said.

"Because we belong to them."

The conversation continued for a while afterward, Dek learning new words and expressions he'd never heard spoken or run across in his online studies. "Corporation. Slave labor. Maximum profit." They sounded so exotic, so foreign. But the one he kept coming back to was "vaccine." There *was* a cure. There had been one for some time now, just not here. How could anyone be so cruel and uncaring? What were they asking God for during National Prayer if a cure was being ignored?

There was another word. He had heard it before but never used the way Mother had last night. "Essential."

"It's how they did it," she said. "Just like corporations used the anti-slavery Amendment to justify their existence, they used essential workers to justify these...Shelters."

It was all so confusing. There was somewhere beyond Outworld where people had a cure and didn't have to live in Shelter but the essential people didn't?

"I don't think they know about us, Dek. Things got pretty bad for a long time and they had to rebuild."

"How do we tell them?"

Mother smiled. "What do you think your grandmother was doing?"

Now, sitting in the living room, waiting for the imminent arrival of the PPD, Dek reflected on that final piece of information. The last coherent thing Mother told him before she started choking on her own fluid. He had cried and yelled and pleaded half the night but now, drained of all that sorrow-fueled energy, he had only logic remaining.

Grandmother had contracted the virus by sneaking into Outworld and trying to contact the cured people. Tag had most likely been killed or forced to work in some horrible factory or mill because he had helped her. The only thing Dek had going for him was the advantage of knowing this while the PPD clearly did not.

When they came for Mother's body and placed him back under quarantine, he would have nothing but time to think and plan. He wouldn't make Tag's mistake and contact anyone. He would do this alone when no one was paying attention. If he didn't do it now, before the second quarantine ended, he was pretty sure he would be deemed essential and forced into some workplace where escape was even more difficult if not impossible.

He remembered Tag saying he wanted to spit in a PPD officer's eye when they came for him and how funny that was to him then. He smiled when he remembered it now for a different reason.

I hope you got your chance, Tag, I hope you spit right in their evil eyes.

As the sounds of the seal being removed came from outside, Dek's smile grew darker, more satisfied. He was going to spit in their eyes, too. All of them.

Soon enough.

CONTACT

NAYAS BANERJEE

About the Author:

NAYAS BANERJEE writes science fiction and fantasy from Kolkata, India. In spite of (or perhaps because of) his day job as a software developer, he is terrified of the impending AI apocalypse. He tweets at @hambasaurus.

Contact
Nayas Banerjee

JEREMY TURNED OFF THE TV, CUTTING OFF THE REPORTER IN the middle of her daily updates of official data about the war effort, looked himself over in the mirror, and sat down on the small stool near the door. His left foot danced nervously as he went over the list of tasks assigned to him today in his head. He glanced at the bracelet on his left wrist, the black metal glistening in the fluorescent light of his living quarters.

6ᵗʰ April, 2056

8:58 AM

Get ready! 1 minute to go.

The same as it said five minutes ago. Someone must be wasting time in the walkways, he thought as he stood up and started pacing in front of the door. Or someone might have died again.

The last death in his sector had been two weeks ago. He had not come across the body during his transit, but it had been all over the sectoral bulletin. That was the third one this year. There hadn't been any for months, and suddenly the death rate had spiked up from the end of last year. They had been rebels though; still determined to overthrow the Government, still failing. They had had a detailed report on the news. Though how much of that could be trusted, Jeremy could not say.

His thoughts were interrupted by the beeping of his bracelet.

Ready to go

He opened the door and stepped out into the walkway.

To the left, the illuminated corridor kept going as far as the eye could see, the dull metallic walls punctuated every ten feet by doors on each side. To the right, after five more doors, was the thoroughfare. It had taken him fifteen years to make his way up from the bowels of the endless corridor to his current quarters. Who knows, in a few more years, he may finally be able to bid goodbye to the corridor altogether. He savored the thought in his mind as he walked up to the thoroughfare and turned right.

He strode along, not looking at the various screens of advertisements lining the walls. They spoke incessantly as he walked, the appropriate voice automatically activating as he stepped in front of the screen. In the background to the cheerful chirping of the actors, he could barely hear the hiss of the overhead curtain of liquid from the ceiling dotted with holes, keeping step with his pace, always twenty feet behind.

He knew it would stop if he stopped to save any of the ads for later perusal, but, even after all these years, there was a part of him that was afraid that its positioning system would fail and it would spray over him as he admired a pair of woolen socks. Death by disinfectant – a particularly painful way to die, he had always thought. These kinds of accidents hadn't happened since the initial days of founding the colony, but the memories lingered. That's why he never dawdled to see the ads during transit. As a result, often he caught up with the spray curtain in front of him and had to wait while the person on the other side sauntered along at a leisurely pace. There was a minimum pace for transit, which the bracelet would notify, but it felt too slow to Jeremy.

Today, though, he couldn't see the leading curtain in front of him. *Good*, he thought; they had better make up for the delay they had caused him in starting. The government should really start banning advertising on the thoroughfare. *Everyone had state-sanctioned TVs, why couldn't ads there be enough*, he wondered as he made a turn and –

Jeremy's face crashed into the cool metallic floor.

Stars erupted in front of his eyes and pain surged through his head. As his senses came back to him, he rolled on his back and lifted his head. The spray curtain stood ominously behind him, still twenty feet back. Even then, he unconsciously dragged himself away as he sat up. His bracelet was beeping now, glowing bright red letters said

EMERGENCY

Respond for assistance

He touched his nose gingerly. A new wave of pain washed over him. His bracelet started beeping louder. His fingers came down bloody.

He looked at the floor between him and the curtain – smooth as ever. What had he tripped on? he wondered.

He sat on the floor, brought the bracelet near his mouth, and spoke into it.

"Jeremy Snader. ID 22856." His voice sounded wrong like he had cotton stuffed in his nose. But that didn't matter to the bracelet.

"Jeremy Snader. Do you need assistance?"

"Yes. I think I might have broken my nose."

"Noted. Do you have any other injuries?"

"Not as far as I can see."

"Noted. Do you see a medical socket near you?"

Jeremy looked around. A few feet ahead, lodged between two screens, was a small red box with the white plus symbol on it. He walked over to it.

"Yes, I see it."

"Please open the box and plug in your bracelet."

Jeremy lifted the lid up. One small red cable protruded out from the wall. He attached the cable to his bracelet.

Connected.

Transferring.

As he waited, he thought he could almost feel the liquid being injected into his artery. But that could just be his imagination.

Injection complete.

Please unplug.

The bracelet began talking again. "A medical pod will be with you shortly. Please follow these instructions. Do not panic. Help is on the way. Sit down on the floor and lean forward."

The bracelet continued giving him orders to follow. Jeremy stopped listening to it. He leaned against one of the walls, making sure to keep his head pointed down and waited.

Thankfully, the advertisements had been automatically switched off. He had never seen the thoroughfare without ads in the last twenty years. Without their bright flashy visuals, the cold overhead lights made the empty thoroughfare seem different. Spooky. Almost like the last few years before the colony had been formed. He remembered little of those days, he had after all only been a child.

His eyes fell on something. At the base of the opposite wall, like a smudge on the polish of the metal, words had been scratched out.

To anybody reading this,
It's gonna be alright!

Jeremy blinked his eyes a few times, just to make sure he wasn't seeing things. Someone had spent time in scratching that out. But why? Weird. It didn't even mean anything. Maybe they were trying to send a message? But, wouldn't that constitute as interference of traffic flow? They'd be charged for that.

Jeremy looked around as best as he could, trying to keep his nose down. One camera from the way he had come looked back from the corner, another looked out over the direction the thoroughfare led. This was a dark spot.

Someone was trying to avoid the authorities.

Rebels was his first thought.

But surely, they had better means of communication and didn't have to resort to such primitive devices.

A strange feeling washed over him. He went over to the message and ran his fingers over the letters. Letters. Written. By another human.

A voice from behind made him jump.

The medical pod had arrived. It looked its name, shaped like a large pea pod with its glass top now open, revealing a narrow bed inside. No driver, obviously.

"Please lie down, sir," the disembodied voice spoke from the machine.

He walked quickly away from the message and lay inside. The glass dome closed over him and the pod zoomed away. A faint, sweet smell hung in the air.

Jeremy knew what would come next. A series of robotic arms would probe and examine him. His nose might be bandaged, and he would be advised to stay at home for a few days by a speaker in the wall. A doctor would be supervising certainly, but he would never see her.

He felt sleepy. He tried to think back to when he had last seen another person in the flesh. Or even really talked to one. He couldn't remember. Before the ... virus? What was that, again? God, he felt sleepy.

Jeremy lay in bed. His mother hovered over him, fussing over his covers. She sat down at the side of his bed and brushed her hand on his forehead, and with her other hand, took out the thermometer from his mouth. She squinted at it for a few seconds before she turned to him with a smile on her face.

"Go to sleep now, sweetheart. Go to sleep. It's gonna get all better soon."

She stood up and started walking out of the room. Jeremy wanted to call her back, talk to her, tell her he missed her. But he couldn't. He had forgotten how to talk. His mouth flopped uselessly as his mother closed the door behind her.

Jeremy woke up.

It took him a few seconds to realize he was in the Medical wing.

He kept having these dreams these last two days that he had been here. Dreams of people he had once known.

He still hadn't figured out when was the last time he had seen a live person.

JEREMY SAT ON THE STOOL NEAR THE DOOR IN HIS QUARTERS. He looked at his bracelet.

13ᵗʰ April, 2056

8:50 AM

Get ready! 1 minute to go.

He touched the pocket on his coat again, feeling the slight bulge. His left foot danced, trying to keeping pace with his heart.

He had been asked to rest for a week. He had requested his leave to be shortened. He needed to go.

Ever since the accident, Jeremy had been going crazy. He kept thinking back to the days before the colony. Before the virus. When people were allowed to be together. He had been only a child then, but the memories seemed more real than anything since. The simple act of being able to look at the person you were speaking to seemed worth so much now.

He couldn't shake off the feeling that it didn't have to be so. He had almost forgotten, but the promises came screaming back to him.

"It's just a temporary measure."

"The virus will die out in a year or two. We can dismantle the colonies after that."

"Social segregation is necessary for our own safety."

How quickly they had accepted the restrictions.

How quickly they had gotten used to them.

The first few months had been hard. There were a lot of protests and riots and suicides. And again, when they had to separate the families. Those had been brutal. Apparently, the virus had mutated such that it could survive in the air for hours, even days. But then, the restrictions became the norm.

The rebels said they would lead the colony back to the golden days. But Jeremy didn't see how that was possible. They wouldn't be able to kill the virus any more than the government. One way or another, this was life now.

Life.

This was the only way for humanity to survive. He knew that. He could never hope to see another human beside himself. Life, whatever that meant, existed solely inside his head.

The bracelet beeped. Jeremy opened the door and started walking.

Within no time, he had arrived at the turn in the thoroughfare. His heart pounded in his chest. He made the turn and stopped.

There it was. The message.

To anybody reading this,
It's gonna be alright!

He fished around in his pocket and took out the rusty nail he had removed from the bathroom door in his quarters. He stooped down.

He had spent hours deciding what to write. He was wary of writing anything that could lead him to trouble with the authorities. But he desperately wanted to talk. He dug his nail in and started to scratch in the characters.

It was harder than he had imagined it would be.

Finally, he put the nail back in his pocket and appreciated his handiwork.

Hope springs eternal

He had heard that somewhere. Seemed apt.

His bracelet beeped as the blaring advertisement went silent. Jeremy jumped up in shock.

Do you need assistance?

Do you have any medical emergency?

Jeremy took in slow deep breaths. They must have sensed his pulse racing and that he was not moving. Coupled with his recent accident, the alarm made sense, thought Jeremy.

He canceled the alarm and started walking again.

23RD MAY 2056

8:59 AM

Get ready! 1 minute to go

Jeremy looked himself in the mirror one final time before his bracelet beeped. He left his quarters. He hastened quickly through the thoroughfare in a trance, eager to reach the turn in the road. A new message might be waiting for him today.

They had replied.

Two days after he had scrawled his message below the original, he went back to find new words below his.

Hello. Nice to meet you.

And so, it had begun. Every day Jeremy would eagerly rush to the messageboard (A name he had given to the place. Not that it mattered – he could after all only ever tell the name to himself.), hoping for a new message from the stranger. Sometimes he would walk away disappointed. But after every two or three days, there would be a new message.

He had ditched using the nail. Scratching on metal was too time-consuming. He had instead nicked a metal-marker from his office. Not only were the words more legible now, he could also write in smaller font, making the messageboard less likely to be discovered. It was the stranger who had suggested it.

He had discovered a lot about them in this last month, and vice versa. Nothing that could be used to identify themselves, of course. But other things. Things that would be deemed insignificant. Favorite movies, favorite songs, likes, dislikes.

Jeremy believed they were a woman.

There was no logical reason to believe so. Yet, he believed.

She (as Jeremy believed) was also a rebel. For this assumption too, he did not have any proof. But who else would risk so much?

Well, his inner voice would say, *you* are.

He shook the thought out of his mind. He had reached the messageboard.

Even from so far away, he could see that there was a new message.

Vanilla. Yours?

Jeremy smiled at the words.

He took out his marker, erased the message, and wrote,

Butterscotch

JEREMY'S BRACELET BEEPED.

19ᵗʰOctober 2057

8:52 AM

Get ready! 1 minute to go

Jeremy paced in front of the door. Her message would be there today. She *was* a woman – he had found out. Delilah.

Their messages had grown more detailed, more personal. He had told her his memories from before, about his mother, his school, his friends. She had told him about her parents. They had lived in a minor town about 500 miles away. Both her parents had died of the virus. She had survived because she was living in the city to study at that time and was lucky to have been selected as one of the earliest residents of the colony.

She would be older than him, Jeremy knew. But that didn't matter. It was not like they had a romantic future ahead of them. The closest anybody ever came to romance was during the weekly semen-collection-special shows on TV.

No, it wasn't romance. It was something more primal, more urgent. He remembered studying that humans were social animals. He had stopped believing that. Or maybe just forgotten it.

He knew they were heading into dangerous territory. Jeremy didn't know if there was precedent for interpersonal communication in the colony, but he was sure that the authorities wouldn't view it with sympathy. But he knew that he was hooked.

As the beeper went off, Jeremy set off for his destination. Funny, how he didn't think of his workplace as his destination anymore. His work had suffered in these last few months. He had been pushed farther away from the thoroughfare.

He passed the door that had been his quarters two months back and turned into the thoroughfare.

Soon, he had reached the messageboard. But instead of the paragraphs of text that they had now started writing each other, this time there were only a few words scrawled on the wall.

In trouble.
Don't reply.
I'll contact.

6ᵀᴴ JANUARY 2057

8:48 AM

Get ready! 1 minute to go

This was it, Jeremy thought to himself. Today was the day.

He slung the small backpack he had prepared over his shoulder, containing the few personal possessions that he couldn't bear to part with, and stood in front of the door. He felt oddly calm.

Delilah had returned.

Jeremy had almost given up. His work had suffered horribly. He had been pushed farther down the corridor two times since that day. There was even talk of getting him transferred to a different division. Only then had he picked up the slack – a different division might entail taking a different thoroughfare.

But finally, two weeks ago, a message had been left at the messageboard. Jeremy had been right. She was a rebel.

She had been discovered. She had managed to escape, though, and was now completely off the grid. They could no longer be in contact, she said. She didn't have access to the thoroughfare anymore. The message was apparently written by someone still undercover.

Goodbye, Jeremy, she had finished.

Jeremy had erased the message and written back his own reply.

I'll join you.

She had implored him over the next few days to reconsider his choice, to give up his hopeless madness. She reminded him that rebellion against the colony was punishable by death.

But Jeremy had already chosen. Delilah.

Two days ago, a message with the details was left. He would request an emergency transport pod when he reached sector 3, a little after of the messageboard. Normally, an emergency transport pod cost an arm and a leg, which would be docked from his salary. But that was the least of his concerns now. The pod that came would be hacked, and would take him to ... wherever rebels go. Jeremy did not know what to expect. He hadn't asked Delilah about that. But he knew it was what he wanted.

When the bracelet beeped, he stepped out. He walked along the corridor, wondering if this would be the last time he would see these paths, these horrid advertisements. Would he miss them, he wondered?

But, at least he'd have Delilah.

He walked along, his heart pumping. Sector 1, then 2, then 3. The messageboard. It was clean today.

He walked a few yards and stopped. As good a place as any, as good a time as any. He held up his bracelet, navigated the menu till he found an emergency transport pod and clicked it.

All the screens around him went black.

He waited

It was haunting, this silence. The spray curtains seemed uncomfortably close to him.

Curtains, he thought. He had been walking slowly and didn't

remember reaching the leading curtain. Were they moving closer?

Soon the pod would arrive, Jeremy reassured himself. He felt a pinch on his wrist from the bracelet, followed by a cool liquid sensation under his skin. That's weird, he thought. There was no ETA for the pod on the display.

The screen directly in front of him lit up. A man stood there with an expressionless face.

"Hello, Jeremy. I am the one you know as Delilah. It is unfortunate that you chose to be here today. Our great Colony was established for the continuation of the human race. For humanity itself. For you. Sure, we may have had to give up some privileges, but that is the cost for survival. The virus forced our hand. The Colony has given us everything we could ever have wanted. We must be thankful to the government for their vision and benevolence.

"But today, you have chosen to leave the Colony. Chosen of your own free will. You were given multiple chances to redeem your errors. But you chose to abandon the Colony. For something as base as ... companionship?" He spoke the last word as if it was particularly distasteful.

"We have known you had secessionist tendencies for some time. Your biosensors don't trigger appropriately for the TV content you watch. You rarely buy Colony merchandise. You were efficient, no doubt, but efficiency is not everything. What the Colony needs above all is obedience.

"We do not want to punish the citizens. We need every person capable of helping us survive. But the Colony comes first, people come later. Your ... punishment ... will once again prove to the people the strength of our Colony and the dangers of the rebellion. Long live the Colony. Goodbye, Jeremy."

Jeremy stood staring at the screen. His backpack lay on the floor beside him. His head was buzzing. He couldn't stand anymore. He leaned against the wall as he lowered himself onto the floor. His vision was going dark. He couldn't breathe. The spray curtains had almost closed him into a small rectangular block now, the two separate curtains now sharply turned to merge together. Half the thoroughfare was being opened to traffic. The show must go on.

His mind was running at the speed of light. Delilah, the conversations, everything. All an elaborate trap, a test. He could almost imagine the news headline in a few minutes, similar to the hundreds he had seen before on his TV. He thought of his mother's hand on his forehead.

The curtains were coming closer. They would pass over him soon, disinfecting his body for commuters to see. They would see and they would believe. And they would obey.

He looked at his bracelet one last time as the life drained out of him.

Goodbye, Rebel.

COFFEE OR BUST

GRACE MILLER

About the Author:

GRACE MILLER lives on a farm in Texas and when she's not wrangling Longhorns, chasing chickens, and cuddling rabbits, she's writing. She has been published in a few online magazines. She is thrilled to see where her relatively new writing career will take her. She invites you along for the adventure!

https://instagram.com/gracemiller.author?
igshid=10tkx7uxvicou

Coffee Or Bust
Grace Miller

I GLANCED AT THE PRECIOUS COMMODITY AND THEN AT THE backdoor dealer. His frame was large, and eyes darker than the dimly lit room stared down at me. Sweat ran down my back, almost as if someone had poured a bucket of water over me. I needed this deal to work out, the consequences of failure were too grave.

"I'm not going down on price." His gruff voice took several seconds to register in my brain.

"I understand." He had all reason not to charge the high price. Coffee wasn't something growing on any local trees, and the shipments had stopped months ago. But I needed it. I needed bad, like one day without my beloved beverage and I couldn't function. Even my rickety toaster did better than me that day.

"Well? Is this happening or not?" The man looked anxiously at the road behind him. A small dog-like robot walked down the road and I felt my knees give out beneath me. The "dogs" were meant to keep people in their homes. And I was not in my home.

"What are you doing?"

I felt my shirt tighten against my throat, and before I understood what was happening my back was pressed against the wall. I opened my eyes and looked at the man with horror. Had he, did he, just touch me?

"Alright it's gone now," he pulled his hand away from my collar and squirted hand sanitizer over his ridiculously large hands. "We better make this fast. I'll give you the coffee for the mascara, basil plant, ten rolls of toilet paper, and your disk of *Away Into The Night* by Ronald James. So, do we have a deal?" After using the liquid cleaner he stood up to his full height. He towered over me as I pulled the objects out of my backpack. I was eager to be rid of the mascara that my ex had left a few months ago, but the plant, toilet paper, and music seemed to stick to my hands. I placed the goods on the ground and took a few steps back.

"I'm sorry Molly." I whimpered as my dear basil plant was roughly jerked off the concrete by the giant of a man. He placed my medium can of coffee down then began to walk backward. "Nice doing business with you kid!" He said as he pulled the hood of his jacket down.

"I'm twenty-seven," I said to his retreating figure. After the man was gone, I suddenly became aware of the noises of the night. Slight shaking sounds, water dripping, and the scattering of little feet became very real to me as I jogged to my little town car. "I really need to get to my apartment before—"

"What do you have?"

An unmanly screech left my lungs as I jumped high in the air and clutched my coffee can. A small form could be seen against the brick of the wall on the other side of the aisle. It seemed to be lifting its head up and down almost as if it was, smelling me?

"I won't repeat myself." It hissed.

I looked at the end of the aisle where my little car was waiting for me. I doubted that I would be able to make it to my vehicle. I felt my hold on the container slip as sweat streamed out of my palms. What if this creep followed me until I was out of gas? I had read about it on a Facebook group, could I be the next victim?

"I just want to say," it lunged from the darkness, a missile from the hidden world of shadows, "HELLO!"

"EEEEEK!" I made for my loyal car and tried my best not to slip on the trash. I heard the creature bounding behind me and the hair on my neck stood up, almost as if it wanted to leave me and my situation.

Three yards away from my car, I slipped on some street filth and crashed onto the ground. Something flew over my head and I lifted my eyes to see that the creature who had chased me had rammed its head into my car's metal rim. I took the chance to jump up and reach for my keys, but they weren't in my pocket. My breath barely slipped in and out of my gaping mouth. I was so close to safety, but just far enough from it to be in range of the thing's hand.

It had a grip on my ankle, desperately I flung my other foot at its wrist. In the millisecond that it had taken me to react, I didn't consider that by kicking with my supporting foot I would fall. I fell.

The hand on my leg retracted as I tumbled to the shadowed ground. I wanted to call out for the authorities but they would be of no help in the dark world of sketchy trade deals. I pulled myself away from the moving form and tried to hide in the shadows. Maybe it would be disoriented and leave, then I could find my keys and get out of the godforsaken aisle. All I wanted was my coffee and peace, but apparently, it was too much to ask of the world.

"Nasty trick." Its voice sounded like a machine that hadn't been run in years, crumbly and with an edge that pierced the listener's ears. It began to hobble up from the ground and looked around wildly. The eyes of the beastly thing were a blue that did not have any warmth; only a cold and numbing shade, not unlike an iceberg.

"YOU ARE—" It started but was cut off by the sound of another voice.

"...out of your home. Please return to your home."

A robot dog repeated its chant to the fiend and a sharp sound emitted from its metal body. If I'd had any breath in my lungs, I would have screeched when I plugged my ears to keep the sound out of my throbbing head, but I didn't.

I forget to breathe when under stress, and this was the only time in my life that it had helped me.

Shoving his fists to his ears, the odd human (if that is what it could be called) wailed and ran into the night, away from my car. The robot followed, and I waited until I could no longer hear their cries before standing again. I needed to find my keys and leave; there was simply too much danger in this city. At any moment someone could come around the corner and report me, or even worse, sneeze.

I frantically looked around for my keys, and when I saw a small shine of light reflect off a smooth surface, I lunged for it. Never before had I felt relief like I had experienced in that moment.

"Come on," I whispered as my fingers repeatedly pressed the unlock button. When it finally opened, I jumped in faster than I knew I could move. I turned the keys and pressed my foot on the gas pedal.

The lights were off and I crept along the roads as silently as I could. The last thing I needed to be was caught in the final stretch. As I drove along, I opened the can of coffee, if after all this it was empty, I didn't want to think about it.

My concerns were relieved as the lid popped off and the smell that I had been dreaming of wafted out.

"My love, how could I ever part from you again?" As I made my way back to the apartment I thought about all the things I could possibly have to sell. If going through all that meant getting more coffee, then bring it.

My car pulled up into the parking spot and I put a bandana around the lower half of my face. Sneaking past the other apartment doors I twisted my key in the lock of my own door, trying to make as little sound as possible. The sound of light footsteps caught me off guard, I whipped around and saw a young woman with a mask and sunglasses hiding her face. She looked at the coffee can in my hand as I looked at the bag in hers.

"Lillian?" I breathed. My neighbor was always the perfect example of humanity, following every rule and never once getting out of line. Back when we were allowed to socialize, I never had to worry when she had guests over; they were never too loud. And when people were sick, she used to make them soup. But there she stood in the middle of the night, holding a bag overflowing with bread and other pastries.

We looked at each other for several moments. She could report me, and then I would have to spend the remainder of quarantine in a jail cell. And who knows how long that will be? She glanced at the coffee container and smelled the air rapturously. Then she looked at her bag of bread.

"One loaf for a plastic bag worth?" She asked, holding out the tempting bread.

I scoffed at her offer. After all, I went through? No. I was at least getting five. "Five or nothing Lillian," I answered her.

Through the mask, I could see her shock. She placed one of her hands on her chest and replied, "Will you not even give me a discount? I made you chicken broth last summer when you were recovering from your surgery. Will you not be kind to me in my time of need?" Her voice pleaded with me, and for a brief second, I felt guilt at even suggesting such a price. But then I remembered all the chaos that I had endured.

"I can't help you, Lillian. They stopped the shipments months ago, and I really don't know when I will be able to get more." I lifted the canister up and examined it. "You might be able to have enough for a cupful for one bag of cookies." I brought the can down and hid it behind my hands. I had read an article about how to trade, and one of the tactics was to take away the desired object.

She took a deep breath and her brows furrowed. I couldn't see her eyes clearly behind the glasses, but I saw them move and her fingers twitched as if she was doing math in her head. "Fine." She opened a bag of chocolate chip cookies and placed them on a napkin in her pouch. She then laid the cloth with treats between us and next to it she placed the plastic bag. I scooped up the cookies and held the napkins four corners to keep anything from falling. Then I poured some of the valuable beans into the bag and laid the coffee on the ground.

She lifted the beautiful beans and smelled them again. I was unable to see through her mask but I was sure that she was smiling. I leaned against my door frame and said, "You wouldn't believe what I went through to get that."

She lifted her sunglasses and I almost got teary-eyed when I saw the natural twinkle that couldn't ever be caught by a screen. I had really missed people.

"I beg to differ. You may be surprised at some of the stories I have myself." She nodded her head and something that looked like pride sown in her green eyes. "Yes, I have become something of a bad girl."

I tried to hold back my laughter as I looked at her. She was all of 5'1 and there wasn't a bad bone in her whole body. "You bad? Oh please!"

Her body stiffened a little. "Well, yes, me! This pandemic has brought out my naughty side, and I do say that you better pray that this all ends soon, because I don't think the world wants to know all that I am capable of."

I chuckled to myself but didn't challenge her on the topic. Looking at the window by my door I noticed that she had one exactly parallel to it. "You know, maybe if you're interested, we could talk through the windows tomorrow," I said looking down at my feet.

"I would love that." She said quietly. "I have to go, though." She pointed at her bag full of baked goods.

"Oh yeah of course." I shrugged and without saying another word I flung my door open and shut it behind me, then I let my body slide down the wood.

I had never been on an adventure before, but I loved whatever that night was called. And it was most certainly not the last time I snuck out and broke quarantine rules to trade or talk.

FLIGHTS OF FREEDOM

MORGAN BARBOUR

About the Author:

MORGAN BARBOUR is an American circus artist, movement director, model, and writer. Her work has been featured in publications such as *Insider*, *GenderIT*, *Al Jazeera English*, *The Journal.ie*, *Circus Talk*, and *HuffPost*. *Forbes* called her movement direction on the 2020 October!Collective short film "Obsolete" 'disturbing but beautiful.'

Her European debut play, *By the Bi*, was recognised by Amnesty International UK as a production inspiring audiences to think about human rights and was awarded the Doric Wilson Award for Intercultural Dialogue at the International Dublin Gay Theatre Festival. She has been a vocal advocate for victims of sexual assault and has publicly criticized the legal system's handling of such cases in the United States, United Kingdom, and the Republic of Ireland. She is a former lecturer at University of Nebraska-Lincoln, a visiting lecturer at Central St Martins, and a flying trapeze instructor at High Fly Trapeze.

At the time of writing "Flights of Freedom," she is

quarantining with fellow displaced circus artists and a growing number of houseplants in London. www.morganbarbour.com

Flights of Freedom
Morgan Barbour

SALOME HAD NEVER KNOWN A LIFE OUTSIDE OF THE CIRCUS. Her mother had strapped her to her chest for her first flight on the trapeze before she could walk, nestled securely to her breast as she flung their bodies through the air. Salome would let out a frightened squeak at the peak of the swing so her mother would dutifully release the bar; they would fall free through the air with a whoosh in her stomach only to be gently swaddled by the net below, mother and child both held protectively in the maternal embrace of the cotton webbing. Every time they let go Salome would fret, and every time they landed, she would coo and cackle in delight. Salome would eventually ask her mother if they would ever fly without a net.

"Never," her mother explained. "There is no flight without falling, and there is no falling if there is no net." Falling soon became as natural as flying; certainly, more natural than walking proved to be in the start.

Salome learned to fly on her own at the ripe age of two, dangling haphazardly off the trapeze, her tiny waist held secure in an even tinier safety belt, her mother controlling her body through the air like a daring marionette. This was in the before times, when their big top was still packed with bodies full of sweat and joy and wonder. Her mother would sing her lullabies after the evening shows, tucking her safely into the top bunk of their cosy caravan. Salome would listen to the hustle and bustle of the audience leaving, drink in the gasps and giggles and despairing sighs that the evening was already finished, and would sleep easy, knowing in her heart of hearts this would be her world forever. The circus was constant.

The first lockdowns happened when she was five years, five months, and twenty-nine days old. Salome had been obsessed with becoming old enough to join her mother and the troupe in her first show – *"When you're eight, sweetheart,"* her mother promised – so half-birthdays were celebrated religiously to earmark the passage of time. With the curse of hindsight, she would come to understand that there had long been whispers, rumors circulated throughout the acrobats that people were falling ill and being buried in mass graves. Her mother did her best to shield her from it, ushering her away from doomsday talk. *"People fear what we do not understand, my pet,"* she had assured her. *"You are safe here."*

And yet it came to pass that three days before Salome's five-and-a-half-year birthday her mother returned to the caravan with sallow cheeks and an empty smile and informed Salome that for a while they would have no more shows.

"It's to keep us all safe, sweetling," she assured her daughter.

Salome spent the afternoon disappointed that she would no longer get to sit on the side-lines and watch her mother flip through the air like an angel in flight. Her mother had assured her that they could stay with the circus, that the big top would remain erect for the company to practice and that their caravan would stay safely on site. Salome did not understand that no audiences meant no income and what a slippery slope that was to empty bellies and sleepless nights. She just knew that her mother suddenly spent much more time holding her close and telling her stories and hoisting her through the air like a pixie, and that was the best half-birthday gift a girl could ever receive.

There was optimism at first. Gratitude from the equilibrists that they were locked down with the means to keep training, enthusiasm from the motorcyclists that they could now spend their mornings racing endlessly round the globe of death and still be drunk by noon; what did time even mean anymore? In the early days there were rich smells and a cacophony of tastes created in the mess tent, energies redirected into creating meals for the whole hodgepodge family. Lenny the Illusionist would often sneak Salome an extra slice of cheddar and a Granny Smith during the hustle-bustle changeover between supper and clean-up; they were supposed to be adhering to rationing, but he would press the treat into her tiny palm with a wink and whisk off to the kitchen within a blink.

They would be unable to procure more apples, six months into the lockdown. Money would dry up within the year.

Initially the government had promised that the lockdown would be lifted within a month. Then three. Eventually the estimate was drawn up to eighteen months, two half-birthdays and one full birthday after the initial lockdown. Salome made a mental note that she would be seven by then, only a year younger than her projected starting age with the circus as a proper grown up performer. While the already proper grown-ups were burrowing worry lines into their brows as money dashed away through the sieve of time, Salome made a plan to train and become strong enough, quick enough, daring enough to get to perform when they were released at age seven.

On the morning of her birthday her mother gave her a kiss and a drawing of a cake. *"We must play make believe this year, my love,"* her mother told her. Salome had become acquainted with the familiar aching want within her belly, had taken note of the concave nature of her mother's abdomen, watched as arms that had once been corded with muscle had been reduced to autumnal twigs. She smiled dutifully and raised the drawing to her lips, smacking them loudly, declaring the cake was rose and cardamom and thanking her mother profusely.

The fatness of her tears was the only healthy roundness that lingered on her mother's body.

The government had promised its people money but gave it to the banks instead.

The government had promised free testing yet refused anyone but the dying.

The government had promised freedom by the time Salome was seven, yet her birthday came and went and they remained just as caged as the lions.

The government would insist they were doing a fabulous job.

When Salome was seven years, three months, and five days old Lenny the Illusionist disappeared. *"Lenny's just left to visit his mother,"* her own assured her, but Salome knew they weren't supposed to leave. There was a chill that hung over the circus following the departure of the illusionist, a quiet knowing that change was upon them, that the unspoken gift of safety provided by the isolated nature of the circus had been revoked.

Salome remembered the rumours of mass graves. On her sixth birthday she had learned they could fit as many as one hundred and fifty bodies. She wondered which number had been assigned to Lenny.

It was announced that they had found a vaccine. The scientists who appeared on her mother's square box television had trepidation on their lips but relief in their eyes. Perhaps there was hope after all.

Folks lined up for miles to be stuck like pincushions. Injections full of quicksilver miracles.

The ringmaster requested that they stay in quarantine. Wait and see what happened.

A month after they announced the new vaccine the first immunized child died. A week later more graves were dug, but the smaller bodies meant they could accommodate more tenants. Salome wondered what it would be like to be nestled up against so many children, questioned how many would have to be stacked on top of her before her bones cracked like glowsticks.

The vaccine worked for the adults, it was reported, but the babes were falling like flies, their bodies hosting a coup against a mind with no defence.

The scientists would have to return to square one.

On Salome's eighth birthday there was a riot in the capital. Buildings were smashed like Legos, homes lit aflame. *"This is not freedom,"* one man yelled as he detonated a homemade bomb just outside the hospital. There weren't enough bits left of him afterward to bother with a grave.

The IMMUNITY ACT was passed shortly thereafter. Anyone who tested negative for antibodies would be relocated to a newly constructed city to ride out the mania until a successful vaccine was discovered. Anyone who tested positive was assumed to possess immunity. They could remain where they were, phase out the lockdown slowly, get the economy running again.

A week before they were due to be tested Salome's mother developed the sort of wild fire fever everyone feared. She was gone with the morning sun.

The strongmen helped Salome dig a grave fit for one a mile away from her caravan. They sunk her mother into the arms of Mother Earth and patted the grave over with soft soil. Tears would not come no matter how desperately she prayed for them; instead she found solace in knowing that, in the end at least, her mother would not be crushed to dust under the weight of nameless strangers.

Salome tested positive for antibodies. The exhausted doctors in weathered masks explained she was what was called an asymptomatic carrier. Sick without ever having known. Death personified.

A few of the acrobats were swept away from the circus for the next phase of quarantine. She would never see them again.

That night, Salome nestled up in her caravan and stared at the window at the big top; by now its red stripes had been bleached pale by the sun, an albino exoskeleton hovering over a field of muck. She slept in fitful bursts, guilt clenching at her gut as she wondered if the kisses she had painted on her mother had been laced with the quiet poison growing inside her. She tugged at her hair until her scalp relinquished custody. She would wake to bald spots speckling her head like a Dalmatian. Xiomara the Contortionist would help her shave her head and promised the hair would grow back right again.

At nine years old, Salome took up smoking in secret, lighting up nubs discarded by the crew in stolen moments of solitude.

She would take three puffs – *all – your – fault* – and extinguish the butts on her thigh. *Murderer.*

She would shave her head for the rest of her life.

The circus remained closed for a year after they ended lockdown for those who had tested positive. It quickly became apparent that some of the results were false positives. More graves were filled, the dead engaging in the sort of skin to skin touch the living could only dream of.

Eventually the numbers tapered off. Six months in, a wild fire fever raged war in Salome's body. For three weeks she lay in her caravan weak as a kitten, and for four months after she could barely hold her own body weight when hanging from the trapeze. No one else from their crew had died, so Salome told herself that it had just been a dramatic cold that refused to vacate. As time dragged on her thighs became riddled with scars.

The seasons passed on like quicksilver. Restrictions were lifted for the immune and the circus resumed. At first the audiences came in droves, desperate people drunk on human contact and the thrill of watching the performers defiantly mock death. Salome had formally joined the troupe and flew like a sprite across the net to her catcher, a quiet woman called Bess who had come to them after the lockdown. Bess had a face frozen in a permanent scowl and shoulders that could emasculate a footballer. She was quick as lightning in the air, whisking away her flyers show after show, tossing them about like ragdolls, retiring just as swiftly after their bows without a word. Salome never asked where she had come from. It was common courtesy to never speak of the Before Times unprompted.

Salome was fifteen years, nine months, and three days old when the announcement was made: the illness had mutated, and the trial vaccines they had been running on the still-isolated had been unsuccessful. Rumours circulated that riots were raging behind closed walls, that the military had been called to keep those at without immunity contained. *"For your safety,"* they were told. A pregnant woman made a break for it over the line. Bullets were swift-footed. The government called her a biological terrorist. She would have called her child Marlene.

As the years dragged on the audiences within the circus dwindled. Long gone were the days of relief and joy at a false sense of freedom; they had been replaced with a sense of dulled complacency. There were no longer thrills at watching a faux dance with death. What interest was it to the audience to see strangers throw up smoke and signals when they were still separated from loved ones, when those who were left to rot in the ground were not afforded the common decency of the autonomy of solitude? *An insult to those who lost their lives,* read one review. *A hoax, a rip off, a sham.*

Our livelihood, thought Salome, but she pushed those thoughts down as far as her mother and smiled out at the sparse faces.

When the lockdowns first ended there had been promises that the economy would bounce right back, be stronger, even, backed by a united front of a people who had weathered hell. Stimulus plans had rolled out and had made for a brief moment of falsified hope. Wine flowed freely, people posted photos online of rustic homemade bread, bellies briefly found the soft roundness of comfortable white collar living.

But the money quickly dried up. Salome found herself returning to her childhood ways of endowing nothingness with the flavor of food, felt as if she were seven once more, smiling up at her mother and declaring a drawing of a cake to taste of rose and cardamom. She burned more calories than she could consume. Although she was reaching womanhood, she was scrawny as a youth, a malnourished giraffe taunting gravity.

She was seventeen the first time she fainted. She had taken off the platform to a rush of trumpets, swept back with all the power she could muster, and then blackness. Bess would later tell her how her body had flung limp through the air, a broken missile flying straight at her face. The bruising on Bess's face and arms would tell her how her catcher had not dodged her body, how she had used her own flesh to break her momentum and try to put her safely onto the net.

The next town they moved to was met with a packed tent. The ratings had never been higher. The reported near death of the young acrobat had travelled around. People were hungry and violent. They would happily let money trade hands if it meant they might actually glimpse death that evening. Trauma can be a villain to the mind, wrapping round the brain like a snake practicing a fatal hug. Retribution.

Salome could not remember how old she was when the news of the isolated stopped reaching her. The news reports of riots and bodies turned to cheesecloth by bullets had grown old quickly. The protests to liberate the isolated had subsided; the counter-protests, claiming those without immunity were a danger to society, fizzled out just as quickly. The new normal simple became normal.

The circus began to purposefully stage falls and blackouts for their audiences. A taste of death, an erotic tease. *We are mortal*, the bruises that peppered Salome's body said. *Take our pain as penance.*

And then, suddenly: a moment of hope. The government announced that arenas were being built, massive cities with reinforced glass walls, a human zoo for the immunized and the vulnerable to safely convene. A decade of separation abruptly ended with a calcified promise of unity.

Salome could not remember the names nor the faces of the acrobats who had been taken. When they were told the circus would travel to the wall to perform for those imprisoned to survive, she felt none of the tumbling anticipation that was shared by her fellows, only a muted sense of dread.

It took a week to arrive to the nearest isolation city. The circus rolled up haggard, a fraction of the size in the Before Times. Gone were the days of lions and horses; the beasts had been turned to supper before the stimulus money had been distributed. The Reunification Space was a sweeping structure of glass and concrete, functional rather than aesthetic. Older members of the troupe said it reminded them of big city shopping centers. Salome thought it looked like a prison.

There was an electric energy as they were brought into the performing arena the size of a football field, fully flanked by glass panels from the ground to the heavens. A man in fatigues and a gun thicker than Salome's scarred thighs explained that the isolated would convene to watch the show behind the safety of the glass. Salome could not shake the feeling that they were the ones in cages.

Their setup was quicker than ever; the big top was not needed in the arena. When asked if they would have time to practice, the performers were told no.

"This is the safest place on earth," they were told by the man with the gun, and they had no choice but to accept that as gospel.

Crowds emerged in quick succession. Even in the Before Times, when their tents were packed full to bursting, there had never been so many bodies watching them, all mashed together shoulder to shoulder. Salome could not help but notice how round their faces were, how bright their eyes. Where her ribs still stuck out from continued post-quarantine rations their middles were rounded, curved with a lack of want. Their plump faces were alight with smiles, joy dancing in eyes that she had been led to believe were deadened by a loss of hope and forced imprisonment. Was it just the thrill of seeing the outside world again that made the vulnerable look so healthy?

Trumpets announced the beginning of the show. The ringmaster bellowed his welcome. The vulnerable cheered their thanks. There were whoops and hollers for the jugglers and fire dancers, gasps as the motorcyclists raced round and round the Globe of Death. Painful anticipation as the clowns played distraction to allow Salome and her troupe set up the rigging for the flying trapeze.

Where the hell was the net?

A pause from Bess as they realized their net had not been

rolled out. A glare from men with guns guarding the arena. A moment of clarity as they understood what was being asked of them.

"This next act, ladies and gentlemen, is a spectacle to behold. Watch as this daring group of women fly through the air with the greatest of ease, defying death on their flying trapeze!"

A punch to the gut as Salome looked back at the ringmaster, and he gave her a nod. Sweat on her palms as she joined her fellows ascending the ladder to the platform suspended thirty feet above the ground. A fall at this height meant death.

More trumpets as the bar was passed to Salome. The ringmaster was speaking but the rush of adrenaline in her ears made it impossible to understand his words. What she did understand was the manic cheering from the imprisoned crowd, the ravenous hunger to watch a show that had transcended smoke and mirrors and entered the true realm of taunting death. She remembered how their shows had spiked in popularity after she had fainted mid-act. She thought of the bodies riddled with bullets who had attempted to escape and could not help but think that, after a decade of isolation, these people wanted to see the immune suffer, as well.

With a rush in her gut Salome jumped, swinging out and back again over the ground below. *Don't look down*, she told herself as she whipped her body around the bar to remount on the board. A *thunk* of a landing and the crowd exploded with cheers.

Bess took the bar and swung out as well. With a grunt she threw her body off the bar into oblivion and for a moment the world stopped and held its collective breath to see if her hands would find the catcher's trapeze. And find they did, if only just. With a heavy swing she flipped up to sit on the bar, began to pump backward and forward like a child on a massive swing set.

The trapeze was passed to Salome again. *"Lista,"* she called to Bess. She watched as the woman dropped to her knees and flung her legs around her bar, hanging upside down. Salome jumped.

She had flown longer than she had walked. Flying was all precision and calculation, as reliable as the tides. And so, she released on instinct, tumbling round once, twice, thrice in the air, opening with the same secure faith as the scientists all those years ago.

As a child, her mother had told her that if she ever needed to fall, she must twist to her back. *"That's why we use a net,"* she had told her. They were performers, not suicidal.

Instinct took over when Bess's hands were not there to hold her wrists. She twisted, back plummeting to the ground. The fear of falling that had once possessed her as a child returned and she felt a swoop in her belly as her eyes met Bess's. Through sheer mercy her world went black before her mind could process the impact of the fall.

The applause drowned out the screams.

ONE FOR THE ROAD

CHRIS WHEATLEY

About the Author:

CHRIS WHEATLEY is a writer and musician, from Oxford, UK. He has an enduring love for the works of R A Lafferty, Jack Vance, and Shirley Jackson, and is forever indebted to the advice and encouragement of his wife and his son.

One For the Road
Chris Wheatley

OWEN AWOKE WITH THE CRIME FORMING ON HIS LIPS.

The hour was late. Day blared through the thin curtains. A faint hum of traffic. Birdsong. Owen watched the dust motes dance and play in a shaft of sunlight.

He had been dreaming, as he often did, of the act. The thing. The deed. It was dirty, dangerous, and mad. But other people did it, didn't they, and if other people did it, then Owen was neither a saint nor a sinner, just a normal human, with normal desires.

He could almost believe it.

As he showered, he thought of the process itself. In his mind, he cycled through every step. The phone-call, payment, booking the transport, the examination, suiting up, the ride, a short walk, the door...

He had been right up to that door, once, on a cold day, back when the days *could* be cold, but at the last he had turned back, back to the noisy street, where traffic lurched and rushed and people strode, made polite yet futile attempts to keep their distance. The shops had been open then, the restaurants, the cafes. Tables nudged apart. Floors marked off with tape. *Keep Your Distance. Please Respect Our Staff And Other Customers.* All gone now. All gone.

As was his habit, Owen delayed the moment of testing for as long as possible. He towelled himself dry, combed his hair, trimmed his beard, applied creams, and did as many other little jobs as he could find. At last, he could put it off no longer. Owen removed the cover from the hateful black box, turned on the power (that sickening whirr) pressed his thumb upon the sensor and, when the little flap rotated back, placed his finger inside. A terrible pause. A prick of pain. The tedious, uncomfortable wait, while the machine tested his blood, logged and communicated the results. Red light turns to green. No sickness today. Not yet.

But what did it matter? The machine caught advanced stages. A man could grow unwell in two hours or two minutes.

Which made the crime more serious, still.

Desire welled up. Fear. Owen willed himself to quell the buzzing in his body and in his brain, the sharp wildness of adrenalin. Slowly, deliberately, he made himself breakfast. A cup of tea. Sat for a while, in the silence of his sitting-room, staring at the plastic token on the coffee-table.

The plastic token was an excursion ticket. A prized possession, dating back to before the double-lockdown but still valid. Owen had been nursing it for a long time. It kept him going, on many days, that warm, secure knowledge that an escape lay in store, should he ever need it. But having the thing and spending it were two different matters. How would he cope, without that safety net, without that warm fuzzy promise? Then again, what else was it for, if not for using?

The unexpected and very loud sound of his phone ringing made Owen start violently. The phone lay on the kitchen counter. He did not remember leaving it there. Another breach of protocol. You Must Keep Your Mobile or Alternate Device On or Very Near Your Person At All Times and Keep Location Tracking On.

Surely not in your own home, thought Owen, but he was well aware that the official position stated otherwise.

Owen was surprised and dismayed at the incoming ID, and irritated to see that it was a video-call. Dutifully, he held up the phone and connected. The woman on screen was large and cumbersome and jowly. She wore a plain black sweater and no make-up. Her hair, by contrast, was glossy and immaculate, extravagantly styled. Owen imagined that he could smell Florentina's sickly-sweet perfume. She sat at an untidy desk, behind which were untidy shelves.

"I'm not working today," said Owen, and at once regretted the hostility in his voice.

Florentina screwed up her face. "Did you book it?"

"Yes. Yes, I did."

Florentina shrugged her heavy shoulders. "Okay," she said, but made no move to end the call.

Owen breathed.

"So," Florentina smiled, "what have you got planned for your day off?"

"Nothing," said Owen, too quickly, he felt.

"Don't you have pro bono to do?"

Owen unconsciously glanced to the pile of cardboard boxes next to the dining-room table. Coarse, blue material spilled out of the topmost. The hated sewing-kit lay where it had been roughly shoved, poking out of another box like the prow of a sinking ship.

He sighed. Suppressed a pulse of anger. "Is there anything else?"

Very slowly, Florentina shook her head. So slowly that it made Owen grind his teeth.

"Bye, then," said Owen, and pressed the off button. Florentina had begun to speak. The silent echo of her broken words lingered in Owen's mind. What had she started to say? It didn't matter, he told himself. It didn't matter at all.

To his relief, the excursion ticket was accepted by the system. A half-dozen times, during the wait, Owen felt compelled to cancel, but each time he sank back too easily, into the coldness and blankness of willful in-action. When the notification chimed, he settled his mask on his face.

The car stood panting and sparkling at the end of the drive, in the blazing heat; a large blue thing with the official yellow cross sticker on its side. The interior was blessedly cool, the seats clean. The driver, slab-faced, masked and gloved, turned only once to stare through the partitioned window and ask, "Where?"

There was little traffic, almost none. The car glided easily along roads Owen had travelled a thousand times, roads which once had been full, absurdly it seemed now, of throbbing, jostling cars and trucks, buses, and bikes, of teeming life, packed so close, rubbing shoulders, exchanging air. Familiar sights of the city rolled by, squares and buildings and malls, made somehow unfamiliar and novel by their emptiness.

In front of St Angel's Hospital, cordons had been erected, ten meters high and a quarter mile from the building. The cordons were of sturdy plastic, tessellated for inter-locking. Where do such things come from, thought Owen? Who builds them? What mistrust of man, what cynicism, to devote one's life to the building of barriers. But they were right, weren't they, in the end?

Too soon, they reached their destination. The car pulled smoothly up to the curb. The engine died. The uncomfortable quietness prodded something unpleasant in Owen's mind.

"Twenty minutes," said the driver, without turning.

Owen pushed open the door and angled himself out and onto the pavement. The heat of the sun stung his face and his arms. Very few people were about. Those who were, dressed in PPE, from latex gloves and facemasks up to full suits and rubber boots.

Owen hustled along to the corner. He felt the driver's eyes burning into the back of his head. He must know, he thought, he must. But Owen could deny it. He used to live around here. If the authorities came calling, then he would tell them that he had just wanted a walk, that he had just wanted to visit the old neighborhood, to see the house where he had been born.

He took the first left and then left again, almost immediately, between two low brick walls to the anonymous gray door. His heart trembled. A terrible fire burned in his stomach. He reached out a hand that did not seem to be his hand, knocked loudly, took a half-step back.

No-one came. There was no sound of movement, no sudden, irrevocable opening of the way. Owen waited some more, was about to knock again. At that point he noticed the little intercom, the hand-written sign beneath: *Ring For Entrance.*

Owen felt a fool. This tiny misstep was almost enough to make him turn back. Almost.

He pressed the buzzer, and was expecting to speak, but instead came a short click. Owen pushed and the door gave, just like that, swinging back into the shadowed interior.

The corridor was dark and dusty and smelled of disinfectant. Something else, too. An unpleasant, tangy odor that Owen could not place. The room beyond was well-lit and full of shelving, like a normal, regular shop. The products upon the shelves were not normal, or regular. In the center was a booth, shielded by plastic.

The man behind this plastic screen was obese. Rolls of fat hung down from his flanks as he sat, perched upon a swivel chair that groaned and creaked with his movements. Owen felt sorry for the chair, felt certain it must buckle and break. He dreaded the coming of the sharp snap, the fall of the man, not for the man's sake but for fear of becoming *involved*.

The man looked up. His face, too, was large. Big ruddy cheeks, small, deep-set eyes, a thick brow.

"Name?" he said.

"I've an appointment at 2pm."

"Name."

"Owen Jones."

A puffing of cheeks. A turning of paper upon a clipboard. The clicking of a pen.

"Hand-holding, right?"

"No, no," said Owen. "No. I booked for a full embrace. I've paid."

The man shifted in his seat. The chair sent out a sharp moan. "Alright, fella," he said, unkindly. "No need to take that tone."

"I'm sorry," said Owen, who wasn't. "I just want what I've paid for."

"You'll get it," said the man. "Take a seat," he gestured, and turned back to his paperwork.

Owen took a seat on the dirty, red-plastic sofa. He sunk down into it uncomfortably, kept his hands upon his knees and stared straight ahead, stared at nothing. Tried his best to think of nothing. He could still get up. It was not too late to back out.

Another door opened. A woman in her fifties. Thin, with long, dark hair, white slacks, and a pink crop top. She wore a full white facemask, with built-in filters, and blue gloves. She nodded.

Owen rose and followed. "Are you...?"

"No," said the woman, sharply.

They walked down a carpeted corridor. It reminded Owen of the chain hotels he had stayed in, back before all this. Anonymous. Sterile. Every door looked the same, but each one had a number.

The thin woman stopped outside door nine, unlocked it with an old-fashioned key. "She'll be in soon," she said. "You get fifteen minutes. You'll hear a buzzer."

Owen stood, helpless.

"In there," said the woman, annoyed.

Owen found himself in small, square room, carpeted in the same dull beige. White painted walls, chipped and scarred. There was a single bare lightbulb, a window, shuttered and bolted, and another door, besides the one he had come through. He wondered where the buzzer was.

A little time passed. Owen found himself strangely elated and excited, in a distant sort of a way. Fear, now that he had hurled himself headlong, had receded a little. The line had been crossed. He had waded into the waters and there was nothing left but to experience it. He *was* a fool, he knew, a damn fool.

The interior door opened.

Not yet, was Owen's first thought, *I'm not ready*. The woman who entered was short and of medium build, with straight, brown hair. What could be seen of her face above her mask was pretty, fresh, with a sprinkling of freckles beneath brown eyes. She wore a modest dress of dark blue with white print. She breathed deeply and quickly.

For some awkward moments they stood in silence, then:

"Hello," said the woman, and her voice seemed very young. Innocent. Tender.

Owen immediately thought of his daughter, as she had been when she was a child, a teenager. When she had been not much older, at the hospital, at the end. All the desire, all the yearning leaked out of him. It was like letting go of a heavy, heavy weight.

"Shall we hug?" said the woman.

"How old are you?" said Owen.

The woman paused. "Seventeen." Another pause. "Sixteen." She shuffled her feet, ran her eyes across the room, slowly reached her hands up to her mask. "You can kiss me, if you like."

Owen screwed up his eyes, held up his hands. He felt faint, dizzy. "No. No, don't."

The woman's fingers froze in their motion.

"I can't," said Owen. "I'm sorry, I can't. I can't," he repeated, as he rushed for the door, tore it open and staggered out into the hallway. Back along the corridor, he went, through the office, without giving the obese man time to speak, back into the entranceway, back to the exit. Here, he found himself held up for some moments, while his shaking hands worked the locks. Then he was out, out into the heat and the soft sounds of the day.

Around the corner, he almost ran, certain that his shame must be written large upon his face.

The car was no longer there.

Owen froze. Sickness lurched into his stomach. He looked up and down the street, walked a few paces along it, stood impotently, hands by his sides, chest heaving. The car must be here, surely, somewhere. Had he misremembered? Was it that one, over there? No. Had he somehow gotten turned around and come out on the wrong road? No.

Gradually, his mind came to acceptance. The car had gone. He was alone. Stranded. It was at least a five mile walk back. Someone would challenge him. The police. So far from home. He would have to tell them, tell them that the car had not waited. They could check, couldn't they? He hadn't done anything wrong, after all.

Owen began to walk, stopping, now and again, to stare back, lest the vehicle miraculously materialize. At length, though, he gave that up, and walked on, his stomach coiled in knots, his feet aching already, the unbearable heat pushing down. He was thirsty, tired. Every step seemed to carry him such a paltry distance forward.

He thought of the girl. He thought of his daughter. Thought of his home. The waiting boxes, the empty rooms, the quiet and stillness of the days and of the nights.

Abruptly, he turned aside, into a park entrance. Owen had thought them all closed, but the large iron gates stood ajar. A padlock on its heavy chain hung limply. He squeezed through the gap. It didn't matter, now. He wanted to sit. He just wanted to sit.

Owen could not recall the moment at which he became aware of the singing. It was so quiet, at first, that Owen doubted he even *did* hear it. But, as he followed, past the rose bushes, out into the green grass, up the slight rise, the singing grew louder, until there could be no doubt. Voices. Dozens. What was the tune? The words were half-familiar.

...swift to close ebbs out life's little day, Earth's joys grow dim, its glories pass away...

Owen crested the rise. There, in the hollow, they sat. Perhaps a hundred people. They sat and they sang as one man led the song, calling out the words before each phrase. Old and young, men and women and children, too. None of them, not one, wore a mask, or gloves, or protection of any kind. They sat close. They hugged and smiled. They laughed.

The man who led the singing, an older man, with long, flowing grey hair and a bright, open face, noticed Owen and, without pausing from his task, gestured warmly that he should come. People turned, smiled, waved Owen forward.

"Come join us, friend," called the grey-haired man, as the others sang on. "There is no distancing here."

Owen took his place among them, picked his way, slowly, numb and delirious, into their ranks. He took a seat upon the grass near a laughing woman who held a little baby in her arms. The song ran its course, the voices stopped. "Let us bow," said the grey-haired man, "in quiet reflection and give thanks."

Owen pulled down his mask and closed his eyes.

The sun bore down, the birds called, the grass wavered as a soft breeze blew.

Somewhere, toward the middle of the group, a man began to cough.

THE MORTICIAN'S BOX

DORIAN WOLFE

About the Author:

DORIAN WOLFE is a young lawyer (and former concert pianist) obsessed with speculative fiction. She loves cats, sugary things, and Tom Hiddleston's Loki. Her home on the net is dorianwolfe.wordpress.com.

The Mortician's Box
Dorian Wolfe

DENISE CHEWED HER FINGERNAILS DOWN TO THEIR SALTY, raw nibs as she snuck repeated glances at the box. The morticians had delivered it to her father's porch almost six days ago; Mom had, after all, been her father's legal wife.

"Stop that, Denise," The Stepmother said as she stalked onto the sitting room's yellow carpet—a carpet so stained by Denise's wild childhood experiments that it looked patterned in paisley. The Stepmother's sky-blue satin dress hissed around her bony ankles and taut ligaments. She stopped six feet away from Denise. The one-percenters prided themselves on being able to measure the so-called "ViroSpace" unaided.

Stop that, Denise, is it? Not even a faint word of consolation. Denise chewed her fingernails with renewed intensity. That was petty, especially for a woman of thirty-two, but it was better than slapping the woman.

She hated The Stepmother for coming, today. Her father should have been here, not his new wife (ah, that was the difficulty, wasn't it? So very new a wife). They had married five days ago in the virtual presence of the Santa-faced Justice of the Peace, to the thunderous applause of thousands of virtually-connected friends, each of them blinking in and out of focus on the ninety-six-inch screen. As if her father and that woman hadn't been in and out of each other's bedrooms ever since Denise's mother left.

Denise would have hated her father, too, if he had come.

The tired, old grandfather clock struck noon. Something rattled in the loops and gears of the mechanism, sounding like a shower of coins.

Almost no one bothered to wait out the full six days to the minute, not anymore. That had been the original rule: six days between the morticians leaving the deceased's personal effects on the next-of-kin's porch or delivery hutch, in a complimentary leather-bound box, and the next-of-kin opening the box. Nobody knew what the deceased had touched—or worse, what (or whom) had touched the deceased—so it was safer to wait. Not everything could be sanitized to perfection. The rules had relaxed a bit, though, especially after the fourth viral outbreak. Scientists now claimed that the disease didn't last but three days on surfaces, making the strict postal-and-package rules unnecessary.

But Mom had been a woman for tradition. She had especially loved the post-epidemic traditions; they were *hers*, not her mother's or her grandmother's. And there were so many of the new traditions, a veritable cornucopia. Postal-and-package rules. Pet rules. Cell-phone sanitation rules. And so on, so on.

Denise could almost see Mom now, sitting alone with loosely clasped hands on the squeaky red love seat, waiting for the digital numbers on Denise's alarm clock to flip to 10:37 AM. It had been six days to the minute after the morticians had brought the effects of Denise's favorite uncle Jerry, Mom's brother, to the porch. When 10:37 silently arrived, Mom had risen and opened the screen door, leaving Denise to follow a ViroSpace behind. Mom had approached the box, her long graying hair swinging and releasing a faint scent of cherry- and orange-blossom shampoo. She had swung the supple brown lid open and studied the meager belongings found on Uncle Jerry's corpse. His clothes, and a tarnished gold locket wreathed in old-fashioned filigree. Inside the two-sided locket, crumpled photos: Denise on one side, her mother on the opposite.

Denise's father had not been there that day, either.

That had been six years ago, before Mom had slammed the door of her ancient Chevy pickup hard enough to make the windows shudder, and left. And never returned alive.

Denise got to her feet, stepped forward in her pinching black pumps. She felt as if she was recreating that scene from six years ago. Her own hair, not gray at all, swung in a fine mist over her back. If she were not so used to the scent of her own shampoo, she would have smelled a hint of lavender. She opened the screen door to the porch, trailing her finger over the square inch of sharp, broken wires—the legacy of a suicidal bird—that hadn't been there six years ago. She approached the box, swung open the supple, brown lid, and studied the belongings the morticians had found on Mom's—corpse. She swallowed back the treacherous salt of tears. They weren't *meager* belongings at all.

Mom hadn't exactly been planning to die that night. Up close, the clothes she had worn to *Raymondo's!* were almost garishly bright, sparkling with sequins; her faux-diamond earrings were equally loud. They had found her slumped, twisted over the glass plate that separated the bartenders from the presumably virus-laden drunks. Her finger was still stirring some unidentified drink. In the dim restaurant lighting, where six feet (more like eight feet; restaurants couldn't be too careful) separated her from any other patron; where servers hid behind curved glass face-shields (no one wanted another round of shutdowns), she wouldn't have looked like a clown. She would have looked exactly as she had always wanted to: poised, calm, in a moment of endless hope.

Denise wondered what Mom had eaten for dinner. The last meal. So final. She hoped Mom had gotten arancinis. The balls of crispy rice and gooey cheese had been Mom's favorite.

She pawed at the pockets of the garish dress. Surely the receipt was here somewhere. But nothing. Maybe *Raymondo's!* had just let the bill go. She choked back a sob. She wanted *so much* to know what Mom had had for her last meal.

AS SHE LEFT, SHE TOOK A DEEP BREATH, CLOSED THE GLASS-paneled door behind her with a gentle shove, and slipped on slick, purple rubber gloves with a satisfying *snap*. (Almost. At the moment, her stomach felt as though it was filled with waterlogged sand, and she thought nothing would ever be satisfying again). When she looked up, she saw Felipe standing on the eighteen-foot wide sidewalk. He was wearing a gray hoodie, over-washed jeans with a stray hole over one knee, and pristine blue sneakers. His green bike snuggled against him.

"Hi, babe," he said. He laid his hand over his heart in a tender gesture.

"Hi." Denise tried to swallow her croak. If there was any time she missed hugs, this was it. But legally, they couldn't be within a ViroSpace of each other until the wedding day. Then, she could touch him, and any ensuing minor children. How messed up was that, huh? Dreaming about her wedding the day before Mom's funeral?

"Sorry about your mom." He dragged his right foot across the pavement. The shoe *scritched* on the uneven cement.

"Yeah. Well." Denise thought she would be able to actually talk and cry if Flips held her, letting her head find that hollow under his chin where he rubbed his *Mad Raccoon* cologne, that "perfume" with a stench powerful enough to reach four ViroSpaces away. She could *be* a mess. Instead, all she could do now was stand here, muttering nonsense-ities and, like Flips, drawing invisible patterns on the pavement with her shoes. "Um. Well, The Stepmother's probably looking out of the sitting room window. Wanna walk me home?"

"Yeah, yeah, sweetie. Of course." He dragged his bike into the third pedestrian lane, the one nearest the road. Denise walked over to the second one, the one in the middle of the sidewalk. Flips reached an arm out straight from his shoulder toward her, as if his desire to hug her was an instinct not to be denied. Then he yanked his arm back, shaking it as if it were an alien limb.

"Hey, eight years in, you'd have thought I remembered the hygiene rules! No *hugs*, no *this*, no *that*...How do you do it, sweetie? How'd you get it down so pat?" He twisted his lips up on one side and down on the other. Denise knew he only ever did that to make her laugh—and maybe she needed a laugh right now, a laugh that left her whole chest aching—but somehow his contorted expression seemed immature. Like a little boy dancing around in a too-loose tuxedo during family dinner (or during a funeral; sometimes the two were hard to distinguish), begging for unearned attention.

"Please, Felipe," she said. His face fell into its proper lines.

They walked the two miles back to her apartment. The roads were no longer big enough for cars (which made all the anti-emissions folks happy), and Denise despised bikes. They belonged to those for whom every moment had to be productive, who couldn't take a moment to smell the flowers in the breeze, or to taste the pelting rain, or to watch squirrels as they chittered in the leaves. (Felipe wasn't like that. Of course.)

"What do you want to do on Sunday?" Flips asked, when they came within sight of her building and their silence stretched taut enough to shatter.

She shrugged. "Mom's being buried tomorrow."

"Look, I'm sorry, Deni, so, so sorry, but the chapel will be too small even to hold you and all the rest of her relatives with their own ViroSpaces. I can't be with you. Sunday is three days from now, and I think you can—"

"I know you can't come with me. I just wish..." Her wish trailed off into something nebulous, something she couldn't catch. She spotted a little lavender butterfly hopping in the half-withered summer grass, pausing to land on the bowed crown of a daisy. *That was my wish, whatever it was. It just flew off.* She smiled and waved at the butterfly.

Flips whipped his head back and forth to check his ViroSpace. "Who's there?"

She laughed now, and the laugh rocked her chest, and she found herself on her knees in the pedestrian lane, rocking and squeezing herself in her arms to contain that great laugh. "Butterfly, Flips. Look at the butterfly."

"Butterfly."

She calmed herself enough to point.

"That little tiny one?" One of his dark eyebrows rose about an inch above the other.

"It's purple, don't you see?"

"I see." A breath. "When we're married, I'll make a butterfly garden just for you. And we can kiss and drink limeade there." He scratched the skin just above his knee where the ragged hole bared it.

Denise climbed back to her feet, her savage breaths slowing. "Maybe we can go fishing on Sunday. It's three days away, you're right, and we're probably just in time to make reservations."

In front of the house, the sidewalk curved into an equally broad gravel path, which then broke into two smaller ones. The twistier of the two branches led to Denise's housemate's half of the house; the straight branch led to Denise's half. Flips' bike jerked and jolted as they walked along, and gravel fragments pinged against the spokes of its wheels. Denise's side of the yard was barren, but for a few potted succulents resembling fleshy green rabbit-heads. She planned to put in a few more, if she ever had the time. Her housemate's side blushed with roses in colors bright enough to dizzy unsuspecting visitors.

"Actually," Flips said as they reached the tan, stucco portico, where Denise reached under her coarse blue-and-white rope mat for her key, "I *hoped* you would want to go fishing."

"Good," said Denise, as she hefted the key and clunked it into the lock. "Great minds think alike."

Flips shifted from his right foot to his left, opened his mouth, closed it again. Looking very much like a fish. *So juicy sweet...*

"What is it, Flips?"

"Well, that is, I've already reserved the boat."

Denise dropped the key. It landed on the mat with a dull thud, and a small metallic ringing where it struck a bare strip that caressing feet had worn down. "You what?" She suddenly noticed a headache worming its way around her skull. It had probably been there all along. "Today's not the best day for surprises. Just in case you didn't understand that."

Flips looked even more awkward. As if that was possible. "It's a three-seater."

Denise huffed and yanked the key up, flipping the mat almost upside-down in the process. The mat flopped back down and lay askew. She shoved the key, its metal already warm from touching her hand less than a minute before, back into the yawning lock. "I don't have time for this. I don't have time to meet any of your friends, Felipe. Even your sisters. I know you want to cheer me up, but you...we...need to communicate better." He was such a child. A child with a degree in electrical engineering. Also, a boat three ViroSpaces long was hard to row.

"Uh. About communicating better." He cracked his knuckles, and Denise's headache spiked. "I thought you and...okay, the third seat is for your dad."

She paused with the key half-turned. *My father. My dad.* For some reason, the image that sprung to mind was the fluffy mustache, prematurely white even during her childhood. It framed a gentle, laughing mouth. And she was suddenly seven years old, and laughing, and Mom was young with hair like a dark mist, and laughing. Denise was sandwiched between them, holding a slurried mix of banana, ice, cocoa, and cream in a pink princess-themed cup. Mom had declared it an abominable concoction—there, one of Mom's favorite words, abominable—but seven-year-old Denise had declared it "pretty good, Dad."

"Denise?"

She let go of the key and, almost instinctively, reached her hand out toward Flips.

Flips reached his hand toward her.

"You know," she said with a brittle laugh, "you'd think after eight years, we'd have given up."

They both checked the landscape around them, making sure no neighbors were peeking out from behind ruffled window-curtains, (sanitized) cell-phone in hand to call the cops. Then they let their pinkies touch for one covert, warm, wondrous second.

Denise, back in her own ViroSpace, unlocked the door. It opened, whispering past the pink furry welcome mat. Her face burned as she entered. Staring straight ahead toward the kitchen, she said, "Eh, a three-seater might not be the worst thing in the world. I think we can handle it."

BLACK MARKET BLUES

SHAUN AVERY

About the Author:

SHAUN AVERY has been published in many magazines and anthologies, normally with dark tales satirising celebrity culture and worship, of which "Black Market Blues" is a proud example. He has won competitions with both prose and scripting work, and was shortlisted for a screenwriting contest. A lifelong fan of comics, he has also co-created a self-published horror one, more details of which can be found here: http://www.comicsy.co.uk/ dbroughton/store/products/spectre-show/ He is currently hard at work on several projects, many of which he expects will cover similar themes to "Black Market Blues." As long as there are bad TV shows to mock, he promises he will continue to do so.

Black Market Blues
Shaun Avery

THE KNOCK BROUGHT HER FROM TROUBLED SLEEP. KAREN rolled out of bed and padded to the window in her underwear and looked down into the garden, trying to see who it might be. Whoever it was, he stood too close to the front door for her to see.

So, she stomped over to the clothes closet, grabbed her dressing gown from where it always hung, belted it up, and headed for the bedroom door. She caught a sideways glance of herself in the mirror as she passed and was shocked by what she'd seen. No, not what she'd *seen,* exactly, more realization that she dared to answer the front door looking like this. Eyes puffy, bags beneath them, hair a mess, not to mention a victim of numerous home cuts since all the salons were shut – she knew people who'd sneaked hairdressers into their homes, who didn't care about the risk, but no way was she about to do *that*.

Saw, too, no make-up on her face since she'd just woken up, slid her eyes down and saw her toenails were not even painted, for whoever was about to see them. But who cared, right, these days? Still, once upon a time, it would have been unthinkable for her to let people see her this way. Not even the rare lovers she took when the urge grew too great to resist. Whenever they'd had sex, she'd made guys leave her house had not let them stay over, had not slept over if she'd gone to *their* house for sex. The thought of actually *living* with someone else had always disgusted her. So, to allow some random *stranger* to get a glimpse of her in this state? Forget it.

It had *to be stranger, too*, she thought as she walked out of the bedroom. *Delivery guy, maybe.* She didn't think she was expecting anything, but it was hard to keep up with deliveries sometimes.

There came another knock.

"All right," she cried. "All right, all right, I'm coming!" Then, as she walked down the stairs, she remembered the last conversation she'd had with another person. When she called her best friend Nina a few days ago . . .

"I JUST CAN'T LIVE WITHOUT THEM."

"I know." Nina sighed. "Me neither."

"Do you . . ." She almost couldn't bring herself to voice this question. It had come to her last night and kept her awake until morning. It's what made her video-call her best friend. But Nina seemed to be expecting her to say something more, so she went ahead and finished. "Do you think we ever took them for granted?"

"What? God, no!" Nina seemed shocked by the question. "Why would you even *think* that?"

"I don't know." Karen shrugged. "It's just, all this time without them, it's really made me think." She paused, thinking, remembering. "Sometimes we could be a little *harsh* on them. Well, some of them. Sometimes." She looked into Nina's eyes through the phone. "You know?"

"Yeah." A look of regret seemed to pass across those eyes. "I guess I do."

"I wish I could take it back," Karen went on. "All that stuff I said . . ."

Nina nodded. "Me, too."

Karen said her goodbyes and hung up the phone then, and as she did, she found she could almost cry, so vibrant were the memories stirred up by the call. It was only now, having asked the question, that she *truly* realized just how much she missed them, missed being around them. Now that it hit her how much her life, her world, was incomplete without the ability to be *near* them, to breathe the same sweet air as them.

Celebrities.

. . .

THE WORD "CELEBRITIES" STILL RUNG IN HER HEAD AS SHE swung the door open. She'd allowed herself to hope, for just a second, that it might be one of *them*. The stars, the famous. It had been so long since she'd been near one . . .

But no. The guy that stood there was completely ordinary. Obeying the distancing rules, too, which was a relief. The way she was feeling, had he not been, she would probably have taken a swing at him.

Instead, she said, "Yes? Can I help you?" Continued to look him over as she waited for a response. The guy was in his twenties, she guessed, young and fresh-faced, slender, in shape, and celebrity or no, there was something kind of nice about the grin he was wearing. In other times, she thought, she might even have . . . but she cut that thought short.

These were *not* other times, not since the virus, not since the lockdown. Not since a lot of bad things happened to people, and many had to learn to live without certain things. Things they'd become accustomed to . . . things they'd come to depend on.

For some, that meant family members. For others, it was friends. When she thought of Nina, she could kind of understand that. Yet still others – singletons – missed sex. That didn't bother her, though. Sure, she'd had one-night stands back in the day, but it's not like she missed snuggling up with someone, someone to wake up next to.

No, all she really craved, all she really wanted, was celebrities. And she found herself remembering the first time she came close to one . . .

THERE WAS THIS GUY ON ERIC PRICE'S FORUM, MYSTERIOUS 2-6. He'd said he worked on the outskirts of the singer's inner circle, that he knew the hotel the star was staying at when he played his big show at the North Star Arena. Karen wasn't sure she believed it, but she wasn't sure she *dis*believed it, either.

So, she asked Nina: "What do you think we should do?" They were nineteen then, had been best friends since high school.

Nina grinned. "We go take a look."

Which they did. First, though, they went to the show itself, screamed their lungs off, belting out the lyrics to all of the star's songs, loving every minute of it, looking across at each other throughout the gig and grinning. But even more exciting was what was to come. Then, finally, making their way to the hotel named by Mysterious 2-6.

That was a fun journey, too. Trekking there in the huge high heels they both wore. Nina slightly behind her, slower, her heels a little bigger, huffing out, "I hope . . . that he'll . . . be worth this."

"He will," Karen replied, not looking back. But even as she said this, something she'd never thought before had occurred to her. Namely, that it wasn't Eric Price *himself* that captivated her so. Not really. It was actually his *fame* that attracted her. And, handsome and fit though he was, it could be anybody, any man at all. Just so long as they were famous.

But Eric it was this time, and they eventually reached the hotel. Were both surprised to not see *more* fans there, trying this same thing. Either no one else had seen Mysterious 2-6's comment – it hadn't been up for long before being removed – or no one else had taken it seriously. Karen had always known that nobody else liked stars, or fame in general, the way they did.

It was nice, just the two of them. So, they went to the corner of the huge parking area, the hotel looming above them, a building so huge and fancy-looking that she was suddenly sure Mysterious 2-6 *had* been telling the truth, that the star really *was* staying here tonight. Then, keeping to the shadows so they wouldn't be seen, the girls waited until the early hours to see if any limos turned up...

Finally, one did. Eric must have gone clubbing after the show, and who could blame him? The guy had put on an awesome show, full of crazy choreography and blazing pyrotechnics.

Mind, if he had gone clubbing, she supposed, *we could have pulled the same stunt there, gone to the biggest club near the Arena – probably* Smooch *– to wait for Eric.*

But a big star like him, he would have probably gone straight to the club's VIP area, bypassed the normal folk altogether. *Besides,* she told herself, *this meeting will be more intimate.* They'd emerge from the shadows and approach him when the limo door opened, ask him for an autograph, tell him he was their favorite singer, that they were his biggest fans. Then he would say *thanks,* and he would take them by the hand, lead them into his hotel and show them his room, where – yeah, she could see that. She would share him with Nina. Maybe, in time, she'd share *many* stars with Nina. But only her. No one else.

As if hearing her thoughts, Nina gripped her arm in excitement. But when the door opened, it was like something from a nightmare. A surreal image, one that made no sense. For it was indeed Eric Price that stepped out of the limo. But he was not alone. No, he had somebody else with him. Some other *woman.*

Karen's mouth dropped. Beside her, Nina gasped.

Eric Price and the woman on his arm walked past, never seeing Karen and Nina, the two of them still hidden back in the shadows. The couple walked into the hotel, ignoring them. Like they weren't there at all. There was a brief silence while they processed this.

Nina said, "Did you see that?"

"Yeah." In the darkness, Karen's eyes narrowed. "That bitch."

They walked away from the hotel, disappointed and dejected. Went back to Nina's place, and all the time Karen had just one thought in her mind: *That should have been us, there with him.* Kept on thinking this in the days that followed.

And the years.

"Ma'am?"

She snapped back to the present. Saw the guy still standing there. Let her eyes trail down his body – as she'd done with her own earlier – and noticed he was wearing gloves. Safety-conscious, then, which was good. Still, though, what did he *want* here, with her?

She wondered if it might be something to do with the briefcase in his right hand.

"Ma'am?" he repeated. "Are you quite all right?"

But he had this look in his eye like he knew the answer already – like *that* was why he was here – and Karen felt herself softening to him slightly.

That might have been this morning itself, though, doing that to her. It was sunny, and birds were chirping in the trees and in the grass, and in other houses along the street kids were playing in their gardens. Kids seemed a lot happier these days, and definitely more relaxed, with schools still closed and digital learning, "study-at-your-own-pace" classes being all the rage. She got that from talking to the neighbors, something she and everyone else, according to the news, did a lot more now.

Some of the kids were even cute, most of them sporting the same sort of homemade haircuts as hers. Adults, too, were on the whole happier, not having to work, instead, collecting the government payment of a percentage of their wages. Sure, it was *only* a percentage, and everybody had less money now – but when you couldn't go anywhere for fear of catching a bug and dying, who cared?

Only her. And Nina, she supposed. Following the phone call with her friend a few days ago, she'd spent a lot of time on her computer, searching online for other people missing stars. But she'd found nothing. Some of the people she'd spoken to about it were even downright hostile, had told her she was being selfish, that there were more important things out there than the famous.

Others pointed out that celebrities posted online now more than ever since there was nothing else they could do, no other way they could reach and entertain the public. And Karen knew this was true – she followed thousands of them, too many of them to name, too many to count. But it was not the same as actually being *near* them. At a concert, at a PA, at a book or album signing. No, it did not feel the same at all.

"What do you want?" she said to the man, good mood vanishing, irritable now.

"Just to talk to you, ma'am," he replied.

"What about?" she asked, crossing her arms before her.

"About what I have," and he lifted up the briefcase, "in here."

She went to shut the door, thinking, *just another salesman.* "Not interested."

"Not interested," he replied, "in celebrities?"

She paused. "What?"

"Not interested, not interested in celebrities?"

There seemed something strange about the way he'd repeated himself there, something almost robotic, like he was a program that had just missed a beat, and Karen started to feel uneasy. But not enough to shut the door.

Instead, she said, "I don't know what you're talking about." But she did. For she'd been tossing and turning in bed these last few nights, ever since that question had started to plague her, that suspicion that she and Nina had taken their celebrities, their beloved celebrities, for granted.

Yes, she tossed and she turned and she saw faces and – *Little V, the British rap star* – she remembered times when – *Philip Venice, the romantic comedy actor* – she'd ignored posts from people she loved and worshipped and – *Roger Butcher, the reality TV god.*

Worst of all, she'd actually *insulted* stars. Both to her friends – well, just to Nina, really – and on the Internet itself, with snide comments and the odd death threat. But she knew now she would take it all back. Just to touch one, once more. Just to be near one, once more. To do that, she'd give everything.

"I think you do," the man replied, cutting into her thoughts. "And that's why . . ."

He placed down the briefcase, opened it up for her to see.

"We thought you might like *these,*" he finished.

Karen was curious. But she hung back in the doorway, a word that he'd just spoken making her feel uneasy.

"We?" she repeated. "Who's we?"

She was expecting him to dodge the question. But instead, he replied with:

"I represent some people that are . . . missing out on vital funding at this time."

"Oh really?" She met his eyes, and though they looked good she now thought that they looked *too* good. Not quite right. Not quite human. Not *just* human, anyway. "So why have 'some people' come here? To me?"

"We've been . . . listening," he explained. Shrugged slightly, appeared more human for a beat. "Nothing is private in this world, not even now." Karen almost gasped at that, but the man went on, not giving her a chance. "We've heard certain . . . conversations you have had. Both in real life and via your computer."

Karen blinked. Remembering again the conversation with Nina. Plus, the ones she'd had with people online, asking if anyone else missed celebrities. And her gaze slowly moved down to the briefcase. Thinking to herself, if what this man – or whatever he was – said was true, then what else could they be trying to sell her, what else could they have for her?

Her eyes widened.

She crouched down, amazed, not believing what lay before her. Saw small circular holes drilled into the case at random intervals, couldn't help but think they looked like *breathing* holes. And between the holes, stuck down to the velvet lining of the case with some sort of tape, she saw six little shapes, roughly the size of the action figures she often saw the neighbor's kids playing with. But these were no inanimate objects. Oh, no. No, these ones thrashed against the tape that bound them. And one of them, a man, shouted up at her.

"Help me!" he cried. His voice was louder than she'd expected, surprising her. "These people, they came in our house with these weird-looking guns and they shrunk me and my wife!"

"Us, too!" another cried, just as loud.

Karen looked up from the case, ignoring their words. "I recognize him," she said, pointing at the first shouting man. And she did. Small though he was, she'd recognize this star anywhere. It was Bryan McLain, action movie star. The one beside him was his wife, the equally famous Sarah, also an actor, though she made romantic comedies.

The man smiled. "You a fan?"

She said nothing. But she knew she was. Not a fan of him. Not a fan of any single star in particular. Just a fan of fame. Of celebrity.

"See," the man went on, "what those people told you online, well, it was right. *They* were right," and he shook his head like he was correcting himself, reminding her again of something robotic, something malfunctioning slightly. "There *are* more celebrities posting online than ever now. But some, you see," and here his tone grew quieter, more conspiratorial, like he was inviting her into some massive secret, "are doing exactly the opposite. They're trying to be more *private!* Can you imagine that?"

The man laughed, and Karen shivered, thinking there was *definitely* something inhuman about that sound, something *programmed.* "And that's a shame, isn't it? Don't you think that's them wasting their fame?" He paused. "One good thing, though: it'll be a while until they're missed. And there's plenty more there." His eyes met hers. "Did you ever realize just how *many* celebrities the world held before all this?"

She thought of all the ones she still followed, and she guessed he was right, this strange man. But for her, there could not ever be enough. No, never.

Thinking this, Karen looked down at the figures once more.

They stared back at her. What seemed to be fear in their eyes.

"Can I . . . can I touch them?" she said.

"Sure," he replied. "Sure, you can, Karen. They've all tested negative for the virus, were just going along with the quarantine to make sure they stayed that way. They're safe."

"Okay," Karen said. "Thanks." Then, she grabbed the one called Bryan, ripped him away from the briefcase's lining. Pulled the man up to her face, examined him. He squirmed a little against her, but he was no match for her – not when he was so small, and she was so big.

As soon as this thought hit her, she realized she liked it. No more was she that girl hiding in the shadows. No, now she was the one in charge, and it struck her that she could just bite this star's head off right here, and there'd be nothing he could do about it.

But she didn't want to do that. Not yet, at least.

"How . . . how much?" she asked instead.

He named a figure. One that seemed reasonable, especially since she, like her neighbors, like most everybody else these days, were still getting the majority of their pay without being able to go out and spend it anywhere.

"For all six?" she said.

He nodded. "To start with."

She looked over the shrunken man's struggling form. "There are more?"

"Yep." He sounded proud of the fact. "Being made as we speak."

She glanced down at the other five. So many stars to work with, to touch, to do whatever she told them to. She could make her own movies, her own dramas, her own anything. And that was just for starters. Who knew what *else* she could come up with, given enough time in lockdown?

"Someone will send you the details for payment," the man

said, his tone suggesting he was wrapping up this deal. "You can keep the briefcase." He turned to leave. "Goodbye, Karen."

She watched his movements. Almost human, but not quite. Certainly not something that could ever catch the virus, so Karen guessed now his gloves and his social distancing had been solely for her benefit, to put her at ease, to sell her something she wanted, something she needed.

"Wait!" she called.

He turned back, still smiling.

"Wait," Karen said again. "I have an idea for you . . ."

NINA PICKED UP THE VIDEO CALL, GLAD TO BE SPEAKING TO Karen once more. Even before the call connected, though, she could see something different in her friend, in the image of her face. She was glad. Karen had seemed so depressed in the last conversation, so out of sorts. But now she was smiling, and Nina liked that.

"Hey, girl," she said. "How you been doing?"

"Great! Just great!" came the reply. Nina thought she heard voices in the background, kind of small and muffled . . . her friend must have the TV on or something. It had to be a horror show she was watching, though – voices sounded kind of scared and distressed.

Karen went on. "Something awesome just happened!"

"What?" Nina said, curious. "What was it?"

"You'll see soon enough."

That was when a knock came at the door.

SOCIALLY DISTANCING

DAVID ANNAN

About the Author:

DAVID ANNAN is a working class nobody surviving in Toronto, Canada. He has a BA in Anthropology which has done nothing for him except make him hyper conscious of how nothing's objective. When he's not grinding away for a small hourly rate, he's busy writing stories about labour rights, mental health, class, environmentalism, and whatever else pops up into his head.

He is most well known for the story that you've just read, or are reading right now. Follow him on twitter @annan_thecannon to keep up to date on his work, and for random musings about writing, the world, Star Trek, and constant existential crises.

Social Distancing
By David Annan

1.5 YEARS; 18 MONTHS; 72 WEEKS; 547 DAYS; 13,140 HOURS.

Gregory Oleff was a construction worker who had not worked in a very long time. He had not gone out for drinks, eaten out, shopped, exercised, partied, been on a date, or even strolled through a park in a very long time.

Gregory Oleff lived in suite 3303 on the 33rd floor of 3 Bloor Street West in Toronto, Ontario, Canada. He had not left his building, his floor, or even his suite, in a very long time – 1.5 years, 18 months, 72 weeks, 547 days, 13,140 hours, to be exact. As he did every day, he awoke to the sound of voices: newscasters on his television. He left the news on through the night, the volume reduced, so he did not feel alone.

It was Monday, and Mondays were important – he actually had to be up at a specific hour. To start his day, Gregory did not brush his teeth, shave, or shower. He had not done any of this in a very long time. What was the point?

There was a beeping coming from his balcony door. Gregory climbed out of bed to pad to the balcony. Waiting for him were his rations for the week, a large brown box held by a large metal claw attached to the undercarriage of a large black drone. Four large propellers extended out from it in the shape of an X. The topside of the drone was a smooth and clear touch screen with a blinking green light.

Gregory stepped out onto the balcony barefoot. The drone detected his presence, and a robotic voice gave a stilted message that he must fill out the survey before he could receive his rations. He walked forward and pressed the green light, and the screen came to life with the weekly questionnaire:

In the past week, have you left your residence?
No.

In the past week, have you interacted with anyone showing symptoms?

No.

In the past week, have you interacted with anyone physically?

No.

In the past week, have you come within three metres of someone?

No.

In the past week, have you received items or correspondence from private persons?

No.

Have you shown any symptoms of the virus (diarrhea, bloody vomit, fever, aching joints, loss of taste and smell)?

No.

The screen went black and he stepped back. Several tube-like jets extended out of the drone, some twisting to point inwards, others pointing downwards at the package. As one the jets hissed out a burst of disinfectant spray, obscuring the drone for a moment in a white mist. The spray settled, and the claw released his rations. In a robotic voice it told him the Canadian Government appreciated his patience in this time of crisis, and that he could expect his next delivery of rations the following Monday, at the same time of day. The propellers whirred to life, and the drone lifted off his balcony and sped off to disappear amongst the skyscrapers of Toronto.

Gregory watched it go, resisting the urge to wave it goodbye. If it were not for drones and automation of production, they would all be starving now.

As he gathered up the box, he heard an engine revving down on the street level. Gregory leaned over the balcony and peered down at the intersection of Bloor and Yonge. A single vehicle stood waiting at the lights. It was a black panel van with tinted windows, and a red W painted on the side – it was the Wardens. Half police, half coroner, they enforced the quarantine and removed the deceased. Other than the occasional emergency vehicles, the black vans of the Wardens were the only activity on the empty streets of Toronto. The van turned north, receding from view.

The sight of the van excited him – it reminded him that it was almost 1 pm. Gregory brought his rations inside and packed the paltry contents of the box away. Checking the clock, he saw that it was a few minutes to 1, and he hurried to the door, crouching with his ear against it.

He heard the ding of the elevator, and his heart rate became fervent. His breath hot, he pressed his ear against the door, hard. It hurt, but Gregory did not care. He heard the footsteps, and he stopped breathing. There was only his heartbeat and the steps coming closer. The steps stopped outside of his door, and he put his hand against it. A moment later, the Warden in the hallway outside walked away and the elevator dinged once more.

Gregory exhaled a heavy expulsion of tension. Shivers ran up his back. It was a feeling akin to orgasm. He laid on the floor for a time, enjoying the waves of pleasure from being so close to someone. In his mind he pictured them, constructed a face for them, a height, a wardrobe, and fantasized about talking with them. He imagined a thousand conversations, a thousand jokes shared, a thousand greetings and farewells.

The Wardens checked his door daily to make sure he had not broken quarantine, as evidenced by a strip of tape they had affixed to his door. Gregory had long since stopped trying to speak to the Wardens; they never responded to his muffled hellos or knocks. In the early days they had come to his floor often – he would hear the elevator ding and watch them through his door's spy hole. Men and women dressed in blue scrubs and masks, coming at all hours to answer medical calls and maintain quarantine. When they started to wheel bodies out, they had taped over his spy hole and never removed it. Now they came only once a day, and he was forced to listen to their footsteps – the closest he could come to another living breathing human being.

Finally, he pulled himself up and sat on his couch in front of the television. The highlight of his day was over. He turned up the volume to watch the Canadian Broadcasting Corporation. They were the only people to speak to him anymore. When the quarantine started, he would call friends and family to chat. First his family stopped calling or answering, and then his friends went silent one by one. Now, all he had was the television and internet.

The CBC correspondents were still dressed in their suits and dresses, but they had a dishevelled fringe to their appearance. They broadcast from their homes in front of green screens, and without the makeup artists their appearance had suffered. It was clear that they were the ones applying their own makeup and trying to cut their own hair. Some had stopped trying, it seemed, appearing aged and tired on the screen as they rattled off their news for the day. Today, as with every day, nothing of importance was mentioned. There was a brief comment by one of the hollow-eyed reporters about one of the latest vaccine trials being unsuccessful, but that was not noteworthy.

Gregory spent his day on the couch, flipping through news channels, all reporting the same thing, and old re-runs of television shows from a different era. Some days, he would force himself to exercise or read, or do something productive like clean. Other days he would get dressed in his workman's clothing, hard hat and all, and pretend he was going to a job site. He still had some of his tools in his closet – hammers, drills, chisels, etc. He would pose in front of the mirror with them, lifting his sledgehammer high over his head trying to remember what it meant to work. However, most days were spent like the present one: in his underpants staring at people on screen. Eventually the hours disappeared, as did the light, and he pulled himself from the couch to his bed.

Lying in bed, Gregory stared at the ceiling and thought about the next day. Specifically, he thought about the next check by the Wardens; there was nothing else to think about, really.

Suddenly, there was a noise that came through his bedroom

wall. Gregory jolted up into a sitting position, his eyes wide. It had been like the muffled drag of someone pulling back a chair. Gregory ran to his den where he shut off the television and he ran back to his bedroom, putting his ear to the wall.

After a moment, there was the sound of a muffled creak and a heavy footstep.

Gregory banged on the wall excitedly, giving it two raps, and paused to listen for the response. *Knock, knock, knock*, came the response. His heart exploded in his chest, and he shouted in jubilation. He shouted, "hello" at the wall and banged it furiously. But, there came no further response. Gregory continued shouting and knocking the wall well into the early morning before finally giving up and falling asleep, elated at the interaction, no matter how brief.

When he awoke, it was once more time for the daily check, yet when he pressed his ear to the door and heard the steps approach then depart, his heart did not cheer as it once did. It was like receiving the appetizer at dinner; it was enjoyable, yes, but what truly excited you was the forthcoming steak.

Gregory lifted his ear from the door and returned to his bedroom. There, he spent the day knocking the wall, shouting at it, and listening to it. Night came, however, and his voice grew hoarse, but there was no response to his calls. Gregory lay in bed, tired from hope.

At the edge of sleep, a low murmur brushed against his ear. His eyes shot wide open. Muffled by the wall, Gregory could hear voices whispering to each other. It was indistinct, like the soft whistling of a summer breeze. Elated, Gregory jumped to his knees and banged the wall shouting, "hello." The voices ceased abruptly. Gregory continued his knocking and shouting, however, until after a time he laid back down, defeated. He suddenly felt silly, banging on the wall − who was he? They did not know him; he did not even know their names. Perhaps they were frightened by some unknown neighbor ranting and banging on the wall.

Before the pandemic, Gregory had never made an effort to talk to his neighbors, beyond a hello or a good morning. Lying there very much alone, Gregory swore to himself that should this pandemic ever end, he would make a point of being gregarious to the extreme. Drifting off to sleep, he decided he would change his tact.

The next day, he wrote a lengthy letter introducing himself on scrap paper. He told them everything there was to know about him: he was a construction worker, he lived alone, his family and friends were all gone, and he would very much like to be friends. He apologized for banging on the wall as well, explaining it as just his excitement over having someone so close.

Satisfied with the missive, he folded it neatly and went to the balcony. There was a tall metal divider separating their two balconies which he could not see around unless he climbed out over the railing. Standing on his tiptoes, he tossed the letter over the top and then rapped loudly on the divider.

Gregory waited for a time, but he did not hear the squeaking opening of the sliding door. He rapped at the divider once more, but still there was no sound of motion on the other side. He gave up, telling himself that they would find it eventually, and returned inside to flip through channels.

As the day wore on, Gregory checked the balcony over and over, but found no reply awaiting him on his balcony. Despairing, he fell asleep on his couch with the news playing.

What awoke him this time was not the scrape of a chair, a knock on the wall, or a low murmur – it was the blaring vibrations of loud music, dozens of voices shouting, and the stomping of feet. Frightened at first by the cacophony of alien sounds, the shock turned to excitement. Gregory leaped from the couch and ran over to his bedroom wall—it sounded like a large party was taking place on the other side of the thin drywall.

Suddenly anxious, he shouted at the wall, banging with both fists. So many people, and so close to him! He just wanted to say hello! He would not call the Wardens! He shouted and shouted, but there was no discernible response—the music was so raucous that he doubted anyone could hear him. Desperate, he banged at the wall with a wild fervor. His right fist smashed a hole in the drywall, and he paused, staring at it for a moment. In his ears his heart was as loud as the bass, and he tore into his closet to its beat. With a mad resolve, he returned to the wall with his sledgehammer gripped tightly in his hands.

As he had done a hundred times before in front of his bedroom mirror, he hoisted the hammer mightily above his head. Unlike those hundreds of times before, he brought it down in a shuddering crash. The thin drywall exploded with the impact of the hammer's head. His chest heaving and sweat percolating on his shoulders and brow, Gregory hammered the wall again and again. With every strike, it seemed that the music on the other side grew louder, as though to drown out his own uproar. Gregory laughed as he pictured himself half naked, in his boxers, hammering at a drywall – he was the real life of the party!

HA-ha-HA-ha!

In between his grunts, gasps, and hysterical laughter, Gregory began to shout at the hole he was creating: he shouted greetings, he shouted that they should not be afraid, he just wanted to come party too, that he would fix the wall, that his name was Gregory Oleff, and he just wanted to be friends.

The blows of the hammer obliterated the wall in cascades of drywall. He came to the layer of insulation and soundproofing, a board of green foam, and he dropped the hammer for a serrated kitchen knife. He tore at the insulation like a starved animal upon a carcass, and shredded his way through to the drywall on the other side, whereupon he hoisted the hammer once more. When the hammer fell this time, the music did not increase, but ceased entirely. Gregory shouted once more, telling them not to worry, he was just coming over to say hi. He laughed again, trying to sound friendly. *HA-ha-HA-ha!*

Gregory judged the hole wide enough, and he dropped the

hammer to stick his head through: the other side was an unoccupied bedroom in darkness. There was no sound of the party, or any occupants. He called out a shy hello, but there was no response. They must be hiding, he decided, and he squeezed through the wall, imagining a dozen or so people huddling up outside the bedroom. Sheepishly, he crept to the den and jumped out with a goofy grin on his face – but there was no one there. The furniture, a couch, coffee table, and dining table, all looked untouched. He ran his finger along the surfaces of the apartment, and found them all to be covered in a fine layer of dust – the apartment was unoccupied, and had been for a long time.

Confused, he sat on his dead neighbor's couch for a time. Where had the music come from? And the knocks, and the whispers? Perhaps the sound was carrying strangely, and was in fact coming from the next apartment over. Once more, he took up his tools and tore through the wall to the next unit.

When he squeezed through to the next suite, he found it to be similarly under a layer of dust. The fanatic fervour that had so driven him to a maddened frenzy had been smothered—where was everyone?

Calmed now, he set about demolishing the wall into the next suite of rooms. The hammer strikes were no longer the wild blows of a manic man, but rather the methodical strikes of someone determined to discover the truth. The wall was paper to his advance, and he was soon in the third unit from his own. As with the last two, all he found was dust and darkness. The next wall fell before his hammer.

Dawn had long since broken across Toronto by the time he tunnelled his way into the final apartment on the 33rd floor. There were fifteen total and, except for his, they were all unoccupied. Beds were unslept in, cupboards bare of food, and every surface was dusty from eighteen months of being undisturbed. For 1.5 years—18 months, 72 weeks, 550 days, 13,200 hours, Gregory Oleff had been alone on the 33rd floor. Alone, alone, alone.

His fingers numb, his breath short, he stumbled out of suite 3315, into the hallway of the 33rd floor. Taking short steps back to his own front door, he was overcome with a dizziness that nearly toppled him. He stopped at the elevators, closing his eyes and breathing deeply. It was nearly time for the Warden's rounds. Gregory opened his eyes and waited outside the elevator. Whatever the legal repercussions were, he did not care; he just needed to see another human being.

When one o'clock came, there was no ding of the elevator or the sound of footsteps to excite him. He stood there for another two hours, but no one came. Every day the Warden came at 1 to check his door and make sure he had maintained quarantine. His chest tight and his ears hot, Gregory walked to his door and stopped, a wave of dizziness washing over him. Looking down, he saw that the floor was covered in a thin layer of dust. It lay undisturbed in front of his door – no sign of any one having set foot there in aeons.

Gregory turned the knob and pushed open his door, breaking the quarantine tape along the seam of the door and frame. He walked to the balcony, and stared down at the intersection of Bloor and Yonge.

"Is anyone out there?" He screamed out at the empty streets of Toronto.

But Bloor and Yonge, once so busy with traffic, vibrant commotion, and crowds of people, had no answer to give.

ONLIFE

ELLA ANANEVA

ELLA ANANEVA is a Russian immigrant who resides in Silicon
Valley. She uses her IT background to write speculative science
fiction. Ella's favorite technique for fighting against a writer's
block is lucid dreaming. You can visit her website here:
www.ellaananeva.com.

Onlife
By Ella Ananeva

"Japanese Scientists Made a Breakthrough in COVID-41 Vaccine Development. The vaccine will be on the market by the end of the year, sources say."

Stark chuckled as he scrolled the newsfeed. They promised a cure every February in the past four years, as though someone still believed it was possible. *Just stay home; that's it.* Stark hadn't left his place since the quarantine started and felt perfectly healthy, not counting extra pounds.

His fingers rolled the wheel of the old-fashioned mouse. Stark skimmed the article about shopping automatization but read the next one. 'TES Online: The Long Reign' got 9.8-star reviews. And he still didn't receive the console to play it.

"Miri, where's my PlayStation?"

"It will be shipped in two days," answered the silvery voice of the AI Stark developed as his final project.

"Dammit! Okay, call Liam."

The yellowish face of his best friend popped up on the screen. It was puffy and swollen, but Liam still looked like the successful streamer he was. He earned more money playing games than Stark got from all his freelance programming jobs. *Yep, why not, he makes the girls piss their pants with his almond-shaped eyes and this glowing skin and this fancy mohawk of his. He wouldn't, if he had red pepper all over his face plus extra weight. Video filters can't mask such things.* Stark glanced at the elliptical trainer, resplendent in dust and dirty socks. *Maybe later.*

"Hey bro! What's up?" Liam's voice was hoarse.

"Hey Liam. Got the new console?"

"Yep, but I haven't unpacked it. Been busy."

"Streaming?"

"Chatting," Liam smiled slyly. "Asian triplets. Kawaii!"

"Congrats." Stark clenched the mouse.

"Again? Chill out man! No need to be jealous."

"I'm not jealous. Online dating is not my thing."

Liam laughed. "No such thing as offline dating now!"

"Or anything offline," the silvery voice said.

Stark spilled his water.

"Was that Miri?" Liam pulled away so abruptly the poster with a half-naked anime girl swung behind his back. "Don't remember her talking like that."

"She didn't." Stark's heart pounded. "Can't believe it worked!"

"Been updating her? Seems a bug to me. The AI who doesn't like anything online. Weird."

Blood warmed Stark's cheeks. "She behaves like the original."

"Eh?" Liam's eyes lost focus.

"Miriam."

"And who would that be?"

Stark's mouth dried, his eyes searched Liam's face for the hint of sarcasm and found nothing. "Eighth grade. She was my... well, Miriam."

He saw her again in his mind's eye, a skinny red-headed girl in ugly round glasses on her freckled face. Her knees pressed into each other, Miriam strained under the oversized backpack, clutching a push-button phone in her small hands. Stark cringed at the memory. Where did her parents find such a phone in 2034, he didn't know. Perhaps, they ought to have gone on homeschooling her. She would've still been alive.

"A girl?" Liam glanced at Stark.

A knot formed in Stark's stomach. He spent the whole sophomore year raving to Liam about Miriam. Stark had never shown any sympathy to her, too scared to play in the open with the main school scapegoat. He didn't even trust a messenger with his feelings. In high school, he believed the Secret Service read all web messages, so he shared his secrets with Liam only, mouth-to-ear, in person.

Stark laughed tensely. "You need to sleep more. She was my crush, all along until she... did the thing."

Liam's face cleared. "Now I remember. She caused you trouble, eh? It's bad luck to have a woman on board. Even a miniature one."

Stark stared at his friend. A few chip crumbles were stuck to Liam's unshaven cheeks. Seven.

"You're kidding," Stark said. "Don't joke like that bro."

"Eh?"

Stark jumped to his feet. "Bad luck? What has a quote from 'Pirates of the Caribbean' to do with Miriam? After they beat her with her phone - she jumped - dammit!"

"Yeah. It's bad luck... " Liam's grin became distorted. "Even a miniature one." He giggled. "She caused you... bad luck." His facial muscles burst in a series of contractions. Liam blinked, licked his lips, and sniffed. "A woman on board..."

The connection interrupted. Stark gazed at the black screen for a minute, his heart beating in his throat, his hands trembling. *I need fresh air.* "Miri..." He cleared his throat. "Call Liam."

"Hey bro, what's up?" Liam's stretched his lips in his signature happy-bastard smile.

"Greetings not needed, we just talked," Stark snapped. "What ha..."

Liam's eyebrows slid up. "No, bro, we haven't. Are you alright?"

Stark clenched his fists. "Am I alright?.. What's going on, Liam? Is it because you don't want to talk about Miriam?"

"Who's Miriam?" Liam's face went blank.

"Miriam Foster! My first fucking love!"

"Ah. Brown hair and freckles? She played guitar?"

Stark sat down, hands on the desk, eyes glued to the screen. "Are you kidding, bro? Do you remember what she did to herself?" The shards of her skull in a red-greyish mess. Her carrot-colored hair mixed with rusty blood. The ugly smudge around her young body. Liam and Stark found her together and ran away and never talked about it since. No way Liam forgot something that horrific.

"She caused you trouble, huh?" His face twitched. "It's bad luck to have a woman on board. Even a miniature... B-b-bad luck."

His features distorted; words bouncing between his gritted teeth, Liam smiled. The call got disconnected.

Stark stood up and tapped the desk. He paced around the room until Miri suggested taking a break. Then, he redialed Liam, only to hear, "I don't feel well, bro. Call me later, okay?"

Liam didn't answer any more calls.

"Okay Google, what do I do if my friend goes glitchy on FaceTime" gave zero results. The first post about the issue on Stack Overflow got Stark banned.

The food delivery came, and then the night. No answer. Not a word from Liam. Stark had tried to distract himself with his final project and had almost broken Miri. Twice.

"It's a connection problem," his brother Ned said between two slurps of ramen on their bi-weekly call.

"Don't fool around, do some serious work. How's your final project?" Mom's temples looked greyer than the last time when he saw her. *I really should call her more often.*

"Okay Google, why do my FaceTime posts on StackOverFlow get banned?" returned one hundred and twenty thousand results; useful, zero.

Liam didn't answer Stark's calls but posted on Facebook and streamed as usual. He was decent enough to keep off testing "TES," though. Stark hadn't noticed the new console either.

"What's going on, why aren't you answering my calls?" Stark texted.

"Still not feeling well, bro, will get to you later."

In his gaming stream, Liam was beaming with a smile.

By Friday, Stark got banned not only on AI forums but also in Facebook groups where he was naive enough to ask what was going on.

On Saturday, he found himself staring at his dusty protection suit. He bought it after sophomore year in college. Going out had presented some interest then. Not so much now, when all restaurants, clubs, theaters, malls, museums, and basically everything else was closed. People still managed to get the virus, though. If they decided to have fun, why ignore recommendations to wear a suit?

It felt tight in the middle. Sitting home didn't present many opportunities for working out, although Instagram stars, of course, got their millions with "on-the-sofa" exercises. Stark zipped and winced: the slider pinched his chin. *I'm not going to go out, am I?* His self-driving car was up to the task, and its batteries were fully charged after several years of non-usage, but still...

"Miri, dial Liam." The helmet muffled his voice.

No answer.

His knees were weak and his shirt clung to his armpits under the protection suit as he descended downstairs. He held his breath before pushing the front door. Through his black visor, the sun looked grey. The wind swung bare branches of the wild plums, but no sounds could penetrate the helmet. A squirrel jumped away from his feet as Stark crossed the driveway. At the curbside, he looked around, turning his whole body from side to side. Perhaps, it was safe to take off the helmet. There was no one on the street but five squirrels scurrying around the trees. He checked the straps.

Was he really doing it? Walking around the street as though there were no pandemic? *Man, the virus is so stubborn; on metal, it can survive for months!* He glanced at the rows of cars along the curb. Their steel hoods glistened in the morning sun. Any of them could host a colony of microorganisms, waiting for their next victim.

He hurried to his vehicle. Once inside, he sprinkled the sanitizer all over the wheel and his hands, even though he wore gloves.

The car stopped at Liam's apartment complex half an hour later. Stark hadn't encountered any vehicles but self-driving trucks that delivered food and computer supplies. Everything else was digitized and uploaded long ago.

As he reached his friend's hallway, Stark was red, wet, and hot as a fresh-boiled crayfish. *Only crayfish don't pant like that.* He didn't take his suit off nonetheless.

Stark stood on grey plates, pushing his knees with his hands, when he had a premonition. He stood up.

Stacks of unpacked boxes cluttered the hallway, obscuring Liam's door. A blue-and-black console package balanced on top of the nearest pile. Stark swallowed. Fear sucked the heat off his body; he felt frozen in space. He forced himself to move: cleaned the space, rang and knocked, knocked and rang. No response.

"Miri, dial Liam. Sound to the headphones." His voice trembled.

"Hey bro, how are you doing?" Liam sounded as cheerful as ever.

Stark froze. He hadn't expected the answer. His voice trembled. "I'm at your door! Could you fucking let me in?"

"You what? Are you nuts, Stark? C'mon, the virus is still out there. You..."

"Shut up and let me in."

"You are nuts. Anyway, I'm in the bathroom. That new Indian meal went wrong. Will you wait? Five minutes, maybe?"

"Okay."

In fifteen minutes, all he got was, "Sorry, I'm still here. Maybe you'd better come later?"

Stark pounded on the door. The wall shook under pressure. Liam went on murmuring about Indian street food he streamed eating. Stark stepped back and hit the door with all his weight. Boxes dropped from the piles, peppering the glossy floor. Liam didn't stop.

"Haven't you heard?" Stark asked, breathing heavily.

"Heard what? Really bro, you're weird."

"Me?!"

"Are you here to pick up the boxes?" a croaky voice asked

behind his back. Stark turned and saw a thin lady peeking through a crack in the door to her apartment. Her face behind the protection mask was wrinkled and pale.

"What? Miri, hang up." He looked at her, eyes wide open. It'd been a while since Stark had seen a live person. Online, it was easy to forget that people could be ugly or old.

She sniffed the air. "Something is rotten. Your colleagues pick up the boxes on Wednesdays, and it's already Saturday."

"I'm sorry, m' am, I don't... What do you mean - pick up the boxes?"

The lady cast him a suspicious glance. "If you don't pick up, what are you doing here?"

"My name is Stark. I'm here to visit my friend, Liam. Do you know him?"

She pulled away. "A young one? A blogger?"

"Streamer," he whispered.

She didn't seem to hear. "The virus killed him. Two... yes, two years ago. I saw them take his body."

The lady was wrinkled. Her colorless eyes watered. She was old. Demented. She was mistaken.

"I've just talked to him."

"I told you what I saw." The lady slammed the door.

Stark slid down the wall. He sat still, his gaze skimming the boxes, until the cold penetrating his protection pants made him get up. Stark dialed Liam. He was still in the bathroom.

Stark ran up to the door and pushed it, again and again, until it creaked and he flew into the apartment, struggling to maintain his balance.

The air was stale, and clouds of dust floated in the sunbeams, but the living room looked perfectly neat – something that Liam was never able to achieve. No dirty mugs in the sink, no clothes hanging from chairs and piling on the floor.

Dust covered the computer desk, the keyboard, and the fancy headphones Liam wore for streams. The poster with a busty anime character was bleached by the sun.

It's bright and colorful on his streams.

Stark's lips went numb. He sauntered to the bathroom, leaving footprints in the dust. He knocked. No response. He squinted before pulling the handle.

The bathroom was empty.

"Mi... Miri. Dial Liam."

"Meh, bro, I asked you to come later!"

"You're still in the bathroom?"

"Where else would I be?"

"Okay. Fine. I'll call you later."

Stark didn't remember how he got back to the car. He found himself staring at the steering wheel, the only thought in his head was, "I'm going crazy. I've just talked to my friend who died two years ago. Any tips?" He posted it on Facebook. It disappeared three seconds later.

At home, he loomed around the web trying to share his adventure elsewhere when Miri said, "Good news, Stark. Your console will arrive tomorrow."

"Finally!" Stark felt as though someone sprayed a sanitizer on the dark mess in his mind. *What, I haven't taken off the suit yet?* He undressed – *cool, I can move again* – and loaded himself with two burritos and an episode of a Japanese series. *I won't think about it. If I just wait and sleep on it, it'll all get to normal again.*

One night, six cups of coffee, and two seasons later, Stark finally got to work on his final project. He was hunting a mistake throughout the system when a doorbell made him jump.

"Delivery!" a mechanoid voice sounded in the hallway.

Stark ran outside, dropping his slippers. There it was, his dream console, in the black box with a beautiful fantasy illustration. He squatted and stretched his arms to get it.

A sharp pain pierced his hip. For a few minutes, he saw nothing but darkness. It faded to white, white like paper, like a browser screen, like Liam's smile. He couldn't recall anything white in his hallway.

Stark sat, rubbing his temples, his eyes glued to his bare toes.

Where the hell are my socks? Did I lose them as well as the slippers? He looked up. His jaw dropped. He was in a hospital room, lying on a bed and – *dammit, no protection suit! No mask, nothing!* He pulled a navy blanket up to his chin and threw it in disgust. *Where is my sanitizer?* He checked his pockets and found none on these pants.

"Miri, where am I?"

Stilettos tapped the floor, and a husky voice said, "Please, calm down, Stark."

He threw his head up so swiftly his neck hurt. A tall woman sat on a stool. Her pencil skirt clung to her slim hips as she crossed her legs. Her white shirt ruffling, she cupped her chin with a bare hand. Stark gasped. *She's touching her face!*

She grinned. "The pandemic is long over. There's no need to cover your skin."

"What?..." Stark froze, swallowing the air. Thousands of thoughts scurried in his brain, causing almost physical pain. *Pandemic's over... How can't it be over?.. Why, then?.. the sanitizer... Mom... Bullshit. Who's she, anyway?* His tongue laid heavy in his mouth. He struggled to force himself into speaking. "Who are you?"

"Doctor Laila Ortega, Defense Advanced Research Projects Agency."

"Are you from the police?"

"Almost."

Stark straightened, pushing a soft pillow to the wall. "I don't believe you."

"Of course." She handed him a badge.

He wouldn't take it from her. "Put it on the blanket."

He picked up the ID using his sleeve for protection. The woman in the photo looked back at him seriously. He scratched the eagle on the black stamp, counted the digits of the serial number, squinted at the signature. It looked okay to him, but again, how could he tell if it was fabricated? Liam's twitched face jumped into his mind.

Stark threw the badge on the blanket and rubbed his neck.

"What does the Pentagon want from me?" *Why does my voice sound so chickenshit?*

She picked up the ID and looked at him with a soft smile. "I'm going crazy. I've just talked to my friend who died two years ago. Any tips?"

Stark gazed at her, barely blinking. *Bitch. Bitch.*

Dr. Ortega started pacing the room, her stilettos pattering the floor in rhyme with her words.

"I'm sorry we had to delete your posts, but they could raise panic. We can't afford it." She stood, her back to the window, her black eyes fixed on him. "On behalf of DARPA, I bring you official apologies for the inconvenience a bug in our application caused to you. Onlife is extremely complicated software. Hard as we work, sometimes, accidents happen."

Accidents. She calls it an accident. Stark threw the blanket and put his bare feet down. "I'm leaving."

He crossed the room, the floor unpleasantly cold and rough under his soles. Dr. Ortega gazed at him with a curious smile. He gripped the handle of the door.

"And you don't want to know what happened to your friend?"

Stark turned. Her black eyes flickered.

"Go on." He leaned to the door and pushed his hands into his pockets – *dammit, no pockets!* – and tucked the thumbs into the belt.

She leaned on the windowsill and tilted her head. "His physical body perished indeed, but his personality survived. Do you remember 2041?"

Stark gritted his teeth. *Mom's red eyes. A series of black dresses, he was so sick of them, but he had to wear black, too, at least, online. No job. No money. Six months on rice.* "Of course, I do!"

She nodded. "It was a hard year for all of us. The virus mutated so quickly vaccines became useless before they finished the trials. When the death rate reached fifteen percent, it became clear we'd lost. Millions of businesses closed when everything was pushed online, but even those that survived were doomed to lose workers, clients, and money. No businesses, no taxes. No taxes, no schools, hospitals, or science."

"Fifteen percent? C'mon, it never reached eight!"

"The death rate went up to twenty-five, Stark."

They stared at each other. He re-played her words in his mind, until their meaning struck him.

Dr. Ortega broke eye contact. "We started development before the first million mark and launched in a year. Thank God marketers had gathered all the information we needed! Without it..."

"But you can't! You can't just..." He recalled Liam's glowing face, his sly smile, his cheerful voice as he streamed his games. "You can't make an AI behave like a living person!"

"Can't we? Video processing algorithms have been production-ready since the early twenties. By 2025, everyone had uploaded enough personal data to create their complete profiles. Aging software was on the market long before that. As for the behavior," she shrugged, "it has patterns. Patterns can be analyzed and reproduced. Our Onlifers post, shop, and communicate just as their original personalities would do. We only have to tie up loose ends: pick up the unopened boxes and fix bugs."

"Bullshit." Stark hit the door with his fists. "Post, shop, maybe. But what about work? Liam, he is... was a streamer. You can't recreate that!"

"Oh, but we can." Dr. Ortega folded her arms on her chest. "Only a small percentage of highly-creative jobs are out of our AI's possibilities now. Those people... well, we pretend they lost their jobs and live on subsidies now. The only exception were doctors. We can neither automate their labor nor substitute them with machines. This is the reason you're in a hospital now. They are the most secure places in the country."

"Bullshit," he repeated. "Your application sucks. Liam went all glitchy when I mentioned..." Cold creeped up his spine.

"When I mentioned Miriam. We... I... We had never talked about Miriam online. And she wasn't even on Facebook. Shit!"

"Exactly. You've never discussed this girl online, and your emotional reaction was so bizarre Liam couldn't detect a correct pattern. You accidentally found a critical error in our app. This is why I'm about to offer you a job."

"What?"

"Yes, and a good one for an undergraduate like yourself. We can't let you get away now, you see. The pandemic is over, but we have to keep the quarantine, or our whole economic system will collapse again. If people know the truth, they'll start panicking; panic is what almost killed us when the virus started."

"Yes. I remember." His heart jumped in his throat. Panic killed his dad, even though it took the form of a heart attack.

"So, you'll stay here, in this building." Dr. Ortega drew a circle in the air. "Your life will be the same. Better, actually: even junior testers in DARPA are well-paid, and you'll get all the fancy gadgets, consoles, and software updates. And more..."

Dr. Ortega crossed the room and stood in front of him. She was neither old nor ugly, even though wrinkles streaked along her forehead, and dark spots spoiled her brown skin, and her eyelashes stretched shorter than those of any online girl.

"We could help you recreate Miri."

He stared at her, his jaw slowly sliding down.

She nodded. "Yes. She'll be like Liam. A living young woman, your age now. You might touch her. Make love, even. This is still in development, but with your help..."

His heart pounded. "No."

"In a few years, you'll forget she... did the thing."

He turned to the window. Blinds obscured the view completely. "What are my other options? Are you going to... kill me?"

"No." Dr. Ortega stepped back. "You're not the only one to find our project. At first, it was rather raw, so we were discovered constantly. Some of these people work here now. Others chose what they call freedom."

"And what is that?"

"One of our benefactors donated an island. There is a village there, nothing special, but fully habitable. About three hundred of your predecessors live there. We visit them once a month, perform maintenance and deliver medications, but most of the time, they are self-sustained. Naturally, they have no internet. You could join them, but really, Stark, with your talent, that would be a loss."

Talent. Miri, living and smiling with the smile he remembered, dimples on her cheeks and a gap between her front teeth. He'd never liked that gap. There wouldn't be a gap in his version.

What am I thinking? It was a lie; everything was a lie. Miriam was dead. Liam, too. Maybe, everyone else he knew. The island was the right choice, with a real life, natural, like in survival games. That would be the truth.

What will I tell Mom?

She'd be glad to know I got a job... If she is not... No, he couldn't think about that, not seriously. His Mom was real, of course she was...

"M'am... Doctor..." Stark muttered. "My brother and Mom. Are they... alive?"

Doctor Ortega shrugged. "What difference does it make?"

Stark froze; the answer trembled on the tip of his tongue. He swallowed it. She was right. It made no difference: he hadn't noticed Liam had changed until the Miri talk and wouldn't notice if anything happened to his other peers. What would he do on an island, anyway? Without the Internet, he'd lose everything he had: his work, Japanese series, video games, and his connections, some of which, perhaps, were real.

"I'm in."

ABOUT THE EDITORS

FROG JONES is the acquisitions editor for Impulsive Walrus Books. He's also the co-author of the *Gift of Grace* series alongside his wife Esther, and has appeared in numerous anthologies, including *Straight Outta Deadwood* by Baen Books and *Dragon Writers,* where his story can be found alongside Brandon Sanderson's, David Farland's, and Todd McCaffery's. He has previously edited the anthology *Well, It's Your Cow,* also by Impulsive Walrus Books, and can be found online at http://jonestales.com/.

MANNY FRISHBERG was born in the shadow of New York City but saw the error of his (parents') ways and moved to the West Coast, 40-some years ago. He has held jobs shaping wood, sheet metal and words (not all at once).

Manny has been an independent book editor since 2010. His two previous anthologies, "Horseshoes, Hand Grenades and Magic" and "After the Orange" came out in 2016 and 2018, respectively. He and his partner serve two cats in their home near Seattle.

ALSO BY IMPULSIVE WALRUS BOOKS:

Well... It's Your Cow: An Anecdotal Anthology, edited by Frog Jones

Blackbox Protocol, by Bethany Loy and Frog Jones

Grace Under Fire, by Frog and Esther Jones

Coup de Grace, by Frog and Esther Jones

Falling From Grace, by Frog and Esther Jones (forthcoming)

CPSIA information can be obtained
at www.ICGtesting.com
Printed in the USA
LVHW011240110820
662878LV00005B/537